I would blame myself for what happened. If anyone should have known it would, it should have been I, the best and only sweet Audrina.

When I was just about at the door, I stopped. There was no doubt. I heard the rocking chair rocking. I stepped up and gently opened the door. The sound stopped. I leaned to my left and found the light switch, my heart thumping.

Sylvia looked up at me.

"Sylvia, what are you doing? Why did you come in here? Why are you in the chair?"

She smiled, unafraid, looking at me as though I was the slow-witted sister and not her.

"Papa told me to," she said. "He said whenever I wanted to talk to him, I should rock in the first Audrina's chair, because that was the way you spoke to the first Audrina."

I should have emptied this room. Maybe we could erase the past, if not forever, for years and years, or at least put it so far in the back of our minds it wouldn't ruin our present lives.

V.C. Andrews® Books

The Dollanganger Family Series
Flowers in the Attic
Petals on the Wind
If There Be Thorns
Seeds of Yesterday
Garden of Shadows
Christopher's Diary: Secrets of
    Foxworth
Christopher's Diary: Echoes of
    Dollanganger
Secret Brother

The Audrina Series
My Sweet Audrina
Whitefern

The Casteel Family Series
Heaven
Dark Angel
Fallen Hearts
Gates of Paradise
Web of Dreams

The Cutler Family Series
Dawn
Secrets of the Morning
Twilight's Child
Midnight Whispers
Darkest Hour

The Landry Family Series
Ruby
Pearl in the Mist
All That Glitters
Hidden Jewel
Tarnished Gold

The Logan Family Series
Melody
Heart Song
Unfinished Symphony
Music in the Night
Olivia

The Orphans Miniseries
Butterfly
Crystal
Brooke
Raven
Runaways

The Wildflowers Miniseries
Misty
Star
Jade
Cat
Into the Garden

The Hudson Family Series
Rain
Lightning Strikes
Eye of the Storm
The End of the Rainbow

The Shooting Stars Series
Cinnamon
Ice
Rose
Honey
Falling Stars

V.C. ANDREWS®

Whitefern

POCKET BOOKS

New York   London   Toronto   Sydney   New Delhi

Pocket Books
An Imprint of Simon & Schuster, Inc.
1230 Avenue of the Americas
New York, NY 10020

Following the death of Virginia Andrews, the Andrews family worked with a carefully selected writer to organize and complete Virginia Andrews's stories and to create additional novels, of which this is one, inspired by her storytelling genius.

This book is a work of fiction. Any references to historical events, real people, or real places are used fictitiously. Other names, characters, places, and events are products of the author's imagination, and any resemblance to actual events or places or persons, living or dead, is entirely coincidental.

For Mary and Joan Andrews,
who help keep the faith

Prologue

Papa died with my name on his lips. I would have thought his final words would be a call for my sister, Sylvia, or for Lucietta, our mother, who had died giving birth to Sylvia. For years afterward, I would think about the way he had said my name in those final moments. Was his call to me a plea for help, or was he begging for forgiveness? Was it merely pleasure at having his last thoughts be about me? Did he see my much younger face before him?

Arden, Sylvia, and I were there in his bedroom when he took his last breath. Sylvia and I were sitting beside the bed. Sylvia held his hand, and my husband, Arden, standing beside me, had his hand on my shoulder, his fingers drumming with impatience. He had been on his way out the door to go to work when Papa took a sudden turn for the worse. Of course, he'd thought it was another false alarm, but he quickly returned and saw that this time, it was very, very serious.

The ticking of the dark oak miniature grandfather's clock on the dresser seemed to grow louder and louder, impressing us with every passing moment. I imagined it was like Papa's heartbeat. I would swear that it paused when Papa took his final breath. A cloud passed over the sun, and a shadow rushed in through the windows and fell like a dark sheet over his body and his face. I felt a shawl of ice slip over my shoulders as Arden lifted his hand away.

The week before, Papa had nearly passed out going up the stairs. His eyes had closed, and he'd swayed almost at the top step. Sylvia had been following him up, just as she often followed at his heels, eager to do his bidding, and that had kept him from falling backward. A fatal accident on those stairs would come as no surprise. They'd already had too much tragic history. Sylvia's scream had brought me running. I'd seen her hands on his back. Before I could reach them, he had regained his composure, the color coming back into his pale face.

"I'm all right," he had said, but without admitting that something wrong with him had caused him to lose his balance, he also declared that Sylvia had saved his life.

"We should call the doctor," I had said.

"Nonsense, no need. Everyone loses his balance occasionally. Maybe a little too much blackberry brandy."

It was futile to contradict him or insist. Papa never changed his mind about anything once he had made it up. My aunt Ellsbeth would say, "He's as stubborn as a tree stump when he digs his roots into an argument."

Nevertheless, at his insistence, we had celebrated Sylvia as a heroine at dinner that night. I was told to make her favorite cake, vanilla with chocolate icing. We had champagne and, later, music so Papa could do a little dance with her. While I'd watched them, I'd been reminded of how he would waltz with my mother sometimes after dinner when they were young, and our world would look like a world of eternal spring. Momma's peals of laughter and joy would echo off the walls. The only one who scowled would be Aunt Ellsbeth.

Sylvia had been so happy when Papa called her "my little heroine." She'd loved repeating, "I saved Papa," every morning for days afterward; it was the first thing she'd say to me when I roused her to dress and come down for breakfast. Compliments and applause were rare birds in her nest. Perhaps she thought she could do it again the day he died, save him and keep him from falling into the inevitable grave. She clung so tightly to his hand.

Arden often called her "your father's extra shadow," but he wasn't saying that because he thought what she was doing was cute or loving. No, he thought it was both annoying for Papa and embarrassing for us, mainly for him, whenever anyone he knew from work saw this grown woman still so attached to her father, sensitive to his every move, eager to do the simplest things for him, like fetching his slippers or lighting his pipe.

"He can't even go to the bathroom without her waiting for him at the door like a puppy. Can't you make her see how foolish she looks? Do something!" Arden had demanded. "You're the one she'll listen to."

"Papa doesn't mind," I'd said in Sylvia's defense, "so you shouldn't, either."

Papa never did complain, nor did he ever criticize my sister or make her feel silly or foolish. If anything, he liked females hounding him. I had no illusions about my father. He was always a woman's man. He would always flirt, even with me when I was older. Of course, Sylvia was special. Perhaps he should have tried harder to have her become less dependent on him. A girl can love her father, adore him, but at some point, she has to step out into the world with independence, or she will not mature and enjoy what other love awaits her.

No one, including me, had much confidence in Sylvia developing an independent existence or finding the love of another man. She had been born prematurely and was mentally slow. Once everyone viewed her that way, she'd become comfortable with that image. She liked being babied so much that she never tried too hard to become a mature woman with a mature woman's responsibilities. At least, that was my theory. Everyone criticized me for it. Arden, in fact, once accused me of being jealous of my father's affection for her.

"Maybe you think he'll turn her into 'my sweet Sylvia' or create a Sylvia Two," he said, with that wry smile on his face that usually irritated me. "He thinks he's God and can change anyone to his liking."

But accusing me of jealousy wasn't fair. With the exception of my father, no one ever loved or treated my sister more tenderly than I did. She used to follow me around the way she was then following him. Perhaps that was why I didn't openly criticize her or try to get her to be less fawning. Many times, I was tempted to do what Arden wanted and tell her to stop clinging so hard to our father. *Let Papa breathe*, I wanted to say, but I swallowed back the words. She probably wouldn't have understood it, and if it was explained to her, I was afraid she would go into one of her hysterical fits of sobbing and others would accuse me of the same thing Arden had. I feared even Papa would admonish me.

So when I saw Papa die in front of us, I looked quickly at Sylvia, anticipating an outburst of sorrow from her.

But then I realized she had no idea he was gone. She still clung to his hand. She shook it softly, expecting him to open his eyes and smile at her as he had done only minutes ago.

I put my arm around her. "He's gone, Sylvia," I said, my lips trembling and tears streaming down my cheeks. "Papa has passed on. You have to let go of his hand. He's gone."

She looked at me, scowled, and then looked back at him, but she didn't move, nor did she let go of his hand. The words apparently made no sense to her. I knew what she was thinking: *How can he be gone if he is still here in his bed?* Sylvia always took everything literally, expecting the truth to be straightforward, the way children did.

I looked to Dr. Prescott. He was frustrated because he had come too late, and he sat on the other side of the bed, his hands pressed against his cheeks, his shock of graying brown hair as wild as weeds from running his thick fingers through it with frustration. He was only a year younger than Papa, but lately, he'd looked ten years younger and was far sprier. He wasn't as tall as Papa; few men were. But these last months, he had looked taller.

The kind doctor raised his head to look at us, his eyes swimming in sorrow far beyond what any doctor would experience after losing a patient. Physicians, probably more than anyone, lived with the inevitability of death. It was like dogs barking at their heels. He leaned over and closed Papa's eyes. Then he gently took Papa's hand from Sylvia's and put it over Papa's now-still chest and then his other hand over that.

"I told him he needed a stent. I finally had him convinced to go into the hospital . . . this Monday," Dr. Prescott said, shaking his head and looking down at Papa. "But I knew he would put it off again and again. Stubborn man."

He had rushed over after I called to tell him Papa wasn't feeling well and was weak and pale. I'd mentioned he was having trouble breathing. Dr. Prescott had thought we should send for an ambulance, but Papa had gotten so upset about it I had to call back and tell him that I was afraid Papa's anger would just make him sicker and that Sylvia and I had helped him to bed.

"Okay, I'm on my way," he'd replied. He was more than just Papa's doctor. He and Papa were good friends and lately had spent at least one night a week playing chess, drinking brandy, and talking about their youth. On more than one occasion, I had overheard Papa's conversation drift into a sea of guilt, on which floated many regrettable actions and decisions. Maybe it was the effect of the brandy or maybe because he was getting older, but he'd sought opportunities to confess his sins.

His biggest one, as far as he and I were concerned, was his elaborate plan to convince me when I was a child that I was the older sister of my dead sister, Audrina, the perfect little girl after whom I was supposedly named.

Back then, Papa would often have me close my eyes and rock in the first Audrina's rocking chair, supposedly to capture some of her gifts and memories, the most horrid of which was her being raped at the age of nine. He knew all the memories would return, for they were really my memories. Whether or not I wanted to believe that there were good intentions behind this deception, the result was that it gave birth to more sadness and tragedy than any family should have to bear.

Papa had known that, and the knowledge had weighed on him so heavily as he grew older that his once strong and perfect manly body began to crumble, his shoulders turning in, his back bent more and more, his walk slower and unsteady, his six-foot-five frame looking so much shorter and fragile. Gray had devastated his unique black hair, which used to appear blue in the sunlight but no longer did, and his lively, sexy, almond-shaped dark brown eyes had dulled and begun to look sleepy and forlorn.

He had started to go to work less often at the brokerage firm, finally acquiescing to letting Arden take on more and more responsibility there. Occasionally,

he would argue with and discuss some of the decisions
Arden had made, decisions that would drive him to
return to work more frequently, often to correct them.
However, during the past few weeks, it had seemed to
me that my father had lost interest in almost everything. Lately, he'd spent more of his time sitting on
our front porch, even when it was raining or there was
a thick fog, bitterly staring out at the world as though
it had deceived him. I would try to cheer him up, bring
him his favorite freshly baked cookies or a cup of tea,
even a brandy, but he would show little enthusiasm.
Only Sylvia could bring a smile to his face during
those last days. He'd pet her and stroke her, and I was
sure he would be thinking of our mother. Despite how
angry he could get at her from time to time, he had
surely loved our mother more than he'd loved—or
could love—any woman.

As Sylvia had grown, she did look more like our
mother than I did. I'd spent as much time as I could
helping her develop into someone who could care for
herself. She was so dependent on the kindness of others,
even to this day. Whenever any of Papa and Arden's
clients came to dinner with their wives, the wives always brought Sylvia something pretty, whether it was
costume jewelry, ribbons, or delicious boxes of candy.
On those nights, there was laughter and music, and
no one dared mention a single sad moment from our
past. Good things still could happen in our house, but
that was never enough to drown out the bad completely. Those memories refused to be forgotten or
buried.

Guilt, in fact, hovered in every corner of White-fern, our family home, like invisible spiderwebs trapping every happy thought to make sure that un-happiness dominated our lives. I had wanted to run from the mansion and never set foot in it again when I learned the horrible truths that had been whirling around me all my life. The grave for the so-called "first Audrina" was in the Whitefern Cemetery nearby, a grave I was taken to often to visit and hear about this mythical sister. The grave was, in fact, empty. What an elaborate ruse. Who wouldn't want to get as far away from it all as fast as she could?

I had to find a deep well of forgiveness from which to draw the understanding and tolerance that would enable me to continue to live here, to accept Arden again, to pity my father and even my ruthless, jealous cousin Vera, who, I discovered, really was what she claimed to be, my half sister. She became one of the fatal victims in this house, along with Aunt Ellsbeth and Billie, Arden's mother. They'd all fallen down the stairway to their deaths, every one of them ruled an accident. It was as if Whitefern wanted to dole out justice or attack deception and had the power to do so. Maybe such thoughts had flashed through Papa's mind when he stumbled backward on the stairway.

It wasn't difficult to accept the idea that my fam-ily home was alive and conscious of all the intrigue and pain that went on within it. It was and remained right up to today an impressive Victorian gingerbread house. Arden had organized some restoration, having it repainted white and all the blinds redone, in addition to the outside steps. Recently, a house not unlike ours in the Tidewater region of Virginia had suffered a tragedy when two women were out on a balcony that gave way without warning. They'd fallen three stories, and both had died. This had prompted Arden to get to work immediately on ours, firming things up but adhering to Papa's orders to keep the style.

Years ago, Papa had repaired the roof. He would do what was necessary, especially when he had made more money. But there were areas now that needed refurbishing and remodeling, and Papa wouldn't give permission to do it. It wasn't all about money. Arden had insisted that much of the structure was now an embarrassment, especially because we entertained so many wealthy clients, but Papa had said he saw some of the wear and tear as contributing to the house's vintage character.

He had especially never wanted to change anything about the cupola, which had windows of stained leaded glass with scenes that represented the angels of life and death. It had held too much history for him. I remembered how pleased he'd been to see the sunlight thread through the stained-glass windows and fall in swirls like bright peacock feathers. There was even a long rectangle of painted glass in the roof. Chinese wind chimes hung from scarlet silken cords. It was still true to every original detail. This had been precious to Papa.

Actually, he had fought against changing any of Whitefern's decor, no matter what reasons Arden presented. When my husband would turn to me for support in these debates, I'd always try to remain neutral.

Despite all that Papa had done to me, I couldn't hurt him, even in the smallest way. Consequently, not a single lamp was removed, nor were stronger bulbs put in any of them, even if they didn't provide enough light. It was as if Papa had been too comfortable with the shadows and would not drive one away.

At one point, Arden had wanted to replace our art, to sell some of the older pictures to take advantage of their escalating values and invest the money in stocks. But regardless of the financial reasons, Papa had resisted that, too. Some of the paintings were startling in their depictions of women. Papa had been particularly fascinated by the picture of a naked woman lying on a chaise and dropping grapes into her mouth. It reeked of sex, I thought, and certainly intrigued every dinner guest or visitor. Even as a young girl, I saw the lust in the eyes of the men who stood before it, smiling licentiously. I couldn't imagine the wall without that painting.

Some of the furniture had been replaced simply because it fell apart, but most of it was considered antique. Papa had replaced whatever was fake with the real thing. I remembered my mother proudly describing the bed in her room as five hundred years old. Perhaps it was an exaggeration, but it certainly looked like a bed for a queen. I could never imagine selling it, and whenever Arden talked about refurbishing one room or another, I felt a pang of sadness and regret. It was like giving up old friends. When I told Arden as much, he laughed and called me a hopeless romantic. However, Papa had been happy I felt this way, which pleased me, even though it was a great disappointment to Arden when his wife was unsupportive.

Once I'd told him, "You can't change the past by changing wallpaper or furniture, Arden. You've got to stop trying. We have to live with it as best we can. It's not easy for me, especially, but we must."

And that was what we did, both of us avoiding memories stirred by any references to my mother, to the piano she played, to Aunt Ellsbeth, and also to Billie, Arden's mother. Vera's name was almost a curse word now. If there was the slightest allusion to her, Arden would blush with guilt. His eyes would flee from mine, and he would find a way to quickly change the subject.

Oh, how did this house and the people living in it bear up under the weight of such pain and horror? Surely that proved it had the foundation to continue eternally, strong enough to hold up the world, like Atlas. It was a magnet for the soul, holding us within its radius. There was always a sense of relief now whenever I returned from a trip or even a simple shopping expedition. It loomed before me, its doors and windows beckoning, urging me to get inside and feel the power of its protection against a cold and heartless world.

Sylvia was twenty the year Papa died. She was still like a child, even though she had a more than ample bosom and her body had carved into a figure most women would envy. Her hair was as pretty as mine. I often thought Sylvia had a healthier, richer complexion. She looked as if she might stay young forever, as if her mind not maturing meant that her body would stay frozen in its beauty.

Not socially mature enough, Sylvia had been kept at home during her school years rather than being sent to a place where we'd thought she would suffer at the hands of other students and also some teachers, who would be impatient with and intolerant of her. Instead, Papa and I had decided she should be tutored at home, as I had been for my first years. Maybe because of what had happened to me, Papa had wanted her to be kept close, protected.

Sometimes, when I would watch her with Papa and see the delight in his eyes, I would admit to myself that Arden was right. I was jealous of how much more Papa loved her than he loved me, even when he thought of me as the first Audrina. If I ever dared mention such a thought, he surely would deny it, of course, but anyone would have to be blind not to see the way his face lit up when Sylvia entered the room after I had.

"You must always look after your sister," he had told me often. "Promise you'll never put her into one of those homes for mentally deficient children."

I'd promised. Of course I'd promised.

But the day would come when I would question the wisdom of that, when I would blame myself for what happened.

If anyone should have known it would, it should have been I, the best and only sweet Audrina.

Darkness before the Light

Papa would rest beside our mother, both just a few feet from the false grave that bore my name. Because Sylvia was taking Papa's death worse than any of us, I spent most of my time with her during the days that immediately followed, and Arden handled the arrangements for the funeral. In the course of doing that, he suffered a big shock. He met with Papa's attorney, Mr. Johnson, and learned that Papa had recently changed his will; he had left everything to the two of us and to Sylvia, as expected, but he had given me fifty-one percent ownership of the brokerage.

Arden returned home in a rage after the meeting. I hadn't attended because I thought, as he did, that it was not going to be anything significant.

"Why did he do this?" he ranted, marching up and down in front of Sylvia and me and waving his arms as violently as if he wanted to throw off his hands. He clutched a copy of the paperwork in his right hand. "Why? Why? I'll tell you why. He knew how much I knew about his earlier dealings, the graft and corruption." He paused as he thought more about it.

"Sure, that's it. Of course. He did this to punish me for confronting him with his dishonesty years ago. How stupid to use you for his revenge."

"It wasn't revenge," I said, shocked but feeling like someone had to stick up for poor Papa. "He was worried about the way you were spending money and not concentrating on the work. All those nights you were out drinking while he went to bed early so he could greet the opening stock market."

"That's . . . an exaggeration. I was at work doing what had to be done when it had to be done. You're getting me off the point. You don't really know anything about our business."

"Papa always told me I was very smart. I knew enough to help you start, remember?"

"That was the basics that anyone would know. How can you vote on major decisions? You could count on your fingers how many times you've been there these past few years. You don't even know my secretary's name."

"Yes, I do. Mrs. Crown, Nora Crown."

He paused and glared at me. "Now, you listen and listen hard, Audrina. I want you to go to Mr. Johnson's office after the funeral and sign over everything to me. I'll call him and have the proper paperwork drawn up and ready for your signature so we can reverse this . . . this stupidity."

He waited for my response. I was holding Sylvia's hand, and we were both looking at him, surprised. Even poor Sylvia could sense it, his contempt. This was not the time to rage about anything, especially

Papa. We were in mourning. It was disrespectful to Papa's memory. Maybe I didn't know as much as Arden did about the business that Papa had built and brought him into, but I had Papa's grit and determination. I could learn anything.

"I'll think about it, Arden," I said softly. "When the time is proper."

"Think about it? Think about what?"

"Lower your voice. You're frightening Sylvia," I told him.

He barely gave her a glance. "Lower my voice? You've barely ever looked at the stock market these past years. You've probably forgotten the difference between a put and a call, selling short and buying on margin. The man was obviously not in his right mind when he had our attorney do this. If it wasn't out of some revenge, then it was because he was sick. That's it. He was sick. His brain wasn't getting enough blood, which was why he wasn't capable of thinking straight. Dr. Prescott will testify to that, and Mr. Johnson will agree."

"There was nothing wrong with Papa's mind. And you know that he spent a lot of time with me explaining the stock market when I was younger. It's not something you forget quickly. He thought it was a good way to teach math."

"Oh, boy, teaching a child math through the market. Like that makes you a broker."

"I didn't say it made me a broker. But he did take me to the brokerage and even announced that I would be his partner someday when he had his own company."

"He just wished he had a son to inherit everything. Every man wants that. I became his son. He said that to me after he married my mother. Or at least, I thought I had become his son. What father would do this to his son?" he asked, waving the papers in our faces.

"Stop it. Stop saying those things. I don't like talking about going against his orders while his body is waiting for burial."

"Against his orders? Don't make me laugh. You think you could choose stocks for our clients the way you thought you could pick winners when you were a child? Tying your birthstone ring to a string and dangling it over a list of stocks in the paper until it pointed to the right one?"

"I did that, and Papa made money on the stock. You yourself were not so very good at it in the beginning. Did you forget?"

"Please!" he cried. "I was learning, whereas all you Whitefern women were crazy with your beliefs in magic . . . hoodoo, voodoo . . . paying that psychic to predict whether your mother would have a boy or a girl."

"I'm sorry I told you that story."

"I bet. Well, hear this, Audrina. There's no magic in our business. It takes knowledge and experience. You don't really have either when it comes to the stock market, especially today. It's too sophisticated. You'd do no better than . . . than *her*!" he screamed, pointing at Sylvia.

Sylvia began to cry.

"Don't point at her like that. She doesn't understand!" I shouted back at him. That only upset her more. Anyone arguing in the house put her into a panic.

"You don't understand, either," he snapped back. "You don't understand how I feel being made a fool of like this. You can feel sorry for . . . for that," he said, pointing at Sylvia again, "but not for your husband!"

Sylvia's sobbing increased, and her body shook.

"Look what you've done!" I cried. "I've been keeping her calm. It hasn't been easy."

I put my arm around my sister and began to comfort her again. Since Papa's death, she would break out into crying jags and then howl with pain whenever there was any mention of Papa's passing. Every condolence phone call was like an electric shock. She would barely eat and wandered from room to room, expecting to find him. Every night, she called to him in her sleep, and every night, I ended up sleeping in her bed with her, her head on my breast, her tears dampening my nightgown.

"You know what? This is insane. I can't believe I'm even discussing it," Arden said, and he marched angrily out of the living room, his arms stiffly at his sides, his hands clenched in fists.

We hardly said another word to each other until the funeral. I had my hands full caring for Sylvia anyway. I was terrified of how she would behave at the service, but fortunately, she was in more of a state of disbelief than one of mourning. She even looked surprised that we were there in the church listening to the sermon and the eulogy. Every once in a while, she would gaze around the church, searching for Papa, especially whenever his name was uttered.

There were many businessmen in the Tidewater area who knew and liked my father very much. And of course, there were many community leaders who also knew him, so we anticipated a big attendance.

"Where is everyone? How can they not pay Papa the respect he deserves?" I asked Arden when I saw that no one else was coming and the service was about to begin.

He turned his amber-colored eyes on me. They were sparkling, but not with tears, the way I was sure mine were. His looked more excited than sad.

"Many of his friends and older clients have died. Besides, people always think, 'The king is dead. Long live the king.'"

"What does that mean, Arden? You're the new king, so they don't care about Papa anymore?"

"Something like that," he said. "After all, he can't do anything more for them, but I can." He patted himself on his chest.

Then he smiled, and for the first time, I realized that Arden wasn't as upset about Papa's death as I thought he should be. He was the head of the household now, and he thought he didn't need anyone else's permission to do whatever he wanted.

Then Arden surprised me by getting up to say a few words, honoring Papa for building such a successful business and promising everyone that he would do his best to uphold, protect, and further develop what

Papa had begun. The speech ended up being more of an assurance to our customers that he would keep the business successful than it was an homage to Papa.

When he was finished, he walked back to his seat beside me, his eyes searching my face for admiration and obedience, but instead, I turned away.

"You could put aside your grief for a moment and compliment me," he whispered, "especially in front of these people. I am your husband, the head of the household, dedicated to protecting you and Sylvia. I deserve respect, more respect, now."

"Today is Papa's day," I said. That was all I said, but it was enough.

He turned away and didn't even hold my hand at the grave site. I had my arm around Sylvia, who finally began to realize what was happening.

"Audrina, we can't leave Papa down there," she said when we were about to leave the cemetery.

The funeral workers would fill the grave after we all left. It was far too painful for me, and for Sylvia, to watch that. Arden had thrown the first shovelful of dirt onto Papa's lowered coffin. Although it was meant to be symbolic, it seemed to me he did it eagerly, even joyfully.

I could feel Sylvia's body tighten. She whispered, "Nooooo," but I tightened my arm around her and kept her from charging forward to stop him or anyone else from covering the coffin.

I practically had to drag her away and at one point looked to Arden for help, but he was too busy shaking hands with those who had come to the burial. He was behaving as if he was conducting just another business meeting. I even heard him mention some investment to Jonathan Logan, one of Papa's oldest clients, claiming that before he died, Papa had told him to tell Jonathan about it.

More people came to our house than to the church or the cemetery. I overheard that Arden had Mrs. Crown contact clients to give them the details of the funeral, but also to make sure they knew that if the church service conflicted with something they'd rather do, they were more than welcome to come to the house instead. He was treating it more like a party. I knew that people needed to avoid excessive grief and needed hope more than depression, but the way Arden was organizing things, I was almost expecting a band and dancing girls to show up.

Arden's boisterous conversations and continuous laughter stung. The whole thing confused Sylvia, who sometimes looked as if she might attack someone for smiling. I thought it best to get her up to her room, telling her to change and then lie down.

"You don't realize how tired you are," I said.

She looked afraid to close her eyes, but eventually she did, and she fell asleep quickly.

When I went back downstairs, I was confronted again with loud laughter and conversation that had grown more raucous. More people had arrived. Arden had arranged for a bartender and two maids to serve hors d'oeuvres. I was determined to be polite, not festive. Many of the men greeted me with quick condolences but, thinking they had to, moved instantly to assure me that my husband was capable of carrying on.

"After all, he was trained by an expert," Rolf Nestor, one of Papa's high-net-worth clients, told me. "You can be very proud of him."

Others said similar things to me, and when Arden, standing off to the side, overheard them, I could see his pleased, arrogant glare. Eventually, too physically and emotionally drained to remain, I excused myself.

"Of course, darling Audrina," Arden said, loudly enough for everyone in the room to hear. "You've done more than enough for any father to be proud of you. He died knowing you would be well cared for, and you will be," he vowed.

I saw the way the women were looking at him admiringly, and the men were nodding. It was not too different from the way they would look at Papa when he was younger and more energetic. Ironically, Arden was becoming more like Papa, the man he supposedly despised now.

I said nothing. My heart was heavy. When I went upstairs, I checked on Sylvia first. She was dead asleep. Out of habit, and maybe because I wanted to convince myself that this was not all a terrible nightmare, I opened the door to my father's bedroom and stood there full of wishful thinking. I imagined him propped up with two of his oversize pillows, his glasses slipping down the bridge of his nose, reading some economic charts or some company's profit-and-loss statement. In his final years, although he was working less, he'd kept up the research and preparation to make sure that Arden made no significant blunders in his absence, the way he had in the beginning. In fact, now that I thought about it more, I could understand why he had wanted to keep Arden from galloping off with the company and thought that perhaps having the majority of the company's shares in my favor would make Arden more cautious. Papa always chose to be more conservative with other people's money. He hated to be blamed for losses.

Of course, the room was dark, the bed was empty, and the cold reality rushed back at me. I did all I could to keep from fainting and made my way quickly to our bedroom, changed into my nightgown, and slipped under the covers. Despite my fatigue, I thought I was going to lie there for hours and hours sobbing and staring into the darkness.

Memories flowed freely around me. I could hear my mother playing the piano. I could see Papa's look of admiration and love and also jealousy at the way other men looked at her, even when she was pregnant with Sylvia. I saw him reach for me so I would rush to him and sit on his lap when I was very little. We would both listen to Momma play. Out of the corner of my eye, I saw Aunt Ellsbeth standing in the doorway, holding Vera's hand. Both looked envious but for different reasons. Vera was always jealous of the love Papa showered on me, and Ellsbeth was simply jealous of her beautiful sister, who seemed to possess everything any woman would dream of having. She was always angry that Whitefern had been left mainly to my mother and not to her.

They tried not to say unpleasant things directly to each other. I recalled how they pretended to be Aunt Mercy Marie and used their imitations of her at their special Tuesday "teatimes" to let loose all the venom toward each other that they usually held back. Aunt Mercy Marie's picture was on the piano. She looked like a queen, wealthy, with diamonds hanging from her ears. Aunt Ellsbeth would hold the picture up in front of her and change her voice to say nasty things, and Momma would do the same. I was still unsure about what had eventually happened to my great-aunt after she had gone to Africa. The family thought it was possible she had been captured by heathens and eaten by cannibals.

It was all those conflicting memories that finally drove me to the edge of exhaustion and pushed me into sleep, a sleep so deep that I didn't hear Arden come up much later. What woke me was the stench of alcohol. He was being clumsy, too, and quite inconsiderate, banging into chairs, mumbling loudly, slamming a glass down on a shelf in the bathroom, and then practically falling into the bed so that my body bounced as if I were on a trampoline.

"Are you awake?" he asked. "Huh?"

I tried to pretend I was not, but he nudged me. "What?"

"You heard them."

"Heard who?"

"Our clients. You see how important it is that the business be completely under my control now," he said, sounding sober. "We can't give anyone the impression that we're not as solid as ever. If they so much as suspected someone without real knowledge of today's market was involved in their business, they'd leave us in droves. We have to talk about this, and you must do what I tell you."

"We'll talk tomorrow," I said.

"Ah, tomorrow . . . tomorrow . . . Your father wasn't in his right mind, I tell you. Well? Well?"

I wouldn't answer him.

Finally, he turned onto his side, his back to me. I was trying to fall asleep again, but then he muttered, "Your sister was crying hysterically in your father's room."

"What?"

He didn't respond.

"What did you say?" I sat up. Still, he didn't respond. In a moment, he was snoring.

I got up and found my robe and slippers. Then I went to Papa's bedroom. The door was open again, but when I looked in, I didn't see Sylvia. I turned on a light and even looked into Papa's bathroom, but she wasn't there. Arden must have imagined it in his drunken stupor, I concluded, and I turned off the lights. Instead of returning to bed, I went to Sylvia's room.

For a few moments, I stood in her doorway and peered into the darkness. The curtains at the windows had been left open, but the sky was overcast. There wasn't even any starlight. In fact, I thought I heard the tinkling of raindrops against the glass. I stepped in and immediately saw that Sylvia was not in her bed. I checked her bathroom, and then hurried downstairs.

The living room had been cleaned up halfheartedly. Spilled drinks and bits of food were everywhere; there would be a lot of work to do tomorrow. Sylvia wasn't there.

I headed for the kitchen. Maybe she had gone down for a snack, since she had eaten nothing. There were many nights when I had found her doing just that. Sometimes Papa would be with her, and they would both be having a piece of cake or cookies with milk or tea. I assumed she'd recalled those nights and had gone to the kitchen, driven by memories.

But she wasn't there, either.

"Sylvia?" I called. I checked every room, every bathroom. Growing frantic now, I hurried up to the cupola, but that was empty, too.

The realization thundered around me. Sylvia wasn't in the house! I thought about waking Arden to tell him, but when I looked in on him, he was snoring even louder. He'd be of no help and grumpy for sure, I thought. But where was she? Where would she go?

I went to the closet in the entryway and put on one of my overcoats. Taking an umbrella, I stepped out and looked for her on the porch.

"Sylvia?" I cried. "Where are you? Sylvia?"

The rain was coming down harder, and the wind was now icy. A thick fog had blanketed the grounds and the woods. It was late October, but fall was obviously being crushed by a heavy oncoming winter. I realized I was still in my slippers, so I returned to the entryway closet and took out a pair of Papa's black leather boots. My feet swam in them, but I was able to walk out and down the stairs with the umbrella shielding me somewhat. I had no idea where to look. Over and over, I called out her name. She wasn't anywhere nearby. Where could she be? Then a terrifying possibility seemed to rush out of the bitter darkness and wash over me.

"Oh, Sylvia," I muttered. "Poor Sylvia."

I hurried down the path and through the woods as fast as I could, the rain soaking my face, but I was too frightened to feel the cold now. It was a long walk, a walk I couldn't imagine her taking, but about a dozen yards from the cemetery, I heard it—a shovel—and I broke into a run, clomping along in Papa's oversize boots and nearly falling a few times.

Finally, I was there and saw her, in only her nightgown, digging away at Papa's grave, the rain soaking her so that she looked as good as naked.

"Sylvia!" I screamed. "What are you doing?"

She paused and turned to me. "We can't leave him down there," she said. "Papa. It's cold and dark. We can't leave him, Audrina. Just like we didn't leave you."

"No . . . oh, no, Sylvia. I was never dead. Papa *is* dead. Papa needs to stay there. He needs to stay near Momma."

I reached for the shovel. She held on to it tightly.

"Please, Sylvia, leave Papa to rest in peace. You're going to get pneumonia out here. He would be very angry at you."

"Angry? Papa? At me?"

"Yes, very. And mad at me for letting you do this. He's probably screaming at us now. Come on. Come back to the house. I need to get you into a warm bath. Come on," I said, more forcefully, and I pulled the shovel out of her grip.

She stumbled, and I put my arm around her waist, threw the shovel down, and, holding the umbrella above both of us as best I could, led her out of the cemetery and quickly back to the house. It was raining even harder. It seemed to take longer to get home. A few times, she paused to turn back, but I overpowered her and warned her again that Papa would be angry.

When I finally got her inside, I helped her out of her soaked nightgown and used some towels from the powder room to dry her off. After I had taken off my coat and Papa's boots, I led her up the stairs and to her bedroom, setting her on her bed while I ran her bath. Once she was submerged in the warm water, I washed her neck and shoulders and gave her hair a quick shampoo. She was quiet now, seeming very tired.

I stood up and took off my own damp nightgown. The tub was big enough for the two of us. We had taken baths together occasionally. I ran some more hot water. She opened her eyes when I got in and sat facing her.

"Audrina," she said insistently, "you came out of your grave. Papa can come out of his, too."

I closed my eyes. How would I ever get her to understand when half the time I didn't understand myself? "Not tonight," I said. That answer would have to do for now. "Not tonight."

We sat soaking for nearly half an hour, and after

we got out and dried ourselves off, we put on new nightgowns. I blow-dried her hair and mine, and then I crawled into bed beside her.

Which was where Arden found us both in the morning, sleeping, embracing each other, probably looking like two lovers to him.

"Hey," he said when I opened my eyes. "When did you come in here? Are you going to do this every night? I'll get a bigger bed, and the three of us can sleep together."

Instinctively, I pulled away from Sylvia. "Stop it, Arden. This wasn't funny. It was terrible."

"What was?"

"What she did last night . . . and in the cold rain! It's quite a story."

"Yeah, well, I have quite a story to tell, too. I'm going to work. The stock market doesn't pay attention to personal sorrow. I'll call our attorney, and we'll talk later."

"That's disrespectful, Arden. No one expects you to be in the office so soon, and you certainly should not call Mr. Johnson today."

"Death is disrespectful," he replied, and closed the door between us.

I heard him pound down the stairs, mumbling to himself.

I hoped that strangers would see his rage as a result of his sorrow and not his ambition, not that it would matter to the people our business relied on, apparently. Our wealthy clients probably believed they could buy off death itself.

The business had changed Arden, I thought. It was almost impossible now to recall the young man who was so devoted to his mother, an Olympic ice skater who had suffered from diabetes and lost her legs. So much had happened since, and so much had changed him. Papa must have realized it, and that must have been why he put that codicil in his will.

But how could I defy my husband and bring him to his senses, even if only to obey my father, who was dead and gone?

How could Papa expect me to step into his shoes and be as strong as he was?

What had he seen in me that I had yet to see in myself?

What had he seen looming on the horizon?

What could possibly be worse than the horrors fate already had chosen to rain down on Whitefern?

The Pain of Memory

I feared I would spend most of my days immediately following Papa's death listening to echoes trapped in every dark corner. I resisted as best I could, but it was difficult to shut them out. I had done that successfully for a while when I was a little girl who had been sexually and violently ravaged. But there would be no comfort from amnesia now.

Perhaps this was why Papa had left me the controlling interest in his business. He knew this might happen to me, and he wanted me to have a path away from it all. He finally wanted me to find a life outside of this house and its dreadful memories. There were many times when he was proud of me, proud of my comments and ideas. Maybe he had come to believe that a girl could carry on her father's successes as well as a boy could. Arden simply didn't fit the bill for him.

If I didn't do something more, if I relegated myself only to household chores and caring for Sylvia, the past with all its tragedies would surely weigh me down. I'd grow old before my time, just as Papa had. I wouldn't neglect Sylvia and her needs, but I had needs, too. Arden must come to realize that, I thought. He must learn to see our marriage as more of a partnership. I must convince him that doing so would not diminish him.

He was so angry. He seemed so changed. When he was younger, living in the cottage with his mother, he was sweet and considerate. I never knew then how much of a role his guilt from witnessing and not fighting to prevent what had happened to me played until he finally confessed. Was he still burdened with that guilt? Had he grown tired of it and resorted to anger as an alternative? He did seem to have a chip on his shoulder these days. I suspected Papa never let him forget.

Of course, I had to overlook his affair with my half sister, Vera. His confessions were so heartfelt that I did blame Vera more than him. She was always there, trying to outshine me.

These memories and more drummed at the door, now that Papa had died. It was no longer necessary to avoid reminding him of the past. Death had trounced that concern. I hated the idea that I might spend my days reliving all the pain, that his death had opened the floodgates. Again, I told myself that what was important now, now that I was living in Whitefern without Papa, was finding a new sense of myself while still caring for Sylvia. I would have to be reborn yet again and become a third Audrina.

I realized that I must ignore, even bury, the fragile young woman who had seen and heard more than most could bear. There were many times when I would actually envy Sylvia for being immature and unaware of the significance of most things. How soft and comfortable was her childlike world. Most of the pain she had suffered, a great deal of it at Vera's hands, was lost to her. Back then, she greeted every new day by acting as if yesterday didn't matter. She could smile and expect good things, even from a world that had given her only bad.

Was that simply a result of her immaturity? Maturity meant many unexpected things. When you were an adult, there was no time to float about in a pond of wishes. There was only time to do, to be productive, to overcome obstacles. There were choices that once could be ignored or at least put off but now demanded attention and wouldn't sit patiently waiting for you to act when you felt like it. That childlike world was the world in which Sylvia still lived.

I thought about all this the next day, pausing only to make lunch for her and occasionally playing a board game with her to keep her from thinking. It was clear she still had not accepted Papa's death. I seriously wondered if she ever would. She kept looking at the front door, expecting him to come home and cry out, "Where's my Sylvia? Who's bringing me my slippers?" Sometimes she used to wait at the front windows for his car to appear. When he was late, she would grow fidgety and needed to be reassured that he was coming home.

"Papa told me he wanted lamb chops tonight," she suddenly said while we were playing checkers. I always let her win. I looked at the clock. It was nearly three o'clock, about the time I would plan dinner. Where that tidbit of information came from I didn't know, but it wasn't unusual for her to come up with something someone said months, even years, ago. It was as if words bounced around in her childlike mind like balloons and suddenly found voice again.

"You must try to remember what happened to Papa, Sylvia," I told her softly. "It's important. We all have to be strong, the way he would have wanted us to be. You want to be strong, don't you?"

She looked like she was going to go into one of her pouts but suddenly smiled with the burst of a new idea. "Let's go to the cemetery," she said. I had the eerie feeling that she expected we'd see an open grave and an open coffin. In her mind, Papa was capable of a resurrection, just like Jesus.

I reached for her hand. "Nothing will be different there, Sylvia. I've already asked Mr. Ralph to go there and fill in the holes you dug."

Mr. Ralph, our groundskeeper, was the most trusted servant anyone could dream of having. He bore no relationship to the Whiteferns, the Adares, or the Lowes, but he had been with my family since he was about fifteen. He was more than seventy-five now, although no one would swear to his exact age, even him, and he was a little deaf, with fading eyesight. All his friends were gone or had moved away, he said. His whole life was caring for our property. He had always been fond and protective of Papa, but I thought he was more afraid than fond of Arden.

"We'll visit the cemetery when it's right to do so, and we'll say prayers for Papa at his grave, okay?" I added quickly.

She pulled her hand back, looking angry as only she could, her beautiful eyes darkening into gray, her lips tightening, with pale spots interfering with their natural ruby tint. She liked to put on lipstick whenever I did, but she really didn't need it.

"I have a secret," she said, her body recoiling like a spring. "Only Papa and I know it. Not Arden, not you."

"Then maybe you should not tell anyone else," I said, a little annoyed at her. Her look reminded me too much of Vera whenever she tried to irritate me with some fact that had been hidden from me. Whatever Sylvia's secret was, I thought, it would be something innocuous, something Papa had told her to keep her from being sad.

She continued to look at me hard for a moment, harder than I ever saw her look at me. The thoughts were twisting and turning in her head. I could see her troubling over what she should do, whether to tell me or not. These past few years, Papa's devotion to her was very important. She didn't want to share his affection and at times hated hearing any references to anyone else he loved, including me. That was another way she reminded me of Vera. I supposed there was no way to get around it. There was a little of Vera in both of us. We shared too much blood, having had the same father.

Her eyes narrowed, and she nodded to herself.

"You're right, Audrina. Papa told me never to tell any-one, even you."

I raised my eyebrows at how adult she suddenly sounded. The memories of the various times my father had said something similar to me returned. Sometimes I felt I was being buried in secrets. Someone was al-ways whispering one in my ear, whether it was Aunt Ellsbeth, Vera, or Papa.

Sylvia kept her gaze locked on me, waiting for my reaction, which I thought was quite unusual for her. I pulled back a little and wondered if Sylvia even understood the concept of a secret. Was this some sort of game my father had played with her when I wasn't around?

"Do you have any secrets you can tell me?" I asked.

She shook her head. "No. When you tell a secret, you can't take it back. That would be like trying to put ketchup back in the bottle," she said. I knew that was something Papa had told her, because he had told it to me, too, when I was a little girl.

"Okay, Sylvia, don't think about it. Keep your secrets in your bottle of ketchup." I got up. "Let's go make dinner now. Arden will be home soon, and you know how hungry he is when he comes through that door. He expects everything to be ready for him, just like all men." I recited what I had been told over the years, especially by my aunt Ellsbeth. "They want you to be their cook and bottle washer and their clothes valet and keep the house spick-and-span. And you have to do all that and still be beautiful so they can go about proudly with you on their arm, looking up to them like they walk on water. When a husband says, 'Jump,' you're supposed to ask, 'How high, dear?' "

I paused when I saw she was staring at me with her eyes wide. She really hadn't understood a word, especially couched in an angry tone. Maybe I sounded a little too much like Aunt Ellsbeth, someone she was not especially fond of being around. All our relatives and ancestors popped up occasionally in us, I thought. There was no escaping that.

"Oh, forget it, Sylvia. Fortunately, you won't have to worry about all this business between a husband and a wife," I added, and immediately regretted it. It was surely something Aunt Ellsbeth would have told her. "Come on. Let's be good little housewives tonight. To the kitchen," I said, and pretended we should charge like knights on horses.

She laughed and stood up quickly. Sylvia liked to help prepare the salad and, despite everything else that held her back, was meticulous about how she cut carrots, tomatoes, and onions, making perfect slices. She did have artistic talent. I had recently bought her some art supplies, and without instruction, she produced some interesting representations of our surroundings, the trees and ponds and paths. Or at least, I thought they were interesting. Arden thought her work was just a muddle of shapes and colors, more like a child's finger painting. He never really studied them and saw the way she layered her pictures so that they looked like images fading into each other. They were like dreamscapes with interesting choices of color and shades. She never tried to draw a person or a face, but sometimes I thought I saw the image of someone caught in the fog or in a cloud.

Recently, before Papa grew weaker and sicker, he and I had discussed the possibility of getting her an art teacher. When I told Arden, he said it would be a waste of money.

"How can she learn anything like that? She barely knows how to dress herself and brush her teeth."

"There are people like her who can't do well in school or even in everyday life with common activities but have specific talents, Arden."

"Then what good is it? They can't handle any money they make or go shopping for themselves. She can't even carry on a conversation. Just teach her how to clean and polish the floors and furniture. At least then she'll be of some value," he said, and went on reading his *Wall Street Journal*.

Nevertheless, I promised myself I would look into getting an art tutor once our lives resembled any normalcy. More than any of us, Sylvia needed something to distract her and take her mind off our loss. I knew how her mind worked. When she picked up a thought, plucked it seemingly out of the air like a wild berry, she turned it over and over in her mind for hours if she was left alone. This told me that she wasn't really dumb; she had deep curiosity about everything that was brought to her attention. The problem was trying to get her to think about something else once she hooked onto an idea, whether it was a dead fly she carried around all day or an old photo of Whitefern. She was that way about dinner preparations. No surgeon in an operating room had more intense concentration.

I had decided earlier in the day to prepare one of Arden's favorite dinners, angel-hair pasta and chicken in olive oil, garlic, and basil. I worked on the sauce and started heating the water for the pasta. Everything was going along fine when he called unexpectedly.

"I won't be home for dinner," he said as soon as I answered. "I have a very important dinner meeting with one of our high-net-worth clients who's worried about his portfolio since your father's death. I have to assure him that we are going to be as efficient and profitable for him as ever. Fortunately, no one but you, me, and our attorney knows about this stupid thing your father did, but the danger remains that it will be discovered. Stupid."

"My father didn't do stupid things, Arden."

"Oh. I suppose the whole ruse of creating the first Audrina wasn't stupid, or marrying my mother, a woman without legs, was brilliant. She was happy and safe where she was. I would have provided for her. There wasn't a woman within arm's length that he didn't claim, no matter what."

"You didn't complain about him back then, Arden. You were very grateful, as I remember it."

"What could I do? I didn't have a job, and my real father had deserted us." He inhaled a ragged breath. "But that's not the same as liking it," he added, his voice straining with frustration and rage. "I put up with a great deal to make him happy, to pay him back, and look what he did. That's what I call ungrateful."

"Have you been drinking?" I asked. He was slurring his words a little, and he would never say these things before my father died.

"Of course I'm drinking. You think a teetotaler could survive in this business? I have to entertain clients, Audrina, and not do things that will make them feel uncomfortable. Your father was quite the drinker. If you want to know the truth, he taught me. That's why I've been telling you that you simply do not understand the business. It all doesn't happen over the phone. People need to be reassured about things in person. You don't have the worldly experience I have. You never went to college. You were practically a prisoner in Whitefern. I've given you the important worldly knowledge you have."

I heard him take a deep breath, pausing like someone who was fighting to get control of himself.

"Everything is being arranged to correct what your father did," he said in a softer voice. "It will take two days. I'll bring you to Mr. Johnson's office to sign the paperwork. It has to be notarized."

"I'm not signing anything until I read it and think about it properly. It was how my father brought me up."

"Oh, please," he said. "How he brought you up? Do you really want to resurrect that subject?"

I heard music in the background. "Where are you?"

"I'm in a very upscale restaurant. You don't entertain clients in a fast-food joint. I'll be home late. Don't wait up for me."

"You didn't call all day, Arden, and you never asked what happened with Sylvia last night."

"Save it for my bedtime story," he said. Someone laughed near him. "Gotta go."

"Arden—"

He hung up. I looked at Sylvia. She was watching me, her face full of trepidation. She was always very sensitive to my moods and feelings and would even start to cry seconds before I did when something upset me or made me sad. Maybe there was something to the theory that people who shared blood were more aware of each other's moods and feelings than even close friends would be.

I smiled quickly. "Everything's all right, Sylvia. Arden has to work late tonight, so it will be only you and me for dinner, okay? We like it all anyway. It's not just for him that we cook."

She narrowed her eyes, looked toward the stairway, and then I thought she nodded to herself as if she had heard a whisper. I told myself her behavior shouldn't be so surprising to me. Like me, she had seen too many deaths in this house. She was in the shadow of the Grim Reaper. Vera, in fact, had tried to blame her for Billie's death when Billie fell down those stairs. Vera resented the attention Papa was giving Sylvia, just like she resented any attention he gave me. Jealousy, rather than blood, ran through Vera's veins. If she cut herself, I would expect to see the green slime of envy instead of blood.

Sylvia went about setting the table in the dining room for the two of us as meticulously as ever. That didn't surprise me. I knew her better than anyone, even Papa. I had practically been her mother all these years. When her body began to look like the budding figure of a beautiful young woman, I spent hours alone with her talking about sex, in as much of a scientific, even fantasy way as I could, especially when we discovered baby mice or a nest of hummingbird eggs and she had a child's curiosity about how they got there.

Everything became more dramatic for her when she had her first period. No matter how I tried to prepare her for it, it came as a big shock. Her scream at the sight of blood made Whitefern's walls tremble. I looked at Papa and hurried up to her. I recalled how frightened I had been when I had gotten mine, and I could handle such changes, so I appreciated what she was going through.

She hadn't forgotten what I had told her, but it was always more like a story to her, something that happened to other women. Why did it look so bad? This sort of thing happened only when you hurt yourself, and the cramps, the pain? How could this mean anything good? What did it have to do with babies?

When she questioned me time after time about it, I was thrown back to when my aunt Ellsbeth had tried to terrorize both Vera and me with biblical references, claiming that women suffered so much with their monthlies and the birthing process because of what Eve had done in the Garden of Eden.

"We're cursed!" she would exclaim, her eyes wild with rage. "Men have it so easy. It isn't fair, but think of it as the first alarm bell. Now, sex will be dangerous. Those little sperms that come shooting out of them and into you will make babies, babies you won't want."

"Like you?" Vera had retorted, surprising me with her defiance. "Making me?"

Most of the time, Aunt Ellsbeth wouldn't respond to such an outburst of insolence, but this time, she'd smiled coldly and said, "Exactly. Look at my burdens now. Thank you for being born."

I remember wondering how it could be Vera's fault. Even though she hurt me, angered me, and teased me, I felt sorry for her. I expected she would cry, but she simply looked at Aunt Ellsbeth and smiled back at her with the same icy eyes. I couldn't imagine being as hard and as emotionally insulated as Vera could be. I was too sympathetic, especially when it came to Sylvia.

Someday, I thought the day after she had her first period, she would be alone or I wouldn't be there to protect her, and some boys might come along and talk her into doing nasty things with them. Papa had once warned me about that. Obviously, because of my own history, that sort of nightmare haunted me. If there was one promise I had made to Papa without ever uttering the words, it was never to let what happened to me happen to Sylvia. I didn't have to come out and say it, and Papa didn't have to put it into words, either. We simply looked at her growing more and more beautiful every day, looked at each other, and nodded with the same thought.

Sylvia's innocent beauty wasn't a big secret. I took her shopping with me often, and people saw her at events we brought her to, especially events involving Papa's business when he was still working hard. She always drew compliments but had no idea how to respond. When she lowered her eyes and smiled, however, she looked like she was flirting or trying to because she was shy. On several occasions, young men had inquired about taking her out. Some had called to speak with her, and two different young men, college boys, had come to Whitefern to visit with her. I had turned them all away, on the phone or in person.

Once I considered letting them visit with Sylvia so they could see how immature she was, but then I thought, *Why put her through it?* Worse, what if she liked one of these young men and wanted to be with him, go for a ride or out to eat, anything? How would we deal with that? No, it was easier to shield her, to step in between her and any young man approaching her, and end it before it could begin.

A few local boys were quite persistent, and even though they learned how simple Sylvia was, their lust for her didn't diminish. If anything, I could see in their faces that they thought she'd be an easy conquest because she was unprotected, and I had no doubt that she might just be.

How long could I keep her chaste, I wondered, and should I do so for as long as I could? She had the mind of a child but the desires of a woman now. Was it fair to deny her the pleasures of her sex? Was it possible for her to find someone who would sincerely care for her and love her and satisfy her womanly needs? I never had the courage to bring these questions up with Papa. I certainly couldn't discuss them with Arden. He'd make a sour face or mock the idea. However, I was tempted to discuss these things with Dr. Prescott. He was a trusted family friend, but I hesitated. After all, he was also a man. I couldn't help but feel embarrassed talking about it, and now that there was no other woman in our home, whom could I talk to about my own problems anyway?

I longed for a true friend or a sister who could handle such matters. It was partly my own fault that I was so isolated. So many terrible things had happened to us that I couldn't fathom being close to a stranger. There would be so many questions, questions I couldn't answer or wouldn't ever want to answer, like those about the deaths at Whitefern or the empty grave that once had a tombstone with my name on it.

Nevertheless, I knew I needed advice when it came to Sylvia's problems and my own. I did come close to confiding in Dr. Prescott when I had consulted him about my failure to get pregnant. Arden had resisted being tested for potency, but I did, and the result was such that he didn't have to be tested. My chances for getting pregnant were quite small. It didn't mean it couldn't happen, but it was most unlikely. Back then, Arden didn't seem to be troubled by the news. He was happier that it was my fault, of course, and let me know it.

"I had no doubt that a man as virile as I am would

not be the reason we're not succeeding in getting you pregnant. I don't shoot blanks," he bragged. Of course, I wondered what that meant. I knew that he'd had girlfriends when he was off at college. Did he get someone pregnant? Was there a child of his somewhere?

"How do you know?" I asked, and held my breath.

He just shrugged. "A man knows. Look at how well I make love. I taught you everything you need to know about it, didn't I? If you're not satisfied when I do it, you'll never be." He smiled slyly again. "I never had a complaint from any other girl. Anyway, let's not worry about it right now." I was practically in tears, but he smiled again and told me, "Look at all the money we'll save not bothering with birth control."

"That's not funny, Arden," I told him. Papa was still alive then, and despite what he had told me about Papa considering him his son, I knew in my heart that Papa wanted a grandson with his blood.

To my surprise, Arden did apologize. Maybe he thought I would go running to my father to tell him what he had said. We continued making love, and I continued to fail to get pregnant. He was too busy back then proving himself to Papa and taking on more responsibility. Some nights, he would begin to make love and suddenly stop, claiming he was tired. "And besides, what's the use?" he would say, and I would go to sleep with tears flooding my eyes.

All these memories and thoughts streamed through my mind as Sylvia and I sat in the dining room. I didn't want to bother eating in there. I thought we could just use the kitchenette, but she had dressed up the big table the way she always did, being a little creative with the way she folded the napkins, making little crowns or flowers. Whenever we had guests over, Papa would give Sylvia the task of creating place cards according to the way he wanted his guests to sit at the table. Most of the time, Arden, Sylvia, and I had the same places, but occasionally he wanted someone closer to him. Sometimes he wanted certain other people as far away as possible, too.

Sylvia wouldn't just write the names in her beautifully artistic script. She would color them in and often draw something to complement whatever we were having for dinner. She could draw a small hen or a funny little cow, lamb, or pig or do something interesting with fish. Everyone praised her, and when she looked at Papa and saw how proud of her he was, she would brighten and look even more beautiful. Arden might even say something nice, compliment her, but I always thought it was more to please Papa.

After dinner, again more to please Papa than anyone, I would play the piano. We'd tried to give Sylvia piano lessons, too, but she never took to it. She didn't have the patience and would rather spend her time drawing and painting in the cupola, where Papa had created a small studio for her. During the past few years, before Papa had begun to show signs of weakening, we did enjoy some peace and contentment at Whitefern. Maybe it was unrealistic to think it would last very long, but for a while, at least, it was truly like we were all finally finding some sense of happiness.

The settings at the dinner table were not modified after Papa's death. His place was still there. Sylvia and I sat where we always sat. This was really our first formal dinner since he had died. With all that went on, we'd been eating buffet style in the kitchenette. Here we were tonight, when I thought we would begin again as a family—diminished, yes, but still a family— and Arden was out with clients instead.

I tried not to be too depressed, because I was afraid Sylvia would start crying once we were at the table without Papa in his chair, and my sadness would only intensify her own. But she surprised me with how relaxed and hungry she was. I should have been happy about it, but she looked like someone who really did have a big secret. I smiled at her and asked her what she was thinking.

"I'm not thinking," she said. "I'm eating, Audrina."

That made me smile. I forgot how she could be so literal, but I was still a little curious, even a little anxious, about the way she would pause, look at Papa's empty seat, and then look toward the stairway, listening as if she anticipated the sound of his footsteps.

I had to get her to stop thinking of ghosts. Even Sylvia needed some sort of future now. Keeping her busy with household chores was far from enough. And I could see that she didn't even have the small attention span for my math and science tutoring. Even role-playing to help her be more confident in social settings wasn't working.

"How would you like me to find an art teacher to help you with your drawings and paintings?" I asked her. I had to get her thinking about something else. "He could help you do so much more. Isn't that a good idea, Sylvia?"

"Papa said you would," she replied.

"Right. Papa and I did discuss it. I'll look into it tomorrow, okay?"

"Papa said you would." She repeated it as if he had just told her.

"Okay, Sylvia."

"I'm not going to wait," she said.

"What?"

"I'm going to paint something new tonight right after I help clean up," she said.

"Oh, good. You don't have to help clean up tonight," I said. I really wanted to occupy myself as much as I could to diminish how angry I was feeling. Arden should be thinking more about us now and not clients. He should be comforting me. Papa's death was far too fresh.

"Really?" she asked.

"Yes, really."

She rushed to finish her dinner and then, remembering to excuse herself politely from the table the way Papa and I had taught her, hurried up the stairway to the cupola and her makeshift studio. I smiled to myself, happy to have some respite. She could be a full-time job, especially during these dark days.

I took my time cleaning up and putting things away. I had no idea how much time had passed, but I felt so drained and tired that when I went out to wait for Arden in the living room, I had no sooner sat back than I fell asleep. Hours went by. I was in so deep a sleep that I didn't hear Arden come home. I woke when a draft of cold air splashed over my face, and I looked up at him standing there gazing down at me, a dumb smile on his face. He looked like he was swaying a bit, too.

"Oh. I didn't hear you come in," I said, grinding the sleep from my eyes and sitting up.

"I'm happy to say that I talked Mr. Camden into putting his pension plan with our firm. While you were playing nursemaid to Snow White, I was building our net worth," he bragged.

Now that I was fully awake, I could smell the whiskey on his breath, even though we were far apart.

"Don't call her Snow White, Arden. When you do things like that, she knows you're making fun of her."

"Oh, please. She doesn't know top from bottom. Well? What do you say to what I just told you?"

"You're drinking too much, Arden."

"What? That's what you have to say? After I tell you I've just talked a millionaire into placing his pension portfolio with us? That's your comment? I'm drinking too much?"

"I'm just worried about you. That's all."

"Yes, me, too," he said, turning restrained. He ran his palms over his face. "I'm tired. There's a lot to do tomorrow." He started to turn away.

"The reason I was with Sylvia last night was that she had gone out in her nightgown to the cemetery to dig up Papa's grave," I said quickly. "And although you slept through it, it was pouring cats and dogs. She could have gotten pneumonia."

"What?" He stopped turning and smiled, incredulous. "Dig up his grave? Why?"

"She's confused. You might recall when someone else was buried and then figuratively dug up."

He stared at me, not angry and not sorry. "So what did you do when you found her in the cemetery?"

"I dragged her back, and then I had to put us both in a hot bath. You slept through it all."

"Glad I did," he said. He started away again, then stopped and turned back. "I don't know about her, about us keeping her here," he said. "This might be getting to be too much. I'm afraid to bring some of our clients here now."

"What? What else would we do? She's my sister. We won't put her in some institution."

"Well, that's why I want you to sign those papers ASAP. You'll be spending most of your time caring for a mental case," he said, shrugging. "I'm going up to bed. I need my sleep."

I sat for a while longer, thinking about him, how disappointing he could be. I remembered once talking about him with Aunt Ellsbeth when I was just seventeen and Arden had given me an engagement ring. She and I went for a walk, and she asked if I really loved him. When I said I did, she told me she hoped I would always feel that way about him, but she warned me, "He'll change. You'll change. You may not love him as much as you think you do now."

I didn't want to give her credit for ever being right about anything—she was so mean to my mother and especially to Sylvia—but not considering the things she had said as true or important was just foolish self-denial. It was also self-denial to ignore how lonely I was and how much I longed for the company of another, more experienced woman.

I went up to the cupola to get Sylvia and have her go to bed. For years now, I'd been the one who told her it was time to go to sleep and the one who woke her in the morning. I was her living alarm clock. Sometimes, even though she was very hungry, she would wait for me to tell her it was lunchtime. How would she live without me, especially in this house? If something happened to me, she would surely be sent to an institution, where Papa was sure she would be abused.

When I stepped into the cupola, she was still hard at work on her painting, so entranced by it that she didn't hear me enter and likely hadn't noticed how much time had passed. I watched her for a moment, amazed and pleased at how devoted to her art she could be. Anyone watching her would never believe there was anything seriously wrong with her. She looked so beautiful and so intense, focusing her mental abilities and talent on her work.

Slowly, I inched up behind her and looked at her picture.

I immediately felt a cold chill.

She had made a reasonably realistic likeness of the woods between the cemetery and Whitefern, and she had done a good job of creating an overlay of fog, but coming out of it was the ghostlike figure of Papa.

And the way she had drawn his face made him look like he was desperate either to get away from something or to get to something, get back to Whitefern . . . perhaps to save us all.

A Flood of Emotions

There were many times before this when I thought I could drown in my own sorrow. Often after my mother's death, I had felt lost and alone in our big house. Shadows grew darker and drowned out the kaleidoscope of color our stained-glass windows would normally cast over the patterned rugs and furniture. My chameleon-colored hair, which Papa called a hat of rainbows, was dull and lifeless.

When I was younger, Whitefern was a house echoing with wishes. I wished I could go to school. I wished I had friends and could go to sleepovers. I envied the freedom other girls my age enjoyed. I read about them in books. I even wished the first Audrina was alive and well, an older sister with whom I could spend hours and hours talking, taking walks, and learning how to flirt with boys.

After Momma died, clocks were haunting with their eternal ticking, amplified by the silence around the piano Momma had once played so beautifully. Papa drifted in and out of sadness, anger, and guilt. He went from room to room mumbling to himself. Sometimes, when he stepped out of a shadow, it looked like it had stuck to his face no matter how bright the light.

Aunt Ellsbeth wasn't a great help to my father or me. Later, as talk about Sylvia increased, Aunt Ellsbeth constantly warned me about my father, telling me that now that my mother was gone, despite his permitting me to go to school, he would find ways to chain me to him and Whitefern forever. The most important way he would do that, she explained, was to make me Sylvia's caretaker for the rest of Sylvia's life.

"When she's brought home, that's what you'll be," she whispered, her eyes on fire with warning. "She'll be the chain that binds you forever to Whitefern and your selfish father."

Her warnings tempered my excitement over having a little sister finally coming home after almost two years of special care. In time, I realized her warnings about Papa came from her disappointment at his choosing my mother over her. There was still bitterness in her, a bitterness her daughter, Vera, would inherit, although many times I thought Vera didn't need to inherit bitterness from anyone. She was capable of being vicious and mean all by herself, first to me and then especially when it involved little Sylvia.

Both my aunt and Vera mocked her when she was first brought home to us. They seemed to take joy in pointing out her disadvantages and slow development. I vowed to myself and to Sylvia that I would work with her and make her as normal as I could. It was a promise I made to my dead mother, too, so that instead of feeling put upon as Aunt Ellsbeth predicted

I'd be, I felt responsibility and love. Maybe Aunt Ellsbeth was right to tell me Papa took advantage of that, but I wasn't about to stop caring for my little sister, either to spite Papa or to satisfy Aunt Ellsbeth.

I suppose I should have realized earlier that Sylvia would be attracted to art. When she was just three, I gave her my prisms, and she loved toying with the colors she could create. No one thought she could feel deeply about anything, but I began to realize that there was a real person in that troubled body struggling to have its mind keep up with it as it grew. Now I understood that she wasn't interested in art just because of her fascination with colors and shapes. Art was far more to her than a way to pass the time and amuse herself. She needed it. It was her way of talking to others, of expressing the deeper feelings inside her. Deaf mutes had sign language; Sylvia had art.

I wasn't any sort of an expert about it, but I knew that an art teacher would help her technically and show her how to explore more with the brushes and colors. He or she wouldn't change or add to what Sylvia wanted to say. That came from a place inside her, words and feelings bottled up, trapped by her shyness and inability to say outright what she felt. But if her art teacher improved her techniques, it would help those who looked at her pictures to realize what she was saying, what she was depicting and expressing, and of course, that would make her happier. She would be able to speak to more people and, in a small and different way, leave the confines of Whitefern.

Perhaps most important, art was her way of escaping from herself, because in a real sense, her undeveloped mind had become her prison. All these thoughts crossed my mind as I studied her new picture. Without instruction, she had somehow achieved more, used her colors more effectively, and drawn her outlines of people and animals more clearly. I supposed there was something to the idea that people could develop their talent naturally. Perhaps she could do much more with formal instruction, I concluded.

"Is that Papa?" I asked, studying the picture and pointing to the image of him. "Coming home?"

She turned slowly and looked at me like someone emerging from the darkness. It was as if she had been in a trance while she had worked. "Papa? Papa is home," she said, nodding.

It didn't surprise me to see her come up with this idea. Whitefern certainly had its ghosts. Relatives like Aunt Mercy Marie were referred to so often it was easy to feel they had just passed through a room. Sometimes, when I came upon Papa sitting in his favorite chair and looking like he was dreaming with his eyes open, he would glance at me and say, "You never leave Whitefern. Whitefern is part of you. Even after you die, you will be here."

I was sure he had said similar things to Sylvia, who might not understand what they meant at first, but with repetition, the idea might have taken hold. Even though these past days she looked like she was waiting for Papa or imagining him still alive, I didn't realize how deeply she believed it. Maybe Papa had specifically assured her that he would always be with her. Whatever he had told her privately he made seem like a secret. I was sure of that. So it didn't surprise me at all that the picture she was doing represented her hope. Papa would not be lost to us, to her. As long as she talked about him, painted him, and looked for him, he would never be gone.

Why discourage that? I thought. What harm did it really do to anyone, even to her? It reminded me of the play *Harvey*, the story of a man who imagined he saw a giant rabbit that was his companion and kept him happy. His sister had come to realize that taking away his imaginary friend would only make him miserable.

Besides, maybe Harvey was really there. What harm was there in believing in magic, believing in something beyond the often dull reality that our monotonous daily lives could cast over us like a net to keep us from the joy of our imaginations?

Yes, maybe Papa really was watching over us, watching over Sylvia especially. His soul, so stained with guilt for many reasons, had to cleanse itself or God would send him to hell. He had to help us in order to save himself. I could believe this. I wouldn't tell Arden my idea, of course, but I could believe it.

"It's time to go to sleep, Sylvia. You can finish working on your picture in the morning, after breakfast."

She nodded, stared at her work for a few moments as if she was looking through a window to be sure Papa was still there and wouldn't be gone in the morning, and then put away her pencils, brushes, and paints neatly in the cabinet Papa had bought for them. She followed me to her room. I watched her prepare for bed. She was quieter than usual. I sensed something different about her. She washed her face and brushed her teeth and then fixed her hair the way I had taught her, but every once in a while, I caught her glancing at herself in the mirror and smiling like someone who knew an important secret.

"Do you think you will be able to sleep alone tonight, Sylvia?"

"Yes, Audrina."

"Will you cry out in the middle of the night or go walking around the house?"

"No," she said.

"You won't go outside without me, will you?"

"No. I don't have to," she said. I knew what she meant, but I didn't want to keep talking about it. Maybe I was afraid to think about it, especially tonight. After all, I had grown up in this house with visions and voices calling to me from the deepest places in my mind born out of my rocking-chair dreams. No one could appreciate what Sylvia was thinking more than I could.

"All right. I'm going to sleep, too, then," I said. I kissed her good night and put out her lights, but I didn't close the door. I never did. She never liked the door closed. The sounds the rest of us made gave her comfort.

Arden was still awake when I got to our bedroom. I was surprised that he was sitting up and reading a folder, looking like he had quickly sobered up.

"I thought you were tired," I said.

"I am, but I remembered some work I had to get done. I don't simply work an eight-hour day, you know. Things happen before the market opens and after it closes. There's not much room for blundering, especially when it's someone else's money and your reputation depends on succeeding even with the smallest portfolios. This is a word-of-mouth business. Success breeds more success. It doesn't take many failures to sink the ship."

"You don't have to tell me all that, Arden. I watched my father work for years and saw how concerned he could be about every little detail."

"Not in the beginning," he muttered. "If there wasn't Whitefern money, what would have become of you all? You'd be out on the street, that's what. He had lots of losses."

"Why think of that now? He became a very well-respected businessman. Everyone makes mistakes, even you, especially in the beginning."

"Yeah, well, whatever . . . he didn't have to concern himself with reporting everything he did to your mother, did he?" he snapped back.

So that was it, I thought. He was putting on this show to emphasize again why he wanted me to sign those papers. He wasn't really doing anything important.

"Did it ever occur to you that I might want something more in my life, Arden? I'd like to be part of the work, the business Papa built. I'd like to do things outside of this house."

He put his papers down. "Oh, really? And just how do you propose to do that and continue to be a nursemaid for your brain-damaged sister?"

"She's not brain-damaged. Don't say that."

"No, she's just slooooooow. Call it whatever you want. Well?"

"She'll be taking art lessons. I'll find other ways to keep her occupied and independent. You'd be surprised at some of the progress she's made. She's not as helpless as you think. I'll arrange for more professional tutoring in all subjects. In time—"

"In time, in time . . . what's to say she won't run out and start digging up your father's grave again? Please. You've chosen to keep her here, so you care for her, full-time. So do it. I do the work we need to keep the house and our lives going, and to do that, I need to be in total control. End of story."

He could be so frustrating, I thought. I went into the bathroom and started to wash my face and brush my teeth.

"If we had a child, you wouldn't even hesitate two seconds to do what I ask," he called. "You'd be busy being a real mother instead of a nursemaid to a woman who should be in an institution."

I felt the tears coming to my eyes and put my toothbrush down and took deep breaths. If anyone should realize how sensitive I was to sexual failure, it was Arden, and not simply because he was my husband. He knew the psychological problems I had. He had witnessed why. His own words when we were younger echoed in my mind: "Audrina, I'm sorry. It's not enough to say. I know that. Now I wish I'd stayed and tried to defend you."

Were those words all lies?

I went to the door.

"You know I want to be a real mother, Arden. You know I want that very much. We can keep trying. The doctor didn't say it would absolutely never happen."

"Sure, we can try until I dry up," he muttered.

"Men don't dry up. You were the one who told me Ted Douglas made his much younger wife pregnant, and he's seventy-eight."

"So he says," Arden muttered. "I've seen that young wife of his out and about. Who knows if he really was the one to father her child?"

"Where? Where did you see her?"

"That's not the point. The point is you should think more about being a housewife than a stockbroker. I'm the stockbroker. Get a hobby. Do needlework or join a book club, and have the women over for tea and talk like some of the other brokers' wives I know. I don't know why your father did this, this vengeful thing!" he said, slapping at his papers.

I returned to the bathroom. Neither of us said another word. He had put out his table lamp and turned over so that his back was to me, clearly telling me that he would not be trying for us to have a child tonight. I lay there looking up at the darkness and thinking. Maybe I would give in to what he wanted and just sign the papers. It would bother me for a while that I had defied Papa's final wishes, but I had my husband's wishes to consider. And I did recall my mother telling me not to be too talented, not to be better than my husband at anything: "Men won't approve if it's likely you'll earn more money than they do." Even when I was young, that sounded very unfair to me. Why were men more important than women?

I didn't want to think about it any more tonight, so I closed my eyes and tried to remember happier times, especially the early days, when Arden was so loving and devoted to me.

I dozed off dreaming about a Christmas dinner when Momma and I put up decorations, but something woke me not more than a half hour later. My eyes just popped open. There was a familiar sound in the house, a sound that belonged in nightmares. I turned slowly toward Arden, but he was dead asleep, breathing heavily with an occasional snore.

I sat up and listened harder. It was there. I was not dreaming or imagining it. The sound was hypnotizing. I didn't need anyone to tell me why. It buzzed in my brain. I rose like a sleepwalker and left the bedroom. I thought the hall lights flickered as if the house was sending warnings: *Stay back. Don't go.* The floor creaked, and the wind seemed to be scrubbing the windows. There were many cracks around frames in this old house. The wind whistled through them. Curtains danced, and above me at one point a chandelier gently swayed.

My heart began to pound. Despite all I had learned about the deception under which I had been raised, I couldn't help imagining that there was a first Audrina. For most of my childhood, I would swear on a stack of

Bibles that she whispered to me whenever I was alone. *Be me. You must be me, or I will be dead forever and ever.*

When I told my father about that once, he smiled and kissed me. "Yes," he said. "That's good. That's what we want. Listen for her always."

Practically tiptoeing now, I walked toward the first Audrina's room. It would always be called that, and it would never be used, nor would any of the toys and dolls ever be taken out of it. Arden thought that was sick and sometimes ranted about it.

"We could give all that stuff to the children of poor people. We'll make a big thing of it and have the newspapers take pictures. People will commend us for our charity, and guess what, we'll get more clients, more business. That's the reason most people announce their charitable gifts, most companies. They want more business, tit for tat."

"Just leave it alone," I warned him. At an earlier time, I would add, "Maybe our daughter will have those things."

"Daughter?" He shook his head. "Go call Santa Claus and tell him you've been a good little girl. We'll find a baby wrapped in ribbons on Christmas Day."

When I was just about at the door, I stopped. There was no doubt. I heard the rocking chair rocking. I stepped up and gently opened the door. The sound stopped. I leaned to my left and found the light switch, my heart thumping.

Sylvia looked up at me.

"Sylvia, what are you doing? Why did you come in here? Why are you in the chair?"

She smiled, unafraid, looking at me as though I was the slow-witted sister and not her.

"Papa told me to," she said. "He said whenever I wanted to talk to him, I should rock in the first Audrina's chair, because that was the way you spoke to the first Audrina."

"When did he tell you that?"

"I don't know when. I don't have a watch, and calendars are just full of numbers and days and numbers and days."

"Was this the secret you wouldn't tell me, the secret Papa told you never to tell?"

"Yes, but he said if I came here and rocked in the chair, he would tell me more secrets, Audrina."

For a moment, standing there and looking at my sister, I thought Arden was probably right. I should have emptied this room. Maybe we could erase the past, if not forever, for years and years, or at least put it so far in the back of our minds it wouldn't ruin our present lives.

"Oh, Sylvia," I said. "Poor Sylvia. Come back to bed. Come." I held out my hand.

"You can talk to him, too, Audrina. Just come here and rock," she said, starting to rise so I could take her place.

"Okay. But it's very late, so not tonight. Please, Sylvia, let's go back to bed."

"But Papa's still here."

"He'll always be here, won't he?" I asked.

That pleased her, and, still reluctant, she rose to take my hand. I turned off the light and closed the door behind us.

"Let's try not to wake up Arden," I warned, afraid she would start talking loudly. "You know how cranky he gets when he's awakened in the middle of the night."

She nodded. When we were almost to her room, she paused. She seemed very excited. I looked around. What was she seeing or hearing now?

"What is it, Sylvia?"

"I almost forgot to tell you," she said. "Papa did have a secret for you that I was supposed to tell you."

"What?" I said, so tired I had only inches of patience left for her.

"He said you'll have a baby, not to worry."

"What?"

"He didn't say girl or boy, just baby," she added, and then went into her bedroom.

I followed her, feeling dazed now. I had never mentioned to her that Arden and I had been trying to have a child. She never asked, and she was never in a room when he and I talked about it or my failure to get pregnant. I wasn't confident that she would understand any of the medical information anyway.

I tucked her in and stood there in the dim light spilling through her doorway from the hallway.

"Papa told you I would have a baby?"

"Yes."

"When, Sylvia? When did he tell you this?"

"Tonight," she said. "He was here first in my room.

I knew he was here, so I went to the rocking chair because I knew he had a new secret, and he told me," she said.

"Okay. Just go to sleep now," I told her. I tucked her in, and she turned onto her side, looking very contented. I stood there looking around her room as if I expected to hear or see something.

I went back to Arden's and my bedroom and paused outside our door. For a few moments, I actually debated with myself about returning to the first Audrina's bedroom and sitting in the rocking chair. Regardless of all I knew, despite how the deceptions were exposed, I couldn't completely disregard the power of the rocking chair. There were too many emotional memories. It called to me, not just tonight but many nights, and in the beginning, after I had learned all the lies, I still wanted to feel its power.

It took a great deal of self-control to push these feelings back, but I was in more of a daze than ever, and when I entered our bedroom, I just sat on the bed for a few moments thinking. Of course Sylvia couldn't have gotten such an idea from the spirit of my father while she rocked in the chair. I tried to be logical and decided that Sylvia was more alert than either of us knew, than anyone knew. She might be sitting and looking at pictures or playing with a puzzle, but she wasn't completely shut off from what people were saying nearby. It was wrong to underestimate her. If anyone should know that, I should.

"What the hell is it?" I heard Arden demand. His shout made me jump. He must have turned, opened his eyes, and saw me sitting up, or else he had heard me walk out and back in. "What did she do now?"

My immediate thought was *Don't dare mention the rocking chair*.

"She didn't do anything terrible, Arden. She merely had a dream," I said.

"A dream? Did she scream?"

"A little," I lied.

"Why does that not surprise me? What was the dream?"

"She dreamed I had a baby," I said.

"Oh, she did, huh? Well, that should do it. We don't even have to make love. It will be an immaculate conception. We'll call the baby Sylvia's Wish. Go to sleep, or go back to her," he ordered. "It's the middle of the night. How I do as well as I do under these circumstances is a miracle. Thank goodness I'm dedicated."

I lay back and pulled the blanket over me.

"Baby." I heard him rustling about and then heard him whisper, "Okay."

"What?"

He turned sharply and threw the covers off us as if they were on fire.

"What are you doing?"

"It's baby time. Sylvia has declared it."

"I don't understand, Arden."

"Nothing to understand," he said. "Only to do."

He reached down and pulled my nightgown up and out of his way, practically tearing it off me. I cried out, but before I could say another word, he scooped my legs up and pressed his hardness into me, so roughly I lost my breath for a moment. I was shocked at how fast and easily he could be ready. He didn't bother kissing me or touching me tenderly anywhere. Instead, he hovered above me like a hawk, pouncing.

"Baby, baby, baby," he chanted, as he pushed and prodded, twisting me this way and that so he could be more comfortable. His grunts made it sound like he was lifting a heavy weight. I couldn't stand the sight of him like this and put my hands over my eyes. On he pushed and prodded. I felt like he was tearing me up. The bed sounded like it would crash to the floor. At one point, my head hit the headboard, but he was oblivious to everything but his own animal satisfaction. This wasn't even sex to me; it was anger and revenge.

As so often when we made love, he had his orgasm before I even began to enjoy one, not that I could tonight. It reminded me of our earlier years, even our honeymoon, when he practically raped me because of my fears and hesitation.

"Men will always care more about satisfying themselves than you," Aunt Ellsbeth had told me time after time. "You've got to train them like circus animals. The best way is to insult them."

"Insult them? How can you do that and still have them want to make love to you?" I'd asked her.

"You tell them they have too many premature ejaculations. You'll see," she'd said. "They'll try to prove otherwise, and then you'll enjoy sex."

I had no idea why she thought I would be making

love to many men. Maybe she thought I would be like Vera, who Arden once told me could go through a college football team in a week. Making love to so many different men in a short time was terrifying to me. It actually made me sick to my stomach. He thought that was funny.

Sometimes I wondered if Arden had really seen what had happened to me in the woods. How could he have seen that and not expected me to have negative feelings when he talked like that about sex? But then why would he confess to his failure to help me and cry about how guilty and small that made him feel?

One night, I'd had a terrifying thought that answered that question. What if he wasn't only a witness? He had never turned in any of the boys' names to the police, and he never even mentioned them now. Was he worried they would turn on him? Thinking of that had made me throw up.

I couldn't depend on my memory to deliver the truth about anything on that horrible afternoon. Faces and voices were forever blurred, so I couldn't identify any of them, either. Even the rocking chair didn't bring it all back, but I wasn't going to complain.

When he was satisfied now, he rolled over and turned his back on me. Then I heard him say, "There. Baby, Sylvia's baby," and he laughed.

I lay there, still naked, my body smarting from the way he had rubbed and pressed on me. My legs were aching, the insides of my thighs feeling burned.

"Maybe," I said angrily, "if there was more romance in our lovemaking, it would work, and I would get pregnant. If you would think of me as more than just a vessel in which to empty yourself, the magic of two people making a child would happen as it is supposed to happen. You once loved me that way, didn't you? Or was that a lie? Or are you going to tell me it has withered like a grape on the vine?"

He didn't answer for so long that I thought he had fallen asleep instantly, but suddenly, he turned on me. "You're absolutely right. Romance comes from love, and love comes from respect and obedience. Your father taught me that," he added. "He should have taught it to you better."

I didn't doubt it. How my mother loved my father despite his meanness and selfishness amazed me. When I asked her about it once, she smiled, stroked my hair, and said, "Love is forgiveness, Audrina. That's all it really is, constantly forgiving someone for his weaknesses and hoping that it will bring about some good changes."

Is that what she would tell me now? I turned my back to Arden and tried to think of good things about him, enough so I could find forgiveness. However, before I fell asleep, I thought I wouldn't even dream of becoming pregnant as a result of this lovemaking. There was no baby on his or her way tonight. Sylvia could rock in that chair until daylight. There would be no magic.

No, as much as I wanted to believe it, Papa wasn't whispering any secrets in Sylvia's ear. What she was hearing were my thoughts. When she was rocking in that chair, she was hearing and seeing my dreams. But what would come of it? These dreams were like soap bubbles, capturing the rainbow light for seconds and then popping and dropping like tears to the hard, cold reality beneath them.

I think I passed out rather than falling asleep. For the first time in a long time, Arden was up before me, this time so quiet as not to wake me. That was unusual for him. Normally, because he was the one going to work and I was the one staying home, my having a good night's rest wasn't as important. I could always take a nap later, but he couldn't. When I looked at the clock, I was shocked. I couldn't recall when I had slept this late. My exhaustion from his rough lovemaking must be the reason, I thought, and I got up, wondering if Sylvia had gone down for breakfast. I had taught her how to make the coffee, and there were juices and cereals she liked, but I could count on the fingers of one hand how many times she had woken, dressed, and gone down without me, and that was over years and years.

Now that I was up and recalled how Arden had attacked me, I decided I had to shower before getting dressed. My body still ached in places, and I found scratches on my thighs where he had seized me, clawing at me to mold me into a position comfortable for him. Just washing my face wasn't going to be enough.

There was a chill in the air, and I realized the temperature must have taken a dive during the night. When I glanced out the window, I saw it was raining lightly, the drops sparkling like liquid ice. The wind had stripped many of the trees in the woods of their once pretty orange and brown leaves. The branches looked like the arms of spidery skeletons. I hated this time of the year. It lasted too long for me, and we couldn't avoid it. Our house had woods on three sides.

But at least Whitefern was comfortable all year round now. A few years ago, Papa had upgraded the bathrooms and bedrooms and installed central heating in the old house, except for two unused rooms on the first floor in the rear. Before I took my shower, I put up the thermostat, and afterward, I chose warmer clothes to wear, a pair of heavier jeans and a pink cable-knit sweater. A good part of the morning had already passed. By the time I walked out of the bedroom, I felt certain Sylvia would be up and waiting for me in the kitchen. She hadn't come looking for me. She probably thought I had gone down without her.

I started down the stairs and then hesitated. It was too quiet below. I listened for the sound of the rocking chair but didn't hear that, either. She wouldn't start painting without her breakfast. I went to her bedroom. Of course, my biggest fear was that she had gone out of the house and to the cemetery again. Maybe she had been there most of the night!

I breathed with relief. She was still sleeping, but her blanket was cast aside and she was naked. How odd, I thought. Had it been that hot in here? I looked at her thermostat. She had never touched any thermostats in the house. She didn't understand them. Hers hadn't been pushed up at all, and the room temperature was a little below sixty. I picked up her blanket and put it gently on the bed. She stirred and looked up at me.

"Were you that hot last night, Sylvia?" I asked. Maybe her dreams and tossing and turning had put her in a sweat.

"Hot?"

"Your blanket was on the floor." She looked at herself and then at me, seeming very confused. Then she shook her head. She looked like she was going to cry.

"It's all right. Nothing's wrong, Sylvia. Are you hungry? Let's make a bigger breakfast this morning, omelets and toast, okay?"

"With cheese?"

"Yes," I said, smiling. "With cheese. Do you want to take a shower first?"

"Yes," she said. "Shower."

I picked out clothes for her and set out her shoes and socks while she showered. Then I sat her at her vanity table and brushed out her hair. When I stood behind her and looked at her in the mirror, I thought she was truly beautiful, angelic. For some reason, even more so this morning. Her cheeks looked rosy, her lips full, and her eyes brighter than ever.

What a dirty trick nature had played on her, to give her this much beauty but not enough mentally to have a wonderful life. She could easily attract a handsome, young, wealthy man who would devote himself to her, build her a bigger home than Whitefern and all the jewelry and clothes she could want. Every man like that would turn to look at her now, but a moment later, when he tried to speak to her, he would surely lose his enthusiasm quickly and look for a fast exit.

And she wouldn't even understand why.

"Let's go down," I said.

She put her hand on mine on her shoulder and smiled.

"What, Sylvia?" I asked, smiling back at her.

"Audrina," she said. "Baby. Coming."

A Tree of Secrets

Right after Sylvia and I finished breakfast, there was an early but quick brushing of snowflakes. The rain that had begun falling at daybreak suddenly was captured by a breath of winter. I had intended to go shopping for food but hesitated when I saw the snow. I hoped that it would soon turn back to only cold rain. It did, and the roads didn't freeze over.

Weather of all sorts fascinated Sylvia, especially snowflakes. When she was little, she loved holding up her palms and letting the flakes fall into them and melt. Papa had once told her that rain and melting snowflakes were like the sky crying. That fascinated her. Actually, she loved the surprises of all seasons and the wonder of spring flowers, rich green leaves, and the birds returning after winter. I never appreciated the abundance of nature that surrounded us as much as she did.

Aunt Ellsbeth used to say, "That girl will be a child until her dying day." When it came to her appreciation of Mother Nature, I didn't think that was such a terrible prediction. The rest of us seemed to ignore how beautiful the outside world could be, perhaps because we were so shut up inside our own. Our world was lit with the lights we cast over ourselves with our petty jealousies. Who had time to look at the stars?

Sylvia never paid much attention to what month we were in, and if told, she wouldn't remember when asked later. The poor girl couldn't even remember her own birthday. Whenever I told her it was her birthday tomorrow, she would look astonished. I knew that if I was going to help her develop, I had to work on her memory, get her to associate things. She was improving, but lately I had begun to suspect that the problem was more a question of what she thought was important enough to remember rather than the failure of memory itself.

Anyone who heard this would immediately say, "Well, my birthday is important. How could I ever be expected to forget that?"

But that memory wasn't so simple for Sylvia.

Before she died, Vera was fond of reminding Sylvia that my and Sylvia's mother had died giving birth to her. I caught her saying things like "If you hadn't made it so difficult to be born, your mother would have lived," or "You were so afraid of being born, you tried to stop it, and that killed your mother." Of course, she was right there on every one of Sylvia's birthdays, between the time Sylvia understood what a birthday was and Vera's accidental death, to ask, "How could you be happy it's your birthday? Your mother died on this day. You should spend the whole day kneeling at her grave and asking her to forgive you."

No wonder Sylvia was not looking forward to it

enough to remember it, or if she did remember, she would pretend not to, I was sure. I constantly told her that our mother's dying was not her fault. "A baby can't purposely do that," I told her, after I had shouted at Vera, and Papa told her the same thing in his way, too, although I knew now that he wasn't eager to bring Sylvia home from the hospital quickly. He made all sorts of excuses about her weight, illness, anything he could think of to keep her from being released to our care. It took him quite a while to accept that he would have such a daughter and to look at her and not think about my mother. Nevertheless, to this day, Arden insisted that Sylvia had no concept of what had happened, no matter what terrible things Vera had told her.

"To tell you the truth, I don't think she even understands the concept of death. It wasn't too long ago that I saw her beating a dead bird with a stick to try to get it up and flying again. You've seen her do things like that, too."

I couldn't help wondering if he was right, but the death of your mother was such a deep loss, even a mother you saw only in photographs. How could you not be affected by it, think about it often, and blame yourself?

"I wouldn't worry about it. You have to be an adult to feel guilty," Arden once said as a response to my fears for Sylvia. "You have to develop a conscience, and that takes a little more intelligence than she possesses."

I didn't come right out and ask him the question about him that always haunted me, but I thought it, especially then: *Was that why it took you so long to confess about witnessing what had happened to me and not stopping it or telling anyone else about it so the bad boys could be punished? Is that your excuse, that you were still a child and you didn't have a fully developed conscience yet?*

I did think there was some truth to what he was saying, however. Adults were always warning us not to be in a hurry to grow up. Maybe this was a big part of why. Growing up meant responsibility, and responsibility brought guilt as well as satisfaction. In the end, conscience would always be king.

In any case, I wasn't going to stop trying to help Sylvia grow more mature in any way I could. Educating her was a big part of it. Whether I liked it or not, I had to be as good as any special education teacher in a public school. Papa put the responsibility on me when I was young, and I naturally continued it all after his death. I was motivated by that one big fear Papa had put into my head: if something happened to me, Sylvia would find herself in some institution where she was sure to be abused. I would have let Papa down in a very big way just by dying. I wanted so much for Sylvia to be able to survive on her own, to learn enough of the basics to get by.

Ever since she was fourteen, when I looked at her and realized she had developed a woman's figure almost overnight, I knew she would need special care and protection. I realized she had a beautiful face and a shapely young body. It was then that a girl really became vulnerable and needed to know how to protect herself and what to look for in a man's face that would tell her he was lusting after her only for his own selfish pleasure. I didn't think it was possible to get her to recognize that. She had a child's trusting nature. The warnings and alarm bells simply were not hooked up inside her the way they were for most girls and women.

Of course, she knew nothing about what had happened to me. Even if Arden or Papa had made some reference to it in her presence, it was as if they had spoken a foreign language. For a moment, she might listen, but then it would pass right through her and be gone like a breeze.

Occasionally, when she was younger, Papa would warn her about being alone, especially going too far away from the house by herself. But the smile on her face would tell anyone that she had no idea what terrible things he was afraid would befall her. She would nod and go on with whatever she was doing. He would look at me with frustration but also with a warning that I'd better protect her. I should be her shadow, the way she was his.

I spent almost all my free time with her. I worked on Sylvia's writing, spelling, and math and still did even today. One of the exercises was my dictating our shopping list for the supermarket. She sat at the table and painstakingly copied down the items, sometimes looking at the boxes or bottles to get the spelling right. I was amused at how important that was to her. Lately, she had become much better at it. She had good handwriting, probably because of her artistic talent. If a cashier saw our list, he or she usually had a compliment for whoever had printed it.

"My sister does that," I would say proudly.

Nothing brought Sylvia's shyness out more than when she was given a compliment. She would always look down to hide her smile, and her face would flush with embarrassment. I would tell her to say thank you, and sometimes she did, but usually with her head lowered, afraid to look strangers in the eye.

At the supermarket today, though, she behaved differently. I didn't have to tell her to say thank you, and when she did, she looked at the person to whom she was speaking. She was also more energetic and eager to find the items on the shelves. I stood back for most of the shopping and watched her go down the list, filling our cart without my telling her where to go.

If Arden could see her today, I thought, he wouldn't ridicule her so much or belittle the work I had been doing with her all these years.

Of course, I wondered what had given her this burst of energy and new self-confidence. From the little she had said about the night before, about going to the first Audrina's bedroom and sitting in the rocking chair, I gathered that what she had imagined had made her feel more important, because Papa had come to her and not to me or to Arden. She was eager to get home, help me put away the groceries, and go back up to the cupola to finish her new picture.

"I'm going to speak to someone today to help arrange for you to have an art teacher come to the house to show you things, different techniques and ways to make your pictures more beautiful, Sylvia. You still want me to do that?"

She thought a moment and nodded.

"All right. When I find the right person, Sylvia, I would like you not to talk to him or her about Papa and the rocking chair. Papa and the rocking chair are our secret, right?"

"Yes. I'll never tell," she said, putting her hand over her heart and hooking her pinkie with mine to make a pinkie promise. Like a little girl, she obviously enjoyed the idea of having a secret with her older sister.

"Okay," I said, "our secret."

After she went up to the cupola, I called the first person who came to mind for advice about something like this, Mrs. Haider, the retired principal of Whitefern High School. She had always been very kind to me and had taken a personal interest in me when I finally began to attend the public school. Because Whitefern was a relatively small town, our school was small enough for her to know some private information about her students.

She knew I had been homeschooled, of course, and that I had lost my mother when she had given birth to Sylvia. She knew of Sylvia, but, like most people, she didn't know very much about her, because in those years, Sylvia was rarely seen. After her retirement, I had seen Mrs. Haider occasionally in the village, and she was always quite friendly and very correct about how she asked questions. I never got the impression that she was a town gossip. I had no hesitations about telling her things concerning my family. She always ended her conversations with me by saying, "I hope all goes well with you, Audrina."

Her smile was sincere. She was a pretty woman, always perfectly put together, with coordinating colors and style. Her green eyes were still vibrantly emerald and contrasted nicely with her snow-white hair layered in an attractive bob.

Mrs. Haider was a widow with three adult children, all of whom had families but lived far away, her son in New York and her two daughters in South Carolina. She had seven grandchildren and lived in a modest two-story house on the north side of Whitefern.

When she answered her phone this morning, she sounded absolutely delighted to hear from me. She listened patiently while I described Sylvia as best I could and what I wanted for her now.

"That's very commendable of you, Audrina. I think that's a brilliant idea, and I know just the person for this assignment. As it turns out, Mr. Price, one of our art teachers, retired just last year, and from what his wife has been telling me, he is quite bored. They're not travelers, and he hates golf," she said, laughing. "Why don't I call him for you and, if he's interested, give him your phone number?"

"Thank you, Mrs. Haider," I said. "That's very kind."

"Oh, indeed," she said. "I, too, like the idea that I can continue to be of some use." She laughed again.

After I hung up, I called Arden at his office.

"He's in a meeting, Mrs. Lowe," Mrs. Crown said. "Is this an emergency?"

She sounded annoyed. A woman in her forties and married to a bank teller, Barton Crown, a man Arden called an untrustworthy leech, Mrs. Crown was a little too protective of Arden, in my opinion. I didn't think there was any doubt she'd rather he was her husband. She was a plain-looking woman with one of those complexions Momma used to call "an unripe peach." Her makeup seemed to fade as the day progressed, leaving her looking bloodless, with dark brown eyes. Aunt Ellsbeth would say, "She shows cleavage in hopes you won't look at her face."

"Oh, no, but please have him call me as soon as he's free."

"Yes, I will," she said. "As soon as that's possible."

I didn't say thank you. I just hung up.

Less than a half hour later, Mr. Price called to tell me he would love to be of some assistance.

"When would you like me to begin?" he asked, sounding very eager. I guessed Mrs. Haider wasn't exaggerating when she said he was bored with his retirement.

"As soon as you wish," I said. We hadn't even discussed the cost.

"I could come this afternoon to get acquainted with the young lady. How's three o'clock?"

"Yes, that would be fine," I said. "Perhaps we should discuss the cost."

"Oh, I'm sure we'll come to a mutually satisfactory arrangement," he said. "I think it's important first that your sister be comfortable with me."

He was right. I wondered what he knew about

Sylvia and what he didn't. I didn't want any brutal disappointments to occur. I was afraid of how that might disturb Sylvia, especially if someone rejected working with her because he thought she wasn't capable of learning. Arden, of course, would feel vindicated and say something like "I told you so."

"Do you know anything about my sister?" I asked.

"I know she's been homeschooled?"

"She was born premature and had to remain in an institutional setting until she was about two and a half. If she had attended a public school, she would surely have been placed in special education. She still needs me to look after her, but she is very pleasant and courteous. However, she is quite sensitive," I added, loading my voice with warning. "She can tell when someone is talking down to her or looking down at her."

"I taught special education students," he said. "No worries at all."

"She has taken to art, loves to draw and paint. She can spend hours and hours doing it. I've been doing the best I can with other aspects of her education, but when it comes to art, no one has taught her anything formally. She doesn't have that long an attention span except when she's working on her art, but I'm not sure how she would pay attention to instruction."

"A challenge. Love it," he said.

I had to smile. He was truly a bored man. "Okay, then let's see how it works out today at three."

I immediately started up to the cupola to tell Sylvia and to talk to her about our lunch, but the phone rang before I reached the stairs. It was Arden. Apparently, telling him I had called had become possible for Mrs. Crown.

"What?" he said sharply when I answered the phone.

"What? Can't you at least pretend to be courteous, Arden, and ask how I am first?"

"I'm busy, Audrina. There is no time for small talk here. I know women feed on small talk like birds on grass seed, but it's a particularly busy day. There's been a big drop in crude oil this morning. You know what crude oil is?" he asked, raising his voice bloated with sarcasm.

"Stop it, Arden. Of course I know what crude oil is. I called to tell you I'm arranging for an art tutor for Sylvia. I'll be paying him from the household account."

"Waste of money," he said. "What about the papers I want you to sign? I'll tell you where to meet me, and . . ."

"We'll talk about that later, Arden. I'm just letting you know I have the art tutor coming at three today to meet Sylvia. Unless there's a problem the teacher sees, I will contract with him today."

"Who is he?"

"Arthur Price, a retired high school art teacher."

"How old is he?"

"He's not that old, Arden."

"I'm not worried about him being *too* old." He sighed. "All right, do what you want. I repeat, it's a waste of time and money, but I have to get back to important things."

"This is important, Arden. She's my sister, and

she's your sister-in-law. My father expected we would look after her."

"Oh, spare me. Your father expected . . . Well, I expected things, too. Women can get so emotional. It's like they have a trigger finger on their emotions, which is why they don't belong in business, especially a business like this," he emphasized. " 'Bye," he said, and hung up before I could say a word in my defense.

I was so frustrated that I wished I could strangle the phone and squeeze every last word he uttered out of the wires and out of my mind. Up the stairs I went, pounding every step as if I was stamping on Arden's face. When I entered the cupola, I found Sylvia sitting and staring at a blank sheet of paper, her pencil in her hand, poised in the air like a knife she was about to stab into something.

"Where's your picture?" I asked.

She turned to look at me, her face twisted in an expression of anger and frustration. "Done," she said, nodding to the picture now lying on a long table.

I looked at it and saw that not much more had been added to it. It still fascinated me. I put it down and turned back to her. She had returned to staring at her blank sheet.

"What are you trying to draw and paint now, Sylvia?"

She looked at me, deciding whether to answer, I guessed. "What makes a baby a boy?" she asked.

"What?"

"Boys and girls come from the same mother, so who's first? And why didn't Papa ever have a boy?"

How was I going to explain this? Explain the X and Y chromosomes? No way. "Why do you want to know?"

"Because Papa told me a baby, but he didn't tell me if the baby was a boy or a girl," she said. I nearly laughed at the way she said it. She sounded condescending, like I was dumb not to realize that.

"Why is that important right now, Sylvia? Many people, maybe most, like it to be a surprise. Except for those people who want to paint nursery rooms and choose clothes way ahead of time," I added, more for myself. "So?"

"I have to draw the baby, Audrina. If I don't draw the baby, the baby will not come," she said.

I was beginning to get a headache. How was she coming up with these crazy ideas? Maybe Arden wasn't so wrong. Maybe the time had come for me to find some help with Sylvia. After all, I did have a life of my own, or I thought I did. The truth I didn't want to face was that what was holding Sylvia back from the world was holding me back, too, as long as I was chained to her daily. For a good part of my life, I had spent most of my time inside one house. For a short while, I had broken free of it, but I was right back in it now, its walls hovering around me, making me feel cloistered. Sometimes I felt I had been swallowed. The walls seemed to quiver like the inside of its lungs.

Taking walks outside around the house wasn't enough, and our short shopping trips were all full of purpose, with little or no fun. There was nothing left to explore here but my own demons, and I was tired of that. I certainly didn't want to start down a path similar to the one Sylvia had to follow, taking in everything outside slowly, in small, careful bites, but what choice was I giving myself? I wasn't trying to make friends, and I certainly wasn't joining any organizations that would lead to making friends. Sometimes I feared that someone who didn't know us would look at us and wonder who was the slow-witted one.

"Maybe whether it's a boy or a girl will come to you," I said sharply. It was not unreasonable of me to run out of patience, especially when I chastised myself for using Sylvia to justify my being such a prisoner of Whitefern. "Forget about all that, and listen to me. I have found a good art teacher for you. He used to teach in the high school. His name is Mr. Price, and he will be here this afternoon to meet you. Do not tell him what you want to draw just yet. Let him teach you the things you have to know in order to draw and paint better, okay? He might start you drawing an apple or a banana or something like that. You do what he asks and what he tells you to do. Okay?"

She didn't look happy.

"This is what you wanted, isn't it? To learn how to do this well? I'm not going to spend the money if you don't want to do it, Sylvia. Well? Do you or don't you?" I asked, practically shouting.

"I do."

"Good. Let's have you change your clothes and fix your hair. We'll talk with Mr. Price in the living room, and afterward we'll show him what supplies you have here. We'll get you whatever else you need. I'm sure he'll give us a list, and tomorrow morning you and I can go shopping."

She looked at the blank sheet without answering me.

"Sylvia!" I said sharply. "Did you hear me? Concentrate on what I'm telling you."

I rarely snapped at her like this, but she was making me nervous. Papa, the rocking chair, babies . . . I had driven all the visions and dreams, all the ghosts and whispers, down as deeply as I could in my memory. Stirring it was like throwing rocks at the hives of hornets.

She stood up reluctantly and, with her head lowered, followed me out and down to her room.

"Now, it's important that you make a good impression on your art tutor, Sylvia," I said in a calmer, more motherly tone. "I know you don't meet many strangers, and you're very shy, but I don't want you looking at other things or letting your attention wander when he asks you questions or speaks to you," I said while laying out her fresh clothes. "Teachers think girls and boys who do that are unteachable, and you don't want him to think that, right?"

She shook her head and listened to me as I went on with instructions, but I could see her mind was still elsewhere, pulling her away every few moments to look up toward the cupola, as if she had left a half-baked new baby up there. She could be like this from time to time. Once her mind enveloped a thought or an idea, getting her to put it aside, even temporarily, was like prying open a stubborn clam.

Would she be like this with Mr. Price? He'd see immediately that he was wasting his time with her. I'd feel like a fool, and Arden would strut around with his arrogant, masculine superiority and his infuriating "I told you so" look, which he could put on as quickly as a Halloween mask.

Nevertheless, I remained hopeful. I fixed Sylvia's hair and straightened her clothes to make her as presentable as possible. I had to be ready for anything, but I had to be realistic, too. If Mr. Price thought she was unteachable, even he, a man bored with his present life, would not attempt the lessons. Money didn't seem to matter to him. I hoped he was sincere when he said he welcomed a challenge. She was certainly going to be that.

"We'll prepare some nice biscuits and tea now, okay, Sylvia? I'd like you to do most of that and bring it out when I tell you to, understand?"

"Chocolate biscuits?"

I recalled the last time we had made them and how she had gotten the chocolate all over her dress and had to be continually told to wipe her mouth.

"I think he likes the plain ones," I said. Little lies were often the glue that held more important truths together. Papa had taught me that.

Disappointed, Sylvia followed me out and down to the kitchen, where I put her to work making biscuits while I vacuumed the living room and polished the furniture to brighten things up. Then I went to the powder room to make myself presentable, too. I hated how haggard I could look sometimes. Frustration, worry, and anger were like the three witches of *Macbeth* in this house, toiling and mixing their evil brew.

Promptly at three, the doorbell rang. Being on time was probably embedded in a schoolteacher after as many years as Mr. Price had worked. Part of the daily instruction I gave Sylvia, especially in the past few years, was how to greet people who came to our door. I spent hours and hours role-playing with her to show her how to introduce herself and be courteous to guests. Papa was very proud of the success I'd had. Aunt Ellsbeth, along with Arden and especially Vera, often ridiculed my efforts and said things like "You're trying to put clothes in a closet without any hangers." I ignored them, and whenever Sylvia did perform perfectly, they usually smirked and looked away with the comment that she'd forget next time.

I stepped into the kitchen. "Go answer the door, Sylvia," I ordered. "It's your art teacher. Introduce yourself after you greet him."

She looked annoyed for a moment. I kept my stern gaze on her and was reminded of how Vera could pout and stomp when told to do something she didn't want to do. Petulant, Sylvia went to the front door. I stayed back, holding my breath.

"Well, hello," I heard Mr. Price say. "I'm Arthur Price."

"Hello," Sylvia said. "Welcome to Whitefern. I'm Sylvia."

She did that well enough, but she didn't step back, leaving him in the doorway. It was awkward.

I hurried toward them. "Oh, do come in, Mr. Price," I said. "I'm Audrina Lowe."

"Yes, yes," he said, stepping in. He was short,

barely a few inches taller than I was, with a trim, graying goatee like some French artist on the Left Bank of Paris. He was balding, the patches of gray-black hair over his temples looking pasted onto his scalp. He had a jolly, Santa Claus face with bright blue eyes and was wearing a dark blue jacket and tie.

I nodded at Sylvia to close the door behind him. The afternoon breeze was quite cool and sharp. I led Mr. Price into the living room. He looked about with great interest, like some buyer of antiques who had wandered into one of the biggest discoveries of his career.

"What an amazing house," he said. "These paintings are most interesting."

Like any man, he focused quickly on our famous naked lady on the chaise eating grapes. He glanced quickly at me.

"And the clocks and vases, all family heirlooms, I imagine?"

"Some are," I said. "Please, have a seat." I indicated the sofa Papa had redone only a year ago. Momma had loved lying on it. "Sylvia will bring us some tea and biscuits," I said, and I nodded at her again.

"Thank you," he said, rubbing his palms together. "Winter's coming earlier this year for sure. You can smell the snow."

Sylvia looked at us. "Smell it?" she asked. "Snow? It doesn't smell."

"Well, not snow, exactly," he said, smiling. "It's just . . . I mean, it feels like winter's coming."

Sylvia glanced at me as if we had let a madman into the house and then continued to the kitchen.

"What a beautiful young lady," he said immediately. "I know a lot of artists, some not so amateur, who would love to have her for a model. Those eyes, startlingly beautiful, almost exotic, and a complexion like alabaster."

"She wants to be the artist, not the model," I said, probably too sharply. It occurred to me, maybe for the first time, that I could actually be jealous of Sylvia. It made me a little ashamed. It was like envying a poor girl's single doll when you had dozens.

"Of course," he said. "So is there a special place where your sister would work? Certainly not in here. I wouldn't want to get any paint on this rug." He looked down at the Turkish rug that had been there as long as I could remember.

"Oh, yes. Before my father passed away, he established a room in our cupola as a sort of studio for her. It's two flights up, if that's all right. We don't have an elevator."

"That's not a problem." He patted his ballooning stomach. "Now that I'm retired, I've gained five pounds. My wife is always after me to do more exercise. Artists and teachers sit around too much. So going up and down stairs sounds good." He looked toward the stairway.

Despite how beautiful the balustrade was, it was difficult for me to look at the stairway and not think of it as treacherous. Surely, I thought, he knew of our history, how Aunt Ellsbeth, Billie, and Vera had died on those stairs. If he had any fear, he kept it well disguised behind his appreciative smile.

Sylvia came in carrying the silver tray with the teapot and cups.

Mr. Price stood up. "Can I help?" he asked.

"She's fine," I said. "Please. Sit."

He did, and Sylvia put the tray on the table. I wanted her to demonstrate that she was capable of basic things and could easily grow and learn.

"Biscuits," she said, more as if she was reminding herself, and turned quickly.

He smiled. "Venus," he muttered after her, and then turned to me. "How long has she been interested in art?"

"As long as I can remember her being interested in anything," I said. I began to pour the tea. "Sugar?"

"Maybe one, if we don't tell my wife. And don't tell her about any biscuits. She's got me on a strict diet."

Sylvia returned with the biscuits and put them on the table. "I like chocolate," she said, still grumpy about it.

"Chocolate?" He looked at them.

"We have plain with a touch of vanilla today," I said firmly.

"Oh, I like that." He plucked one off the dish.

"I like chocolate," Sylvia repeated.

I raised my eyes toward the ceiling.

"So, Sylvia, what do you like to draw and paint? Things in nature, people, animals?"

She looked at me. "Whatever I'm told to draw," she said.

I felt my heart sink.

"Told? Who tells you?"

"She means she likes to draw what people like to see. My father used to ask her to draw birds in trees."

"Oh, I see. Well, we'll start with going over colors and then learning perspective. How's that sound?"

"I want to draw and paint," she said.

"That's what he means, Sylvia."

"Don't worry. I'll get her to understand," he told me, chewing on his biscuit. "I spent years in the grade school before teaching junior and senior high. Say, this is a very good biscuit. Homemade?"

"Sylvia made them," I said.

"Did she? Well, if you can make biscuits this good, you can paint the *Mona Lisa*."

"Who's that?" she asked.

"Oh, it's a famous painting. I'll bring a book that has many great paintings in it so you can see all the styles in which artists have worked."

"We have art books, Mr. Price. Sylvia wants to be active. Art history is a little beyond our goals here. How often do you want to give her lessons?" I asked. "And when?"

"I can be here in the afternoon." He leaned toward me. "Probably only an hour at first. I know about attention span," he assured me, nodding. "Say, three times a week?"

"Would you like that, Sylvia? Three times a week?"

"I want to do art every day," she said.

He smiled. "Oh, you'll have homework to do every day," he said.

She looked suspicious but then nodded.

"Why don't we look at your studio and see what you have, and then I'll make a list of things you'll need," Mr. Price said. He thought for a moment and then plucked another biscuit off the dish. "Let's keep this a secret." He winked at me.

Sylvia's eyes widened instantly. "Secret?"

"He means he doesn't want his wife to know he's eating what she doesn't want him to eat, Sylvia. You won't tell her, will you?" I said, trying to insert a joke quickly.

She shook her head. "Is she coming today, too?"

"No."

Mr. Price sipped his tea. Sylvia hadn't poured herself a cup or taken a biscuit. She had yet to sit.

"Let's go show Mr. Price your studio, okay?"

"Okay," she said, and he and I stood up. I nodded at Sylvia for her to go first, and we followed.

"My sister tends to take everything said to her literally," I warned.

"I understand."

We started up behind her. "She has a little bit of a wild imagination," I added, with the same cautionary tone.

"All artists need that," he replied.

"What were you thinking of in terms of cost?" I asked. I was getting mixed messages, wondering now if I was doing the right thing. I hoped he wasn't someone who would carry tales from Whitefern. There were enough rumors about us.

"How's twenty-five dollars an hour sound?"

"It sounds okay," I said. I had no idea whether it

was fair, and I was sure Arden would have something negative to say about it.

"You can pay me every two weeks so it's not a chore," he added.

We started up to the cupola. I could hear his heavy breathing already.

"This will be good for me," he said, aware that I heard it.

"I hope it will be good for us all," I replied.

Sylvia opened the door to the cupola, and we stepped in. Her sheet of paper was on the easel, but I could have sworn it was completely blank when we had left earlier.

Right now, there was the start of a baby's head.

Voices in the Brush

I was still trembling a little when I walked Mr. Price to the door to say good-bye. Sylvia followed closely behind us and stood behind me. When I glanced at her and nodded at Mr. Price, she moved quickly to say good-bye properly, adding, "I'm pleased to meet you."

"To have met you," I prompted, and she repeated it.

"And I am very pleased to have met you, too, Sylvia. I look forward to helping you with your artwork," Mr. Price told her. He offered her his hand.

She looked at it suspiciously and then touched it as if it might be a hot stovetop and quickly stepped back.

He smiled at me and said, "She's precious."

He had dictated a list of supplies, and we had decided he would begin in two days. He liked Sylvia's studio space, his only criticism being that there was not enough light. I assured him that we would bring up two more lamps.

The sun was already losing its grip on the day. Fall twilights were much earlier, so the shadows were thicker in and out of Whitefern. Papa used to call fall the "dying season." Trees were beautiful only for a short while with their brown and yellow leaves. "It's like a last breath of beauty," he had said. "Then come the skeletons."

I waited for Mr. Price to go to his car and wave to me before I closed the door. For a moment, I stood there catching my breath. Without my asking her to, Sylvia began to clean away the tea and the remaining biscuits. She was still mumbling about chocolate being better. I picked up what was left and followed her to the kitchen.

Upstairs in the cupola, she had not said anything about the partial drawing. When Mr. Price had asked her what she was doing, she didn't respond. He had looked at me, and I'd changed the subject quickly. I hoped he hadn't seen the surprise on my face when we had first entered.

In the kitchen, Sylvia was immediately busy putting the leftover biscuits into a plastic container. She was plucking them off the plate as if they were dead insects.

"When did you go back up and start drawing the baby, Sylvia?" I asked.

She ignored me and began washing the cups and the teapot.

I drew closer. "Sylvia, I thought you said you needed to know if it was a boy or a girl before you could start to draw a baby."

She paused and looked at me like a child who had been caught with her hand in the cookie jar. "I thought if I started, Papa would tell me," she said. She returned to the cups and the teapot.

"Did he?"

She shook her head. "Not yet." Her eyes widened with a thought. "Maybe he was waiting for me to learn more art and do better."

"All right." *Enough of this*, I thought. *Why am I encouraging her wild imagination?* "So you like Mr. Price and want to learn from him?"

"He didn't say he likes chocolate biscuits."

"Forget the biscuits, Sylvia. Do you like him enough to want him to give you instruction with your art?"

"He didn't tell me anything to do."

"He's coming back for that in two days. He'll be here at the same time three times a week, remember? Is that all right?"

"Yes," she said. "But next time, I want to make chocolate biscuits, Audrina." She spoke firmly, as firmly as Papa when his mind was made up about something.

"Okay. Make chocolate biscuits, Sylvia. Make tons and tons of chocolate biscuits," I nearly screamed. Anyone could have heard the tense impatience in my voice, but she simply smiled. I wondered if it was a good thing never to realize how much someone was annoyed at you. You went on your merry way, doing whatever you were doing, not feeling guilt and rarely upset with yourself.

On the other hand, I was frustrated. I went to the freezer to take out pork chops and keep myself busy.

"We're making grilled pork chops in plum sauce tonight, Sylvia. Concentrate on that now."

"Can I do the sauce?" she asked immediately.

Gradually, I had been teaching her more sophisticated recipes. She could make a nice cheese omelet or bake cookies, biscuits, and some cakes. Last Christmas, I'd taught her how to make a turkey stuffing and marshmallow sweet potatoes. The more delicate something was, the more intense was her concentration. Ironically, the easiest things bored her.

"Okay," I said. "Get out the bag of plums."

This was another of Arden's favorite dinners. Why it was so important to please the men in this house I never knew, but if you disappointed Papa, you might expect the ceiling to fall and the walls to cave in. It was the same for Arden. As Aunt Ellsbeth often said, "Men are the sun, and we are the planets circling them and held in their grip."

I took out the ingredients for the sauce—ginger, garlic, shallots, soy sauce, and honey. It was a recipe Arden's mother, Billie, had taught me. She had tried to teach it to Vera, but Vera hated working in the kitchen. She hated all household chores. Whenever she was given something to do, she would try to get me to do it for her. Sometimes she threatened me by saying she would break something and blame it on me if I didn't do it.

The memories streamed by like the echoes of nightmares.

Suddenly, I heard the front door open and close. I rushed out of the kitchen and was surprised to see Arden home so early. When he saw me, he raised his arm to show me he was holding a big manila envelope. He waved it like a winning lottery ticket.

"I've brought it all home. Mr. Johnson understands how busy you are here with Sylvia and agreed to let you sign and put your fingerprint on the page for notarization without him being present. He doesn't do this for everyone. He's bending the law quite a bit; it's a special favor for us. Let's get right to it," he said, and sat on the settee. "I want to turn it in first thing in the morning." He put the envelope on the table and began taking out documents and the ink pad for a fingerprint.

"I told you that I want to think about it first, Arden. Why are you rushing me?"

"Why? Why?" He slapped the table with his palm and sat back, folding his arms across his chest like a boy about to go into a sulk. "I'm chasing new, high-net-worth clients, Audrina," he began, speaking with obviously forced self-control. "More than likely, these people will do their due diligence and investigate us inside and out before they place millions of dollars in our hands. They'll certainly question why your father left the majority percentage of the company to you, someone who doesn't work there and doesn't even have a broker's license. That's what we call in the business a red flag. It will drive them away."

"I'm thinking of getting my broker's license," I said.

"What? You're thinking what?" His eyes widened, and he turned red with rage.

"Don't be so shocked at the idea, Arden. I was the one who tutored you in the beginning to help you get your license."

"That was years ago."

"Nothing's changed. The stock market is still the stock market."

"Yes, a great deal has changed. There are new laws, regulations."

"I'll study up on it. You know I'm good at that. Aunt Ellsbeth and even your mother told me I should have gone to college. I was always on the honor roll in school."

He stared coldly. "I can't believe I'm hearing this." He shook his head the way someone would shake water out of his ears after swimming.

"It might be very attractive for our company to have a husband-and-wife team," I suggested. "That, it seems to me, would make new clients comfortable and be a great advertisement."

"A great advertisement? Next, you'll want to wear my pants."

"Stop it, Arden. Don't treat me like a child."

"Then don't act like one."

"At least, let's let some time pass so we can think about it."

"I should think about this? I'll tell you what I think about, Audrina. I think about why I'm doing all this, why we have all this, and why I work harder and harder. We have no children. We have a mentally slow young woman to care for. That's all. And ourselves, of course, but where's the future?"

"We could adopt, I suppose. If I don't get pregnant soon," I said.

"Soon? It's been years. When will you realize it won't happen?"

He looked away for a moment and then turned back to me, his eyes smaller. He looked like he was about to cry, like a little boy who couldn't go out to play.

"And adopt a baby? You say it so casually. What about my feelings? I'd like to have my blood passed on, too, you know. I am not excited about making someone else's unwanted child the heir to my fortune, my heritage."

"I'm sorry, Arden," I said. I really did feel sorry for him now. "Let's take a breath and give everything more thought. I'm not saying you're wrong. Papa taught me that the best decisions come after they're nurtured and turned around and around to check for cracks or dents in your thinking. Every decision is—"

"Yes, I know, like a birth. He said that so much that I felt like checking into a maternity ward."

I smiled. "I'm making one of your favorites, grilled pork chops in plum sauce. Your mother used to make that. She taught me."

He looked down at the papers and then began stuffing them back into the envelope. "I need a drink," he said.

Sylvia came to the doorway. "Sauce is ready," she announced, smiling from ear to ear.

"Sauce is ready? You let her make it?" Arden asked, astonished.

"She's good at it, Arden. You'd be surprised at what she's learned in the kitchen."

"Might be poison, for all we know. I guess I need this just in case."

He poured himself a hefty glass of bourbon. Then he looked at Sylvia, who was still standing there smiling at him. Her right cheek had a streak of plum sauce across it.

"Looks like she was finger painting with our dinner."

"Oh, she just touched herself after handling the plums. Every cook gets a little messy."

"Cook. Artist. Next she'll be CEO of our company," he said, and gulped his drink, his eyes still on her. "What happened with her art teacher?"

"I hired him. He'll be here day after tomorrow. He'll come three times a week at first, an hour each time, for twenty-five dollars an hour."

"Twenty-five dollars? Are you crazy? That's seventy-five a week to babysit. You might as well open the window and toss the money out," he said, and finished his drink.

"If it doesn't help, we'll stop it, but for now, she is happy about it, Arden. You know," I added, "her name is on the estate Papa left, too. We hardly spend any of her money on her."

"I know. I know plenty," he said, and poured himself more bourbon. He looked at us both while he sipped his drink and then turned and headed for the stairs. "I'm going to wash up and get out of this monkey suit that I have to wear every day to be sure our business is a success and I can make enough money for you to waste."

We watched him head up the stairs, pausing to sip his drink. Sylvia looked at me and then stepped toward the stairway, as if she expected she'd have to charge up and save him the way she had saved Papa from falling backward. But Arden continued on, his anger marching him the rest of the way.

"Let's set the table, Sylvia," I said.

Arden came down a half hour later. He did look refreshed and relaxed, but there was something else different about him. He wore the wry smile of some-one who was carrying a secret full of self-satisfying irony. He opened a bottle of Papa's prize red wine, which was to be used only for very special occasions, and poured a glass for each of us. We usually didn't give Sylvia much alcohol of any kind. Arden knew why.

Once, years ago, Vera had gotten her terribly drunk. She'd thrown up over everything in her room—her bed, her rug, her desk. The reaction she was having terrified her, and she flailed about, crying and waving her arms. Vera was hysterical with laughter when I came upon them, and when Papa found out, he went into a rage and beat Vera with his belt until Aunt Ellsbeth stopped him by clinging to his arm so tightly he lifted her off her feet with every attempted swing.

I actually felt sorrier for Vera that day than I did for Sylvia, because Sylvia simply fell asleep after we bathed her and changed her into her nightgown. Vera was off in her room whimpering like a beaten puppy. Aunt Ellsbeth didn't show her any sympathy, despite stopping Papa from beating her to death. She went to Vera's room and told her she had gotten what she deserved. She didn't even look after her welts. Some of them were bleeding. After Aunt Ellsbeth left, I went to see Vera. She was curled in the fetal position on her bed, shivering with pain.

"You need to wash those welts, Vera," I said, "before they get infected."

"Leave me alone. You're happy this happened to me."

"I'm not happy. You shouldn't have done that to Sylvia, but I'm not happy to see you so beaten," I said. I said it sincerely enough for her to turn and look at me.

"Okay. Go get me a warm washcloth and some antiseptic gel and some Band-Aids," she ordered.

When she took off her dress, I saw how Papa had hit her around her waist and thighs. She lay back so I could wash every welt and put on the medicine and bandages where she needed them.

"You know why he hit me so hard, don't you?" she asked as I worked.

"Because you did a bad thing to Sylvia," I said.

"No. It's because he loves me the most and wants me to be the perfect Audrina, not you," she said. Then she leaned forward to whisper, "He even told me to sit in the rocking chair so I could learn her special gifts."

"No, he didn't," I said.

She smiled through her pain and lay back. "He loves me more," she insisted. I watched her close her eyes and smile, despite what must have been terrible stings and aches.

I went back to sit with Sylvia, who was asleep, and brushed her hair off her face.

"I won't let her do mean things to you again," I told her. "I won't let anyone, sweet Sylvia."

The memory drifted away like smoke, but also like smoke, it left a bitter taste in my mouth.

"A toast, then," Arden said now, raising his glass after pouring the wine. "To the baby who is coming, who is always coming."

"A boy or a girl?" Sylvia quickly asked.

"Why, a boy, of course," he said.

"Who told you? Papa?"

He looked at me and smiled. "Of course," he said. "Who else?"

He drank his wine in one gulp and poured another. I looked at Sylvia. She drank hers quickly, too quickly, and he rose to pour more for her.

"Don't," I said. "You know she can't handle it, Arden."

"Oh, a little more," he said. "To celebrate."

"Celebrate what?"

"Sylvia is getting an art teacher, and I'm getting a partner, apparently." He laughed and drank.

I served the salad, and we began to eat our first real formal dinner since Papa had died. I looked longingly toward his empty chair. Arden would never have said these things if Papa were still alive. Arden saw my gaze and read my thoughts.

"Tomorrow night, Sylvia," he said, "you set my place there. It's time we faced the reality. I'm the head of Whitefern now, no matter what our estate documents read. Is that all right, Audrina?"

"No. It's not all right," I said. "But you can sit there.

Maybe it will help you think more of yourself. No matter what happened to him or to people he loved, Papa kept his self-respect."

"Why is it that after people die, we think only good things about them and forget the bad?"

"I think about it all, Arden. Your mother told me to be that way. She knew I was proud of my father, even though there were many times I disliked him, regretfully so. She taught me that none of us is all good or all bad."

"Meaning me?"

"Meaning all of us, Arden, so yes, you, too."

"What about you, Sylvia? Do you think about all this? Do you think everyone is bad and good? Do you think?"

"Stop teasing her, Arden."

"Teasing? Am I teasing you, Sylvia?"

He laughed, and we began to eat in silence. When I looked at Sylvia, I saw how happy she was despite Arden's ridiculing her. At first, I didn't understand why. Then I thought about what Arden had said and why that would make her happy. She was already planning it, I was sure.

She could finish her drawing of the baby.

I saw it in the way she rushed cleaning up after dinner. I didn't want her to be deeply disappointed, even though I wished in my heart of hearts that it was all true, that a baby was going to come.

"You must not pay attention to everything Arden says, Sylvia," I warned her. "He likes to tease you. He teases me, too."

She nodded, holding her soft smile as if I was the one who didn't understand. I helped her finish so she could go up to the cupola to work, and then I went into the living room, where Arden was having a brandy. His face was red from all the alcohol he had consumed.

"You can leave the documents here tomorrow," I told him. "I'll read them."

He widened his eyes. "And?"

"I said I'll read them and talk to you tomorrow."

"Right. Tomorrow." He reached for the *Wall Street Journal*, but I knew he wasn't going to read anything. He was simply going to hold it up and fume behind it.

"I'm going up. I'm a little tired tonight."

I scooped up the envelope and headed up the stairs. I had drunk too much wine myself, deliberately making sure there wasn't too much left for Sylvia—or for Arden. He'd wanted to open another bottle, but I had talked him out of it.

I prepared myself for bed and then went up to the cupola. I didn't want Sylvia staying up there deep into the night. She had no concept of time, especially when she was drawing or painting. She had the outline of the baby completed and was sitting there and staring at it. She turned and looked up at me.

"Is he going to be a pretty baby?" she asked me.

"We're a handsome family, Sylvia. Everyone was very good-looking, as you can see from old photographs. Momma was so beautiful that Papa was afraid to let her out of the house."

"Why?"

"Other men would look at her and want her to be

their wife," I said. "And you're beautiful. Everyone who sees you says so."

"Am I?"

"Yes, but you have to take care of yourself. It's time you went to bed. You need sleep to stay healthy and pretty. Don't forget, we're going shopping tomorrow for your art supplies," I said.

She stood and gazed at her drawing. "I don't know what color eyes he'll have. Or hair," she said, looking frantic.

"We'll worry about it tomorrow," I told her.

She turned abruptly, the way Vera would when she became impatient with me, and marched out of the cupola and down the stairs. I followed her to her bedroom and watched as she prepared herself for bed. I remembered the early years when she could do almost nothing for herself. Papa was convinced that she was severely disabled and would be practically an invalid all her life. Every bit of progress I made with her had amazed him.

I was amused by how much care she was taking with herself right now. Usually, she did nothing with her hair, and I had to brush it and pin it back for her. Both Momma and Aunt Ellsbeth refused to go to bed without first putting Pond's Cold Cream on their faces.

"Your skin dries when you sleep," they told me. "Wrinkles wait in the darkness ready to pounce."

So I put it on, and I taught Sylvia to put it on. Vera made fun of it, but she didn't live to be old enough to see any wrinkles on her face.

Usually, I still had to tell Sylvia to do it, but she went right to it tonight, and then she looked at me and asked, "Am I really beautiful, Audrina?"

"Yes, you are," I said. I smiled, happy that she was taking a female's interest in herself. It meant she was developing a little self-respect, something else Papa had never believed would happen.

Afterward, I returned to our bedroom and waited for Arden. I believed him when he said we would try again to have a baby. He always expected that I would be in the mood for lovemaking whenever he was. Most of the time, he didn't care if I was or not. I would never forgive him for telling Vera some of the details about our honeymoon night, how I had delayed and delayed coming out of the bathroom. If there was ever a time when I wasn't ready to have sex, it was then. But he had waited long enough and demanded his conjugal rights. He actually had tried to break down the door, claiming that a man had a greater need than a woman. He claimed that there was a buildup in him that had to be satisfied and that the same was not true for women.

Those memories always haunted me, along with the horrible memories that had come to me in the rocking chair. I didn't need a psychiatrist to explain my inhibitions now. Lately, Arden had come up with the idea that I was so psychologically wounded when it came to sex that my body might actually be preventing me from getting pregnant.

"Medical doctors like Dr. Prescott don't understand the emotional power a woman can employ without herself even realizing it," he'd said. "I read up on it. Until you really, really want to enjoy sex with me, you'll never get pregnant."

I tried, fearing that he might be right. But even when I thought I wanted it as much as or even more than he did, I did not get pregnant. These thoughts tormented me. Often at night, I would toss and turn in and out of sleep, trying to throw off the haunting ideas and words. I felt like shouting, but I didn't want to make any noise and wake Arden. He'd be angry about it. He might ask why I was so troubled, and he'd repeat those claims about women and about me.

Now, as I waited for him, I wondered if it wasn't the other way around. Because he thought I was so troubled by sex, it was affecting him. He would never, ever admit that he could be affected, but deep down inside his angry heart, those feelings surely twirled about and worried him. What would bother him the most, and what did he fear other men would think about him? That he couldn't satisfy his wife, that he couldn't produce a child? Not Arden Lowe. He wouldn't stand for that.

I turned over in bed and closed my eyes. He was taking so long. How long did he expect me to wait? I fought sleep, but it was heavy tonight and easily forced my eyelids closed. I had no idea what time it was when my eyes snapped open, but I saw that the light beside me was still on, so I sat up, rubbed my eyes, and looked at the clock. It was well after one. Arden hadn't come up. Where was he? Had he started drinking again? Had he fallen asleep on the sofa? He'd be upset with himself, I thought. I put on my robe and slippers and went out.

I had just started toward the stairs when I saw him. He looked like he had fallen asleep in the living room. His hair was wild, his shirt was unbuttoned and out of his pants, and he wasn't wearing his shoes. But he wasn't coming up the stairs. He was coming from the direction of the first Audrina's room and Sylvia's room.

"What are you doing?" I asked.

"What you should have been doing," he said. "Why didn't you?"

"Do what?"

"Come and get her."

"Why?"

"Why? She was making enough of a racket in that damn rocking chair. I thought someone was cutting up the floor. She's lucky she didn't go over backward in it, the way she was rocking back and forth. I heard it above me. I didn't know she would go rocking. It sounded like animals eating away at the roof. You were dead asleep, so I went to check, and there she was, rocking away. Do you know why? She thinks your father talks to her when she's rocking."

"I know," I said, a cold chill rushing through me as I recalled my own rocking-chair memories and my childhood faith in its power to take me into another world. "I'm sorry. Where is she?"

"I got her out of that chair damn fast and practically dragged her back to her room. I imagine she's fast asleep, which is exactly where I should be," he said, and walked past me toward our bedroom.

"I'm sorry, Arden," I said again.

He paused and looked back at me. "I told you years ago that we should throw that chair out, empty that room, and give away all those toys and things. Maybe now you'll listen. I can get someone here to-morrow to take it all away."

"I can't do that, Arden. I just can't."

"Suit yourself. I'm tired, and I have to get up in a matter of hours," he said.

I went to Sylvia's room and looked in on her. She was asleep, her blanket up to her waist, but her hair was down. She always liked it up when she slept. A few times when she was younger, she got strands of her own hair in her mouth and choked on them. I watched her sleep. There was something more about her, some-thing different, I thought, and stepped closer to get a better look at her face.

She was smiling.

Maybe she was having a pleasant dream. I wouldn't want to interrupt that. I fixed her blanket a little better and then returned to our bedroom. Arden was already curled up, clutching his pillow like a life preserver.

The funny thing was, he was smiling, too.

Shadows in the Darkness

Arden was up, dressed, and gone before I got up. I had to wake Sylvia, too. For a moment, she acted as if she didn't know where she was, but it wasn't unusual for her to wake up with a look of confusion on her face. It was almost as if she never expected there would be another morning. I wondered what sort of dreams she might have had.

Did she dream?

Sometimes I felt a little confused when I first woke up, and I imagined everyone did at one time or another. For a moment or so after you awaken, no matter who you are, how intelligent or mature you are, you can feel like a stranger in your own room, in your own house. You have to let everything you know and have gotten used to as belonging to you return, sort of fade in like a movie scene. Sunlight awakens it all, pulls it all out of the shadows, and fills your eyes and your mind with your identity. If you are pleased with who you are, you are happy, grateful, even relieved, but if you are not, you wish you hadn't woken up. You wish you had remained in your dreams being who you'd rather be, what you'd rather be.

Did Sylvia ever hate who and what she was? There were many times when I did. Did she look with envy at me, or had she felt envy toward Vera, especially when Vera had returned from her failed marriage, looking prettier and more sophisticated? Could Sylvia even experience jealousy? She never complained about one of us having more than she had. Vera used to claim that when Sylvia was very young, she was jealous of Billie's wagon, a device Billie used to get around because she had lost her legs to diabetes, but I never believed much in the things Vera would say. She was the epitome of jealousy in this house, her eyes of green envy converting anything beautiful that any of us had.

Once Sylvia realized what was happening when I woke her, she usually broke into a beautiful smile. This morning, however, she looked happier than I had seen her in a long time. She was, in fact, radiant. She wasn't groggy or sleepy and moved quickly to get out of bed. There was excitement in her eyes and an eagerness to start the day that I didn't often see, especially when Vera had come back to live with us and tormented her every chance she had.

When she stood, she stretched and looked at me as if I had just popped out of thin air.

"Hello, Audrina."

"Good morning, Sylvia. I overslept, so it's later than usual."

"Me, too. What do you want to do, Audrina?"

"Do?" I asked, smiling with amusement. She never began a day asking me that.

I remembered when I was a little girl, my mother would wake me and put me through her morning rituals. I had to stretch and then brush down my body before taking a shower so I could get rid of the dead skin cells. After I dressed and she brushed out my hair, she told me to sit before my mirror and smile at myself for thirty seconds so I could immediately think well of myself. She was adamant that I didn't put on a goofy grin.

"Because we're so behind schedule, let's go down first and have our breakfast, Sylvia. Then we'll repair our rooms, shower, and get dressed to go out and shop. We're buying your art supplies, remember?"

"Oh, yes, I need them."

"I know. Mr. Price gave us a list, remember? That's how we know what to buy."

"Is he coming back?"

"Yes, Sylvia. He is coming tomorrow afternoon. I'm going to post the schedule on the wall here in your room. For now, we have to get everything ready. Let's get a move on. It's a sunny day and not as cold as yesterday," I said. "There's much to do first."

"Much to do," she said. "Repair, repair." She repeated it as though she was making fun of me.

I looked at her with a half smile. "Yes, repair, Sylvia. We always repair."

She nodded. Although Arden certainly would be the first one to ridicule the idea, I sometimes looked at Sylvia when she wasn't aware that I was there and thought she looked brighter than she did when she was with Arden and me. She would study a painting or an object, look at pictures as if she remembered relatives she had never met, and then tilt her head as though she was hearing their voices. If I made a sound, she'd go right back to her cleaning or polishing like someone afraid she had been caught doing something wrong. I shook off the impression and told myself Sylvia was just not clever enough to put on an act and probably never would be. Of course, I told myself, she wasn't being sarcastic when she repeated "repair." It was only my imagination.

It was Aunt Ellsbeth who had first used that word to mean clean up our rooms, make our beds, and periodically change sheets and pillowcases as well as vacuum our rooms and wash our windows. The perfection in Whitefern had been broken merely by our living in it. According to her, especially after my mother had died, there was much about our home and our lives that needed mending. In the beginning, Papa had growled after every one of her critical remarks, but in time, he put up with it and made her the lady of the house. Every once in a while, I had to remind myself that I was the lady of the house now. The care and maintenance of Whitefern were my responsibility. Arden simply wasn't as devoted to it as I was. That was understandable, I guess. It wasn't his family heritage, and after all, his mother had died here tragically. Yet he knew I wouldn't live anywhere else, and neither would Sylvia.

Sylvia had more of an appetite than ever this

morning. She ate almost twice as much as I did. I rarely saw her exhibit as much energy, too. She went about our chores vigorously, cleaning up after breakfast. I imagined she wanted to get her art supplies as quickly as possible so she could do a better job on everything she drew now. I should have been happier about her enthusiasm, but I couldn't help feeling there was something wrong about it.

I chastised myself for feeling this way. Why couldn't I simply be happy for her? After all, this was what I had been hoping to see all these years and why I worked so hard to help and educate her. If I was hesitant and suspicious, what could I expect from Arden?

We went into town and bought the supplies Mr. Price had listed. I rarely took Sylvia anywhere but to the supermarket, clothing stores, and the dentist. Today I thought I would take her to a restaurant for lunch. I called Arden before we had left and asked him if he wanted to meet us at Danny's, a simple hamburger restaurant in Whitefern with booths and a long counter. It was like an old-fashioned diner.

"Are you sure you want to do that? We've never taken her to a restaurant, Audrina."

"She's very excited about the idea, Arden."

He was quiet so long that I thought he had hung up. "Arden?"

"I can't. I have to meet a client for lunch. Did you spend the morning reading the papers I brought home from Mr. Johnson?"

"I haven't had a chance yet."

"Well, *get* the chance," he ordered. Then he hung up without saying good-bye.

At the restaurant, we took a booth. Sylvia looked at everything and everyone as though she had just landed from another planet. The conversations and the laughter, the work of the short-order chef, and the music piped in had her turning every which way and gaping.

"Don't stare at people like that, Sylvia," I instructed.

"Why not?"

"They'll think you see something wrong with them, and it will make them self-conscious," I said, which was exactly how I felt when people stared at me.

"What's 'self-conscious'?"

"Aware of something that you think might be wrong with you, like your hair is messy or you put too much makeup on or that you have food on your face like a baby. Understand?"

She shook her head.

"Just look at me and think about your food." Sometimes it was easier to give up explaining something and leave it hanging in the air to be plucked again another time like an apple.

I ordered for both of us, knowing what she liked—cheeseburgers with tomatoes and lettuce and lots of ketchup, which she could have drooling down her chin.

"That man is staring at me," she said, looking toward the far end of the counter.

I turned. There were actually two men looking our way and talking. I recognized the older man. "That's

Mr. Hingen. He's a plumber. He was at Whitefern two months ago to fix our hot-water heater."

"Repair," she said.

"What? Oh. Yes, repair. Very good."

"Should we tell them it's not nice to stare?"

"No, just ignore them, Sylvia. Open your napkin and put it on your lap the way we do at home, so you don't drip anything and ruin your dress."

She did, but every once in a while, she stole another look at Mr. Hingen and the young man with him. I tried to get her attention on other things, talking about some of the pictures in the restaurant.

The waitress brought our food, and we began to eat.

Sylvia smiled after taking two bites. "Better than your hamburgers, Audrina," she commented.

"Well, thanks a lot."

"You're welcome," she said, proud that she had remembered to follow up a thank-you and, of course, missing my sarcasm. Vera was the first to tell me that talking to Sylvia was like talking to yourself. It was true, but I never let her or anyone else see that it bothered me. Most of the time, it didn't.

Before we were finished, Mr. Hingen stopped at our table to say hello, introducing the younger man as his son, Raymond. He was a good-looking, dark-haired man with light brown eyes, probably in his twenties. It was obvious that Raymond was quite taken with Sylvia and had asked his father to introduce him to us.

"How's everything at the house?" Mr. Hingen asked.

"Fine, thank you."

"My son is working with me now, so if you have any problems, just give us a call. This is your younger sister?"

"Yes."

"You're very pretty," Raymond said to Sylvia. "Where have you been hiding?"

"I don't hide," Sylvia said, indignant. "Do I, Audrina?"

"No, of course not."

"Do you go to college?"

"No, she doesn't attend college. She's at home with me."

"There's a lot to do here for a small town. You'd be surprised," Raymond told Sylvia. "Do you like to dance?"

She looked to me. "We dance, don't we, Audrina?"

I shook my head. "Not like he means, Sylvia. Thank you, Mr. Hingen, but—"

"Raymond, please." He turned back to Sylvia. "If you're not seeing anyone, I'd like to call you one day."

"I see Audrina and Arden, and I'm going to see Mr. Price tomorrow," Sylvia told him.

I wondered how long it would take him to realize whom he was talking to.

"Price?"

"He's a retired art teacher, ain't he?" Mr. Hingen asked me.

"Yes. He's giving my sister lessons. Right now, that's all she has time for. Thank you for stopping by," I said curtly.

Getting the idea, he poked his son. "Nice seeing you," he said to us.

"Yes," Raymond said. "Looking forward to the next time," he told Sylvia.

She narrowed her eyes and looked at me the moment they left. "When is next time?" she asked.

"Not ever," I said. "Forget it, Sylvia. It's just something someone says."

"Well, why do they say it if it's not true?"

"Just to make conversation. Most people hate silence. C'mon, let's finish. You need to fix up your art studio with the new things we just bought."

She nodded, but she watched Raymond Hingen leave the restaurant, and I thought she was more than just curious. His smile and the twinkle in his eyes had stirred something in her, something she might have felt for the first time. I was confident she didn't understand it. I remembered when I first had it, actually when I first met Arden. It both frightened and excited me simultaneously. I wanted to understand it, this tingle in my budding breasts, this thrill that traveled through my body, but I didn't want anyone to know about it, especially Vera or my aunt Ellsbeth.

I had brought Sylvia a long way from the disadvantaged little girl who had been treated so poorly by others in our family. Even Papa had to talk himself into accepting her as his daughter at the start. Was I wrong now to assume that she wouldn't ever be interested in young men? Was the idea of a romance, a relationship, as far off as another solar system when it came to her? If she could have a passion for art, why couldn't she have a passion for a man?

Eventually, she might have these feelings; she probably did at this moment, I thought, but no man would treat her well. And even if there was a man who cherished her now, when she lost her beauty, as we all did eventually, he would have far less tolerance for her and would surely cast her aside. Maybe it was cruel of me, but I wouldn't let Raymond Hingen or any young man date my sister, no matter how far she had come. It would only mean deeper suffering for her.

I could see that after I paid the bill and we were on our way out, she was still looking for Raymond. I tried getting her mind off him by talking about her artwork, her lessons, and what beautiful paintings she might do someday.

"We'll hang them on our living-room wall next to the expensive ones we've had in our family for years, Sylvia. Wouldn't you like that?"

She was quiet, thinking, gazing out the window as we drove home.

"Sylvia?"

"The faucet by the washing machine leaks a little," she said. "Maybe we need a plumber to fix it."

Was I astonished? Yes. But was I more fearful than surprised? Yes. "I'll look at it," I said. "Sometimes it's easy to fix."

She wasn't happy with my answer, but I did get her mind on other things when we arrived at the house and brought her new art supplies up to the cupola. She didn't mention Raymond Hingen again. I thought she might say something about plumbers and leaks when we sat with Arden at dinner that night. We had prepared a roast chicken with stewed potatoes. He didn't open another bottle of wine or make any nasty remarks. I was anticipating more about the papers Mr. Johnson had sent over with him, but he didn't mention them. Maybe he had asked someone's advice and had been told he'd get more with honey than with vinegar.

At times this evening, he reminded me of the young man who had courted me when I was a young girl. He was so sweet back then, always worried about me. He volunteered to take me on his bike to my piano lessons and was always waiting for me afterward. He was so protective. When I learned that his mother had lost her legs and that her husband had deserted her and Arden, I admired him even more for doing all that he could to make his mother happy. As insulated as I was, it was probably not unexpected that I would fall in love with the first boy who showed me so much attention and concern.

Tonight, he sounded so much like the Arden Lowe I remembered, giving Sylvia more attention than ever. Suddenly, he wasn't upset about spending money on an art teacher for her.

"You do great art without knowing anything about it. Imagine what you will do when you get all these lessons," he told her. His soft tone brought smiles to her face, even though I didn't think she understood what he was telling her.

Afterward, while she washed the dishes and put

away the food, I complimented him on how nice he was to her at dinner.

He nodded, thinking. "It's important that we bring some happiness back to Whitefern," he declared. "We have to change the landscape, as they say—as your father would say."

He poured himself an after-dinner cordial and asked me if I wanted one. I decided I did, and we sat reminiscing about some of the happier times when his mother had first moved in and taken such good care of my father.

"Sometimes you had to remind yourself that she'd had her legs amputated," I said.

"Yes. She had spirit. I hope I've inherited it."

"You have."

He looked at me with the pain of warm memories lost to time in his eyes. Nostalgia is always painful. You realize you can't bring back the smiles and laughter. In our house, reminiscences of past happiness often brought heartache. Sometimes it seemed better to forget them, no matter how wonderful they once were.

"I'm sorry I always talk about it, but we need a child, Audrina. We need someone who will strengthen our bond and give us more purpose in life. And I don't mean to blame anything on you."

That brought tears to my eyes. "I know," I said. "I want it as much as you do, if not more, Arden."

He kissed me. Sylvia came in and stood there looking at us. "I'm going up to finish drawing," she said.

"Good," Arden said before I could. We watched her go up the stairs.

That night, we made love more softly and affectionately than we had in years. Maybe he was simply testing his theory that if I welcomed sex, my body wouldn't resist fertilization. Maybe if he showed me true love, he, too, would be more potent.

There was no twisting and jerking me around to make himself more comfortable. There was more concern for my comfort and pleasure. He entered me gracefully and waited for me to accept him and open myself to him. There were kisses and caresses to accompany his strokes. I had that elusive orgasm time after time. He laughed about it and then brought himself to a satisfactory climax. Breathless but happy, we lay there holding hands. I thought he was so different tonight that it was like being married to Dr. Jekyll. I hoped Mr. Hyde was gone forever.

We fell asleep in each other's arms. I didn't even worry about Sylvia. When we woke in the morning, I was expecting him to bring up the paperwork, but he surprised me again by not mentioning it. Like the morning before, he was up early, dressed, and gone before I went to wake Sylvia. I remembered he had said he had a breakfast meeting. He was working hard, I thought. I should be more considerate. I promised myself that I would look at the papers and maybe do what he asked. When would I study to become a broker anyway? Wasn't that too much like a fantasy now? How could I leave Sylvia alone?

I was in such deep thought that I didn't realize for a few moments what Sylvia's still-made bed meant. In a little bit of a panic, I hurried up to the cupola. She wasn't there, and from what I could see, she hadn't done much more on her baby drawing. I descended and slowly walked to the rocking-chair room. As I'd feared, she was asleep in the chair. She was still dressed in what she had worn to dinner.

"Oh, Sylvia," I said, and poked her gently.

Her eyes opened, but she didn't look happy to see me.

"What's wrong?" I asked.

"The baby isn't a boy, Audrina. The baby is a girl," she said.

"Okay, Sylvia. You fell asleep here. I'm not happy about that."

She looked around and then stood up. Still very groggy, she let me lead her back to her room. I pulled back her blanket.

"Maybe you should rest a while longer, Sylvia. You want to be alert for your first art lesson this afternoon, don't you?"

"Yes," she said.

I helped her take off her dress and then had her crawl into bed and fixed her blanket. I brushed back her hair. Her eyelids fluttered, and she closed them. She was asleep in seconds. I watched her for a while and then went down to have some breakfast and debate with myself about whether I should give in to Arden's demands and get rid of the rocking chair, clear out the room, and maybe even lock the door.

Perhaps he was right about other things concerning Whitefern. Maybe if it had the makeover he had once proposed to my father, things would change dramatically. When the house you live in is changed, surely you're changed somewhat, too. Why didn't I want to wash away the darkness, brighten the rooms, erase the shadows, and replace the furniture, perhaps going more for a modern decor? We could change the floors, too, sell the rugs, and have most of the rooms tiled. And the kitchen needed new counters and new equipment, too. The stove we were using was the one my grandmother had used.

I couldn't help but recall how adamant Papa had been about not making such changes. He hadn't grown up in this house, but there was something about it that claimed him. Was it simply its history, with its variety of clocks and all its memorabilia? Was it because it held his secrets and still might, secrets he never revealed?

Of course, it wasn't only Papa who had felt something special about Whitefern. When I was no more than seven or eight, I would sit outside on the lawn and admire its grandness. For me, it was always a living thing. As I contemplated some of the changes Arden had been suggesting, I couldn't help being afraid that Whitefern would take some vengeance on us all, the way it had on Aunt Ellsbeth, Billie, and Vera. Maybe it was the wrath of our ancestors who hovered over us in sepia photographs and paintings. Seriously changing Whitefern was almost as blasphemous as disturbing the bones of the dead in ancient graveyards.

Where would the whispers go?

Sylvia surprised me by getting dressed, fixing her

hair, and coming downstairs a little less than an hour later. She said she was hungry and couldn't draw or listen to a teacher if she was thinking about eating.

"We have plenty of time yet, Sylvia. Don't worry," I said, and fixed her some eggs. She said she wanted to make breakfast for herself, but I told her, "Today, I'll be your cook and waitress. You are the artist. You must be spoiled rotten."

I then had to go into a long explanation about what being spoiled rotten meant. Afterward, she did go up and repair her room. Later, we had a very light lunch, and then we waited in the living room for Mr. Price. Sylvia had decided she would behave and warm up the biscuits we had when it was time for tea, without complaining that we didn't have chocolate ones.

Mr. Price was at the door just as our clocks, the ones that were accurate, were announcing the hour. Sylvia surprised me again by leaping to her feet and hurrying anxiously to the door. In her confused and simple way of seeing things, I thought she now must believe that Mr. Price's instructions would help her create the right baby on her canvas and thus do what Papa was telling her to do. How long could I keep Mr. Price from realizing what wild thoughts she had?

He was as jolly as ever and eager to begin. I followed them up to the cupola to be sure it all began well. He was happy with what we had bought and set up the first blank sheet on her easel. Sylvia sat in the chair, and he stood next to it with one of the drawing pencils. He glanced at me and began by explaining what he would teach her first and what was important to a beginning art student.

"I'm an art student," she said, nodding.

"Yes, you are. And I am, too, Sylvia. We are always learning. I'll learn from you," he told her.

She looked at me, astounded. I nodded and smiled, which made her even more enthusiastic.

"Here are the lessons I will use," he continued, now more for my benefit than hers, I thought. "Accuracy of size, how to use basic shapes like circles and squares, contrast and tone, stroke techniques, and pencil techniques."

She looked at me again.

"Don't worry, Sylvia. Mr. Price will explain everything so you understand."

He was patient and constantly complimented her. It was going well, I thought. Sylvia was finally doing something that would give her some self-confidence. I told them I would wait downstairs and have some tea and biscuits ready before he left.

"How kind," he said. "I do love your biscuits."

"Sylvia makes them all the time now," I said.

She was beaming with pride.

I watched for a few more minutes and then went downstairs. While I waited, I read the papers Mr. Johnson had sent home with Arden. There was no question about the end result once I signed them. Arden would have complete control of everything, even of the disposition of Whitefern, because it had been added as a company asset. If Arden made tragic mistakes, the house itself could fall into jeopardy. I knew enough about business to predict that he would leverage it to raise more money to invest in the stock market.

I would never sign this, I thought. It might bring our truce and tender loving to a quick end, but it truly was as though Papa were standing right behind me and reading over my shoulder. I could hear him whisper. *Don't do it, Audrina. Don't sign those papers.*

"Don't worry, Papa," I whispered back. "I won't."

I smiled, thinking that I should never criticize Sylvia for imagining that Papa was still here.

Maybe we were both still children of Whitefern.

Maybe we'd never be anything else.

Awakenings

Arden's upbeat temperament was unchanged for the remainder of the week. He came home from work happy and excited about the successes he was having in the stock market and the compliments he was getting from clients. He practically bounced when he walked and always charged up the stairway with a show of energy that brought smiles to both Sylvia and me. We could hear him singing upstairs while he showered and changed his clothes.

At dinner, he would go on and on about the maneuvers he had made and how brilliantly they had turned out. I had never heard Papa brag as much about his business achievements. Although he'd enjoyed making money, especially after failing so much in the beginning, he never seemed to have Arden's passion for it. Perhaps it was because Arden was younger and was surprising himself with his success, or maybe he thought it was important to impress me.

The pleasure he was getting at work spilled over into everything we were doing at home. According to Arden, our dinners had never been as good as they suddenly seemed to him, especially some of the new recipes I had found. He used to accuse me of experimenting on him and complain about being a guinea pig, but now he even complimented Sylvia on her contribution to our dinners, even if it was something as simple as whipping up mashed potatoes or chopping onions.

He would even pause once in a while, look around, and tell me the house had never looked as well kept. I waited for the inevitable suggestion that it would look far better if we got rid of the old furniture and redecorated, but he didn't say that. He didn't even suggest it by harping on the threadbare rugs.

Any compliment he gave me he shared with Sylvia. Through the years, especially before Papa died, he would avoid looking at her and never spoke directly to her, only about her. According to him now, Sylvia was surprisingly bright, even funny. Sometimes he even gave her a hug and kissed her on the forehead when he came home at the end of the work day.

"How are my women?" he would cry, and Sylvia would look so pleased. "My beautiful women." It didn't sound at all like a false compliment, and truthfully, it couldn't be, for Sylvia was looking more beautiful.

"Those lessons must be doing her a world of good," he declared one evening at dinner. He gazed across the table at Sylvia, who looked as surprised as I was. "You were very wise to arrange for it, Audrina. What a wonderful mother you would make," he added, but not with any note of sadness. "Oh, no," he went on to correct himself. "*Will* make. Won't she, Sylvia?"

"When there is a baby," Sylvia said, and he laughed. I had to laugh, too, at how positive she sounded.

"That's right. You can't be a mother unless you have a child," Arden told her. "You want Audrina to have a child to care for and spoil like you've been spoiled, right?" He looked at me quickly and added, "Any woman as pretty as you two should be spoiled."

"A baby is coming," she said.

She looked at me as if she and I shared a secret, but Arden didn't seem to notice that conspiratorial expression. As far as I knew, she had never told him about her drawing, and if she had, he had never mentioned it to me. All he knew was my saying that she had dreamed about it, not that Papa specifically had instructed her to draw a baby as the way to bring a child to Whitefern.

Every time I sat with her and Mr. Price after one of her lessons, I listened carefully to see if she had said anything to give him any idea of why she had been working on a drawing of a baby. Apparently, she hadn't, because he never revealed anything remotely associated with it. He talked about her natural artistic talent and praised her for how quickly she grasped visual concepts. I went up to watch every lesson for the first week and a half and saw that he was right. He didn't have to show Sylvia something more than once. How I wished Papa had lived to see this. It occurred to me that she really was visually brilliant. How ironic, but how wonderful, I thought.

It had been so long since we had such a pleasant and hopeful atmosphere at Whitefern. I worried that it wouldn't last. Every night, I anticipated Arden's asking me about the papers, whether I had read them and agreed to sign them, and every night, he surprised me by not making the slightest reference to them. Why had something that was so important to him, something that he was adamant and angry about, drifted away? My suspicious mind began to explore the darkest possibilities. Being leery and apprehensive was not an unexpected feeling in this house. If there was one thing Whitefern was fertile with, it was the dark weeds of human wickedness. After all, I grew up with the admonition never to trust kindness or believe in smiles.

I began to consider possibilities. Would Arden have forged my signature, even my fingerprint, or could he have paid off Mr. Johnson to accept it? He would certainly feel confident that I would never take my own husband to court. I wondered if I should call Mr. Johnson to ask. Would Arden be enraged that I even suggested such a thing, especially if he didn't do what I suspected? I couldn't ask Mr. Johnson not to tell him I had called. Why would he keep my confidence over Arden's? I had met our attorney only a few times at social events in the house, and he had spent very little time talking to me. I had the sense that, like Papa and certainly Arden, he didn't think women were capable of doing well in business or even understanding it.

Could it be that Arden believed that if he didn't bother asking me about the papers for quite a while, I would lose interest in them, too, and whatever he had done would go unnoticed? I hadn't mentioned anything about my becoming a broker since I had broached the subject the first time. I hadn't even researched what I would have to do to get a license or asked any questions about it, and Arden hadn't brought it up. Maybe he was simply being cautious. Papa used to say, "If you don't ask questions about things that will upset you, you'll never get upset." He believed that just ignoring something often made it go away. If I remembered his advice, Arden certainly would, for despite how critical he was of Papa, he did respect him when it came to worldly and business knowledge.

Perhaps he was complimenting Sylvia and accepting her being tutored because he believed it meant I would be more involved in her life and, as a result, I would drop the idea of doing anything more than caring for Whitefern, Sylvia, and him. Maybe our lovemaking and talk of a baby were designed to keep me dreaming. As long as I did that, I did nothing to challenge the status quo.

However, the nicer he was to both of us, the guiltier I felt about having any suspicions. I made an effort to put them aside. With Sylvia devoting more and more of her time to her art, I really did have more to do in the house anyway. It took time to get her to prepare herself for instruction, and after the lesson was over, she was too excited to polish furniture or wash a kitchen floor, sometimes even to help with dinner. Whatever assignment Mr. Price gave her for the days in between she took very seriously and devoted all her energy to it. I didn't have the heart to pull her away for menial work.

Often now, I left her alone in the cupola and did my grocery shopping without her. I knew she didn't hear me say I was leaving; she was concentrating too hard. So I put a note on her door reminding her. I felt less insecure about it, knowing she was too occupied to get into trouble like going out on her own and wandering.

Winter, although it came roaring in like a lion, seemed to have calmed down. We had less snowfall than most years I remembered and fortunately few days of sleet and icy rain. There were delightful sunny days when the air felt crisp and fresh. Occasionally, Sylvia and I took walks, during which she was far more talkative than ever, describing her artwork and what she intended to draw and paint in the future. Before she had begun her lessons, she would never pause in the forest and look at a tree or a bush and tell me that it would look nice in her new picture.

Mr. Price, Sylvia, and I didn't have tea and biscuits after every session, but I saw how well Sylvia was getting along with him. She liked being complimented, and he never stopped giving her praise. I concluded that this was because of his experience with special education students. Who else would have such patience and understanding?

It got so I didn't interrupt the lessons by appearing anymore. Although he never said anything about it, Sylvia did. After one of Mr. Price's visits, she surprised me by telling me it was better when I wasn't looking over her shoulder while she learned and worked.

"Why?" I asked.

"You make me nervous when you're there, Audrina," she said.

I was speechless. Nervous? Had I used that word enough for her even to understand what it meant?

I told Arden what she had said, and he raised his eyebrows and nodded in agreement. "I must say, it's all quite a surprise." He thought for a moment and then added, "But perhaps a nice surprise."

I should have thought likewise, but that persistently suspicious mind of mine wouldn't hibernate, not in Whitefern. Sylvia would never before say or do anything even to suggest she didn't want me to be with her or watch her do something. Although seeing her develop some sense of independence should have pleased me, it didn't. Of course, I asked myself, did I want her to be dependent on me forever? Did it make me feel more important? Did it fill my empty moments? Had I used her as an excuse for not pursuing my own ambitions? Was I being unfair to her?

Perhaps it was Arden's continued comments about how Sylvia was changing that kept me wondering about all this. The more he said it, the more I looked at her with unreasonable and unwarranted worry. But I couldn't help it. I told myself that it was a result of my not having a passion for something the way Sylvia did. I was spending too much time thinking about her and not myself. The Vera in me was showing its envious face.

One morning on a day when Sylvia was having a new lesson, I noticed that she was taking extra care with her appearance. I no longer had to hound her about brushing her hair or wearing clothes that coordinated. Colors had become important, and she wanted to be correct about them. She was even good about the shoes she chose, and she did all of it before I had a chance to tell her or make suggestions. In fact, she was waking up on her own and three mornings in a row was up and dressed before I had arrived at her bedroom. There were times when she showed some interest in wearing a little lipstick and even a little makeup. Now that she was learning about colors and contrast and how important that was in her artwork, I could tell that she was looking at herself and thinking about it more and more. Again, I was surprised to see her do anything about her face without my instruction, but she did, and she did it surprisingly well.

When I mentioned it to Arden, he said, "Why are you surprised? Isn't that all part of art? Women paint their faces. They look in their mirrors and sometimes turn pale, homely mugs into faces a man would at least glance at. Of course, when they wash it off, you'd rather not be there." Then he leaned over to whisper, "That's why most men like to make love to their wives in the dark."

Papa would say something like that, I thought. "Then they married them for the wrong reasons," I countered, irritated.

Of course, he simply laughed and went on reading.

All of this was riling up some unexpected anger and discomfort in me. I marched about the house pouncing on things out of place or anything left on tables.

My intolerance for the smallest imperfections, like a vague stain on the kitchen floor, sent me into a cleaning frenzy, mopping and sweeping while I muttered to myself. I envisioned Aunt Ellsbeth observing and nodding with approval. "Repair, repair, repair!" she would chant. It felt like a whip.

One afternoon nearly a month later, I put on my coat and boots when Sylvia and Mr. Price went upstairs to work. I stepped out of the house and looked at the skeleton forest. I felt I had to have some air. All my worried and jealous thoughts were stifling me in Whitefern. I had no shopping to do, no friend to visit, only the outside world around our home to distract me.

It was a partly cloudy day, with the sun playing hide and seek on the forest pathways. I recalled the first time I had gone through the woods to see the new family that occupied the gardener's cottage. That family was Arden and his mother, Billie. I'd still believed there was a first Audrina back then, and as I snuck away from Whitefern, defying Papa, and ventured into the forest, I'd felt myself grow uneasy. Little butterflies of panic had fluttered in my head, and the warnings I had heard for years seemed to echo now, years later: *It's dangerous and unsafe in the woods. There is death in the woods.*

Once I'd learned what had happened to me in this forest, I understood my innate trepidation. How brave I'd been to go forward when I was so young and had been told so many terrible things. The horrible memories thundered around me, but they were blurry now. No amount of time in the rocking chair would bring back the gruesome details. It was still frightening, but it was vague.

Nevertheless, when I walked into the woods slowly, my head down, the darkness seemed to close in on me. Tree limbs devoid of leaves looked spidery, swaying and trembling in the breeze like beckoning sirens, enchanting, hypnotizing, and seducing. Death lay in wait behind cold smiles. Dried leaves between small patches of evaporating snow crunched beneath my feet. It sounded like I was walking over shards of glass. Far off, a dog howled. The scent of some animal that had died in the woods recently flowed over me, churning my stomach.

I paused and opened my eyes like a sleepwalker awakening.

I was surprised to see that I had walked far enough to be near the infamous clearing in which I had been attacked. I could feel every muscle in my body tighten, and the chilled air seeped under my coat to run up my spine.

Suddenly, as if I had been nudged, tapped firmly on my right shoulder, I turned and looked back at Whitefern. There was something in the look of the mansion that alarmed me. I felt two hands on my back pushing me forward. I broke into a run and rushed back to the house. I charged through the front door and hurried up the stairs until I was at the cupola. There I paused to catch my breath and my wits. What was I doing? I didn't want to frighten them or look foolish. Quietly and slowly, I opened the door.

But then I froze.

Mr. Price was sitting in Sylvia's chair in front of her easel, and Sylvia was standing in front of him, her beautiful, full breasts uncovered, her hands clasped behind her head. She wore only her skirt, but it was lowered beneath her belly button. Her eyes were shifted so that she was looking at the ceiling.

I screamed, a scream so piercing that it knifed through both of them. Mr. Price raised his shoulders as if he'd been slapped on the back of his neck, and Sylvia brought her hands down and looked at me in confusion. He rose, turned, and backed away, his hands up and pumping the air as if he thought that would keep me away.

"Now . . . don't get excited. I can explain—" he said.

"Sylvia, dress yourself!" I shouted, and she hurriedly did so.

I turned to him, my eyes feeling like they were popping and on fire. "How *dare* you."

"It's not what you think. I'm teaching her . . . all aspects of, of art, of being an artist," he stuttered. "She's a perfect model, you see, and I'm an artist. This is nothing more than art, you see."

"Get out!" I shouted. "Get out of my house!" I stepped away from the door to give him a clear exit.

He looked at Sylvia and then hurried past me, pausing in the hallway. "I'm an artist," he insisted. "Don't you tell anyone anything else. I can sue you," he warned, and then hurried down the stairs.

I turned back to Sylvia, my hands still pressed firmly on the base of my throat.

"Is that the end of my lesson?" she asked.

I was trembling so hard that I didn't think I could speak or move, but I slipped into the artist's chair and took deep breaths. Sylvia stood there looking at me in confusion but with great interest. She had never seen me like this. I glanced at her and then looked at the canvas. He had finished the drawing and done a remarkably good job of capturing both her face and her body. I reached up quickly and ripped it off the easel, then folded it and stood up.

"Did he tell you to tell me you were nervous when I was in the room?"

She thought a moment, remembering, and then smiled and nodded.

"Get dressed and come downstairs, Sylvia," I said. "Quickly!"

I was afraid that Mr. Price was still in the house, so I descended slowly, but he was gone.

"Sit on the settee," I told Sylvia when she appeared, and I went to the phone to call Arden. That self-important Mrs. Crown had started to tell me he was busy when I screamed, "Get my husband on the phone now!"

She stammered and squeaked out a "Right away."

Moments later, Arden, irritated, said, "What is it, Audrina? You have Mrs. Crown shaking."

I rattled off the details so quickly that I was sure he didn't understand.

He was silent for a few moments. "Tell me that again," he said in a much quieter tone of voice than before.

I went through it slowly this time, even mentioning Mr. Price's threat to sue us.

"Is he gone?"

"Yes."

"And Sylvia?"

"She's in the living room. She doesn't understand what's happened, what she has done, or why I am so upset," I said, and then I started to cry.

"You didn't call the police, did you?" Arden asked.

"What? No. Should I?"

"No," he said, quickly and firmly. "That would be the worst thing for us—and for Sylvia. Can you imagine them arriving to question her? And when it got out to the public . . . oh, boy. Just do nothing until I get there."

"We can't just do nothing. I have his drawing. It's clear evidence."

"I'm not saying we will do nothing, but I'll handle it. Just keep her calm."

"She's very calm, Arden. I assure you that she has no idea why what was going on was wrong."

"Okay, okay. Just have tea or something. Wait for me," he said, and hung up.

I hung up, too, and as calmly as I could, I returned to Sylvia, who waited with the expression of a little girl, frightened but confused, wondering whether or not she had to cry.

"Oh, Sylvia," I said. I sat beside her and took her hand. "This is not your fault."

"Art?"

"No, I'm not talking about art. This man, Mr. Price, he took advantage of you."

She shook her head, not understanding.

"He asked you to do something you shouldn't have done. He was here to teach you art, not to exploit you for his own sexual needs."

I could see that nothing was making sense to her. To her, I was just raving.

"Look, Sylvia, you should never undress in front of a strange man."

"Was Mr. Price strange?"

"Not strange like that. Well, maybe, but what I mean is, he's not family. He's a stranger. He was supposed to just work for us, help you with your art. He used art as an excuse to have you undress."

I thought a moment as she worked at understanding.

"Did you do this before today?"

She nodded.

"Did you undress more?"

She nodded.

I felt a cold chill first and then a hot flash in my chest. "Were you ever completely nude?"

"Like when I take a bath?"

"Yes."

"Yes," she replied.

My heart was pounding. "Did he touch you?"

"Yes," she said.

"Where?"

"In the studio."

"No, where on your body did he touch you? Show me," I told her.

She thought about it and then nodded and put her hands on her breasts, her stomach, her thighs.

I started to breathe some relief until she put both hands between her legs. The blood left my face. I sat back.

"I had to stand right for the drawing and not move."

"Oh, Papa," I muttered. All I could think of was how angry he would be at me, not Sylvia. I had broken a promise. I hadn't protected her.

My mind was a workshop of miserable thoughts. While I had been dumbly cleaning the house, taking walks, reading, and minding my own business, Sylvia was being sexually abused, and the worst part of it was that she didn't understand. I thought about all the times the three of us sat here after the lessons and had tea and biscuits together. I should have noticed something, realized something. How conniving and clever he was. He was probably the one telling Sylvia how to dress, do makeup, and brush her hair. I had stupidly thought she was simply learning to take pride in herself. Perhaps in her limited vision and thinking, she was, but that wasn't why he was doing it. All those compliments he brushed over her, dipping her in the well of ego so that she would appreciate him and never resist his mauling of her beautiful body, now made sense to me.

"Mr. Price was simply another frustrated old man," I muttered. "I don't know why the alarms didn't go off in me. I'm simply too inhibited, too cloistered here, too out of the social world to recognize the clues. It's my fault, my fault. I'm sorry, Sylvia."

I lowered my head and took her hand in both of mine. I couldn't help it. The tears began to flow.

"I'm not mad at you," Sylvia said. "Don't cry, Audrina."

"No, you're not mad at me," I said, smiling and wiping away my tears. "You'll never be mad at me. You're the angel here, Sylvia. I'm mad at myself." I took a deep breath. "Let's have some tea and biscuits, chocolate biscuits."

She nodded and then paused. "But Mr. Price left," she said.

"And he'll never be back, Sylvia. I guarantee that."

"Oh," she said. She looked stunned, worried, and then she smiled. "My lessons are over. That's all right, Audrina. I know what to do."

"Good. That's the way to think of it. I'll try to think of it that way, too."

We went into the kitchen. I was still clinging to the folded sheet on which Arthur Price had drawn my sister half-nude. I couldn't help glancing at it every once in a while, and that made the shock of the scene in the cupola return. Finally, I put it in a drawer by the refrigerator where we had other important household papers. Then I tried to talk about other things. We had our tea and biscuits in the kitchen. Suddenly, the idea of sitting in the living room to enjoy it had turned sour. Sylvia didn't care. I kept talking—babbling, really—and then I started to plan dinner, and she quickly forgot about what had happened. I doubted that I ever would.

A little more than half an hour later, Arden came home. He looked at both of us to see if we were all right, and then he told me to follow him to Papa's office, which was now his. I left Sylvia mixing batter for a vanilla cake.

"What did you do?" I asked as soon as he closed the door.

"Where's the picture he drew?"

"In the drawer by the refrigerator."

"Get it," he said, and dropped himself into Papa's desk chair. His face was flushed with rage. I hurried out and returned with the drawing.

He studied it a moment and nodded. "This is good. I mean, it's important that we have it." He took a breath, sat back, and said, "I confronted him at his home."

"You did?"

"Yes. He tried to keep his wife out of the discussion by taking me to his home studio, but I think she was just outside the door listening. He swore up and down that he didn't mean any harm to Sylvia and that he did not sexually abuse her. I told him I didn't care. That if he came within a thousand yards of Whitefern, I'd press charges. To me, it was the same as abusing one of his students in school. He got the point quickly. He promised he wouldn't come anywhere near us, nor would he say a word. He offered to give back all the money he took. I accepted it." He showed me a check he had in his inside jacket pocket.

"I don't want his money," I said. "The money isn't the important thing, Arden."

"Of course it's important. Money is always important. Consider this to be the fine levied against him, only we didn't have to go to court to sue him and attract all sorts of prurient public interest, get Sylvia—and us—in the newspapers. Can you even imagine what it would do to our business image?"

"I'm not worried about our image. I'm worried about Sylvia."

"The two things go hand in hand," he insisted. He looked at the drawing again and then put it in his desk drawer, the one that could be locked. "We'll hold this as our insurance. Have you had a talk with Sylvia? Does she realize what's happened now?"

"A little," I said. "She's not upset with herself or him, however. She's upset that I'm upset. It's probably better if we don't talk about it anymore."

"Exactly," he said. "Over and done with. She'll be all right." He put the check back into his jacket pocket.

"I'm upset with myself for letting it happen."

"I'm sure you could never have imagined this happening. I did, but that's because I'm a man, and I can understand how the male mind and lust work. If anyone taught me that well, it was your father. So I'm not blaming you. Let's go about our lives with this stuffed away in the cellar of horrors Whitefern has accumulated." He looked at his watch. "I have some calls to make because I left the office in a rush. Fortunately, Mrs. Crown did a good job of covering it up."

"Does she know why you left?"

"Not really," he said.

I wasn't sure what "really" meant, but I was mentally and emotionally exhausted and didn't want to talk about it anymore. "I'll get back to making dinner," I said. "Although my stomach is in so many knots I don't think I can eat a thing."

"You'd better. Don't get Sylvia upset," he warned. "I know her. She'll be the one who gets sick over it."

Suddenly, he was thinking more about her welfare than I was. That made me feel even more guilty. Arden was truly more mature and sensible than I was, I thought. He should be totally in charge of our business and our lives. Look at what a mess I had made of one simple thing.

I nodded and left, telling myself I had to put on as good an act as I could for Sylvia. She asked no questions and went about our dinner preparations as if it was just another day. I wondered how well her memory did work. I knew from the way she had usually acted toward Vera the day after Vera had abused her that bad memories didn't cling to her the way they did to me—or anyone else, for that matter.

But several days after the incident with Mr. Price, she looked up at me while we were having lunch and said, "Something bad happened in the cupola."

"Yes, Sylvia, something bad happened."

She thought for a moment and then looked at me and said, "I liked it, Audrina."

"Liked what?"

She looked like she wasn't going to answer or

didn't know what to answer. I thought I knew what she meant.

"You shouldn't like just anyone touching you, Sylvia. And whoever does it shouldn't trick you into thinking he is doing something else, something you should let him do."

She looked at me and nodded, but I had no false hopes about it. She didn't have any idea what I meant, and maybe she never would.

The day would come when I would wish that this was all I had talked about until she understood.

But by then, it was too late for all of us.

Shadows Do Multiply

Despite how firmly and confidently Arden had declared that the incident in the cupola was over and should never be discussed or even thought about again, I couldn't help feeling a sense of doom about Whitefern because of it. Old demons were roused from their sleep. The devil who liked to frolic about in our lives had paid us another visit. Shadows were darker. Every face in every painting looked angry and accusatory as I walked by. Every clock ticked as though every minute, every second, was heavier in this house than anywhere else. And no matter what anyone would tell me, what had happened to Sylvia was my fault.

"You don't tend your garden, and weeds will grow. And it's not the fault of the weeds!" Aunt Ellsbeth would tell both Vera and me. Her condemning voice echoed in the hallways. "Your father gave you one important responsibility, and you failed him. You failed him!"

Vera's laughter naturally followed, resonating through the hallways in my house of memories. Sometimes I went about with my hands over my ears. But the voices were inside my head, haunting, pouncing, eager to remind me that I was all twisted and beaten down, forever poisoned by the lust of the boys who had killed the real Audrina in me, the little girl her father had cherished. No baths, no shampoos, not even sandpaper on my skin, could scrub away the disgrace. How could my father have any faith and confidence in me? Aunt Ellsbeth and Vera were always there to remind me of that question. They expected failure no matter what I did. Nothing made them happier, because it proved them right.

How did you kill ghosts?

There was nothing in Sylvia's behavior to encourage this. She didn't mope around looking lost and melancholy all the time like any victim of such abuse would. If anything, she seemed to have more energy than she had before. Absent from her psyche was any embarrassment. She was still very interested in her artwork and spent more time in the cupola experimenting with her watercolors the way Mr. Price had taught her. Nevertheless, I couldn't help it. Whenever she mentioned something about drawing and painting, I didn't react with the enthusiasm she expected. I would never ask her to stop her artwork, but it seemed contaminated in my mind now, as contaminated as I believed I was deep down inside. I knew she was surprised and upset by my subdued reactions to everything she showed me proudly. I hated flashing smiles and those terribly meaningless words, "That's nice."

At times, I thought Arden paid more attention to her at dinner and afterward than he did to me. Maybe

I was imagining it, but she seemed to become more interested in the things he said. She laughed at his jokes even if she didn't fully understand them, and when he addressed her now, she seemed to try harder to do whatever he asked. He asked nicely, too, not like before, when he would snap an order at her as if she was a pet hound. When I made a reference to his changed behavior toward my sister, he said, "We've got to do all we can to keep her from feeling guilty, Audrina, feeling like it was her fault. It'll set her back years if we don't."

"Since when did her feelings matter so much to you?" I countered, annoyed at his tone. He sounded like I was the one who was making things more difficult, like I was trying to shift the blame from myself to her.

"Since I realized I was the head of this household and responsible for your and Sylvia's welfare," he replied. "That's since when."

He sounded so sincere that I couldn't contradict him, challenge him, or accuse him of being sarcastic.

"I would have thought you, of all people, would be pleased," he added.

"I am," I said, now feeling a little ashamed. "I'm just . . . surprised."

"Happily, I hope."

"Yes, happily, Arden, happily."

I left it at that, but despite how well both Arden and Sylvia were doing after what I considered a serious and terrible event at Whitefern, I could not simply forget it and go on the way they apparently were. To them, it was as though Mr. Price had never come to instruct her and had never taken advantage of her, while it haunted me. I shuddered to remember what I'd seen when I opened the cupola door. How much further would things have gone if I hadn't made the discovery, if I had continued to avoid going to the cupola because I thought that would make Sylvia more comfortable?

Needless to say, what had happened to Sylvia revived my own gruesome memories. Were all the women of Whitefern under some curse to suffer at the hands of some man? In the days and weeks that followed, I moved about under a dark cloud. I dozed off more than usual and had no sooner finished with dinner than I announced that I was tired and would go up for a hot bath and bed. At first, Arden seemed not to notice the difference in me, but one night after dinner, he ordered me to come to the living room. I thought he was going to start on the paperwork, and I was ready to give in, but to my surprise, he was more upset about me, about the way I had been behaving.

"You've got to stop beating yourself up for what happened, Audrina. Nobody would have expected you to be suspicious of a retired schoolteacher apparently quite well liked at the school where he had taught. Don't forget, the principal recommended him to you."

"I know," I said. "But I'm sure there were clues I missed."

"What clues?"

"The way he spoke to her, admired her, smiled at her, and the little whispering I saw him do with her."

"Ridiculous." He thought a moment. "But I see how heavily your misplaced guilt is weighing on you. You're sure to get yourself sick. Maybe you should see Dr. Prescott," he suggested.

"Why? I'm not sick yet."

"There are all kinds of sickness, Audrina. You might need some sort of medication for this . . . depression. I think they're called mood enhancers. One of my clients was telling me about it the other day. His wife suffers from depression."

"Any doctor would first want to know why I was depressed. He'd want to know why, and I'd be terribly embarrassed, Arden, even with Dr. Prescott, maybe especially with Dr. Prescott. He was here sometimes when Papa told me to watch over Sylvia closely and warned me time and time again how vulnerable she was. No, no, I'll deal with it myself," I said. "Give me time."

"Time? How much more time? I pretended for weeks not to notice, hoping that you would do just as you say, deal with it yourself, but you haven't, and I fear you never will. I'm afraid to invite anyone to dinner or take you out like this," he insisted, raising his voice. "A man with a growing business like mine can't have an emotional invalid for a wife."

I started to cry.

"All right, all right," he said more calmly. "Don't worry about it. I'll see about it for you."

"I don't think I'd like—"

"Stop worrying about it, I said. I'll look after you. I made promises to your father, too, you know, and one of them was to always be concerned about your welfare. Please let me fulfill that promise I made to him."

What more could I say once he invoked my father? The next day, he came home with a prescription for me. It didn't have my name on it, but he said that was because the doctor didn't actually examine me.

"It's a common one," he said. "Harmless. Try it for a while. As you see, it's best to take it in the evening, after dinner."

I turned the pill bottle around in my fingers and shook my head. "I'm not fond of pills, Arden. You know that."

"This is not anything terrible. It's just to help you manage. It's time to do something. Sylvia is becoming affected by your dark moods, too, Audrina. She's even starting to eat poorly, and I fear she's losing interest in her art. She might be blaming herself or thinking we're both blaming her now. She'll get sickly and return to the half vegetable she was. Is that what you want?"

"No, I don't want that, of course not."

"Well, she may be slow about many things, but she's not blind. Anyone, even Sylvia, can see that you're not looking after yourself as well as you usually do. Sometimes you look like a hag, a bag lady wandering aimlessly."

"I do?"

"Yes, you do. I didn't want to say anything, but someone who saw you at the supermarket commented to me about you."

"Who? What was said? When?"

"It doesn't matter who. They were concerned because of how you looked, how void of energy you seemed. They thought you were seriously ill. Why do you think I've avoided bringing anyone here? Half the time now, you don't even put on lipstick, and I don't know if you realized it, but you wore the same dress three days in a row this week."

"I did? Why didn't you say something?"

"I didn't want to bring it up. I wasn't sure if it would do good or add to the bad, but how can we go forward and do wonderful things for Sylvia and for ourselves if you are so depressed all the time?" He pushed the pills back at me. "Take them for a week or so, and let's see how you do. Okay?"

I looked at the pill bottle again and nodded. He was right. I couldn't go on the way I was. That night, I took the first one. I felt a little dizzy and even a little silly. We had wine at dinner and an after-dinner drink, too. He said the doctor had said I could drink a little with the pills.

Arden put on music, and for the first time I could remember, he made Sylvia dance with him. She was bashful and afraid, but he showed her some steps, and then she started to do it. They both looked clumsy to me, and I laughed again. Sylvia beamed, believing she was doing something I wanted her to do and that she was bringing smiles back to my dreary face.

Arden got me up to dance, too, but I didn't have the energy to go on and on. Finally, I collapsed onto the sofa while they went back at it. I closed my eyes, my face frozen in a silly smile, and fell asleep. I had no idea how long I slept. I woke with a start and looked around. There was only a small lamp lit, and both Arden and Sylvia were gone.

When I stood up, the room started to spin, and I fell back onto the sofa.

"Arden?" I called. I looked at the nearest clock. It was two in the morning. "Arden?"

I struggled to my feet, made my way to the stairs, and started up. It seemed to take me ten times as long as usual. Every once in a while, I paused, listened, and took a deep breath before continuing. When I turned to head toward our bedroom, I felt the hallway spin and pressed my palm against the wall to steady myself. In the room, there was a nightlight on, but Arden was in bed, facedown, asleep. I stood there looking at him and desperately tried to remember what had happened. Everything was so vague.

I went to the bathroom and looked at myself in the mirror. My hair was wild, and my eyes looked terribly bloodshot. I washed my face and struggled to get undressed and into bed. Arden moaned and turned over with his back to me. I wondered about Sylvia, but I was just too tired to go check on her. In moments, I was asleep again.

The dream I had that night was so vivid that when I awoke, I questioned whether it was really a dream. In it, I had sat up in bed because I was sure I heard whispering in the hallway. I had turned to wake up Arden and realized he wasn't there. So I'd risen and slowly made my way to the doorway to listen. There was definitely someone whispering. Confused and intrigued, I'd stepped out and made my way down the hallway toward the rocking-chair room. I'd stopped when I saw Arden outside the doorway, the door half open, talking.

What was he saying?

To whom?

I'd drawn close enough to look through the doorway and had seen Sylvia in the rocking chair, half naked the way she had been in the cupola, her head back, her eyes closed, rocking.

"What are you doing?" I'd cried out.

Arden had turned to look at me, and when he did, he had my father's face.

My father was looking at me, and he was angry that I was disturbing Sylvia in the rocking chair. His face had been full of such fury that I gasped.

"Papa?"

My legs had turned to water and floated away as I sank into the cool darkness beneath me.

But when I opened my eyes again, I was back in my bed. The morning light rushed in around me, and the bedroom exploded in a kaleidoscope of colors from the stained-glass windows, the same colors that had turned Momma's and my hair into chameleon hair because it was sometimes flaxen blond with gold. There were strands of auburn, bright red, chestnut brown, and copper. And sometimes in a passing ray of sunshine, our hair looked white. Papa had loved the strange prism-like color of our hair. He loved the way the light played on everything in Whitefern. I was seeing it all this morning the way Papa would see it.

It was as if time had not passed and I was a little girl again.

I turned onto my back and looked up at the ceiling. What exactly had happened last night? When did I pass out? Why did Arden leave me there? And the dream, the dream . . .

When I looked at the clock, I was shocked to see that it was nearly one in the afternoon. I had never slept this long.

"Sylvia?" I called. I listened but heard nothing. Of course, Arden would have gotten up, dressed, and been long gone.

I groaned as I got up again, scrubbed my cheeks with my palms, and went into the bathroom. The face I saw in the mirror looked like it belonged to Rip Van Winkle, the face of someone who had slept for years. There were spidery creases in my cheeks, and my hair was like a garden of weeds growing in all directions. My eyes were gray and lifeless.

There was no point in standing there and waiting for the memory of the night before to return. I threw off my nightgown and stepped into the shower, deliberating whether to turn on cold water to jerk every sleeping muscle in my body awake. When I got back out, I felt more like Lazarus, happy to have stepped out of a grave. I quickly dried myself off, then hurriedly dressed and started down the stairs.

"Sylvia," I called. "Are you downstairs?"

At first, I heard nothing, and then I heard her answer me, but from above. She was in the cupola. I turned and went up to her. She was seated at her easel and leaning over her work. She sat back, and I saw the baby she had begun to draw now completed and painted in watercolors. Only she had painted his eyes a flaming red, so bright they looked like a fire was burning behind them. Every little detail of the baby's face was just as vivid, from the twist in his mouth that gave him a ridiculing smile to the thinness of his slightly pointed nose and the gauntness in his cheeks. She had drawn a baby, but it looked like a man in a baby's body.

"Why did you paint him like that?" I asked, my voice breathless.

"It's how Papa told me to paint him." She paused. "He's coming."

"That's not a pretty baby, Sylvia. You told me you were going to draw a pretty baby."

She looked up at me angrily. She hadn't looked at me that way for a very long time, since when she was a little girl and I would tell her she couldn't have something.

"It's Papa's pretty baby," she insisted.

"All right. All right. Draw and paint what you want. Did you have your breakfast?"

"Yes. Arden and I had breakfast."

"Arden and you? You got up yourself when he got up?"

She looked back at her picture. "I think the baby is beautiful."

"Good. Look, I'm sorry I slept so late. I don't know what happened. It was probably that pill I took," I said. She had no idea what I was talking about, but

I continued. "I shouldn't have had anything alcoholic with it. I guess I just passed out. I'm surprised neither of you woke me. You left me downstairs."

She continued to stare at her picture. I didn't know if she even heard me or if she understood why I was upset. She slowly turned and looked up at me, her eyelids narrow as she focused on her thoughts. "Babies are grown first inside you. When it's time for them to come out, God pushes them gently, and they flow out," she recited. "They have to be delivered to you. That's the man's job. Afterward, you carry the baby around like a mailman carries a letter in his pouch, and then the letter has to be opened."

"Who told you all that? Did Mr. Price tell you that? Well? Answer me. Did he?"

"Papa told me," she said.

"When? When?"

"I don't remember," she said, and looked back at her picture. "Maybe he never told you, and that's why you don't have a baby yet." She smiled. "But you will. There's a baby coming . . . see?"

"Not that baby, I hope," I said. "Did Mr. Price ever take off his clothes when he was with you, Sylvia?"

"I don't remember," she said too quickly.

"It won't be your fault if he did. Did he?"

"I don't remember," she said. She smiled again. "I made you lunch. Egg salad. Is it time for lunch?"

"Oh, Sylvia," I said, shaking my head. I glanced at her baby painting. "Yes, it's time for lunch. I hope you'll work on a prettier baby now."

Looking at the image, she simply said, "If Papa tells me."

Feeling exhausted again, I started out. She followed me, babbling about her egg salad, describing every step of the process the way I had taught her. I made myself some coffee and toast and actually ate the egg salad. It was delicious. She ate some, too, being as messy as ever.

Arden called a little while later to see how I was. "I tried to pick you up, but I wasn't exactly in a steady enough condition myself," he explained. "I figured you'd come up when you were ready. We had a good time, though. It's been long in coming. Good to hear some laughter in our house, wouldn't you say?"

"If I could remember it, yes," I said.

He laughed. "That's all right. You drank a little too much. I'll make sure that doesn't happen again."

"I don't think I want to take another pill, Arden."

"It did what it was supposed to, Audrina. Your sister was happy again. It felt good. Let's try to keep our house pleasant now. This coming weekend, I'll take both of you to Don's Steak House. It's a bit of a ride, but the food's great."

"You will?"

"Yes, I will. As long as you make an effort, too. Okay?"

I paused, thinking. Could he be right?

"Okay?"

"Yes, Arden, okay," I said.

I continued with the pills. It wasn't that they made me happy, exactly, but they kept me so subdued and calm that I didn't do or say much to change the new atmosphere Arden wanted in our home. I found myself falling asleep faster and earlier and waking up confused. What was worst of all was that dream. It returned. One time, Arden was naked, and so was Sylvia in the rocking chair. I watched the whispering and then saw Papa's face, and the dream ended.

I was afraid to mention it. I was beginning to believe that one of the side effects of the pill was nightmares. I did tell Arden that without going into detail.

"Okay," he said. "Maybe you'll do fine now without it. Put it aside for a while. Besides, I want you fully alert and hungry for our night out this weekend. Why don't you take Sylvia to buy a new dress and buy yourself one, too?"

"Yes," I said. "That sounds good. Oh, Arden, I'm sorry I've put you through so much."

"I'm not upset. Ups and downs are part of marriage, part of life. If anyone should know that, it's you, Audrina Lowe."

He kissed me, and I felt happiness surging back. I did what he suggested, went shopping for new clothes for both Sylvia and myself. I got us matching shoes, too. Despite her poorer eating habits for a while after the incident with Mr. Price, I noticed she had gained weight. She didn't look too heavy; it wasn't anything like that. In fact, she looked like she was blossoming, filling out. Even her breasts looked somewhat larger.

On our way home, Sylvia talked more than usual. She asked many questions about the stores, the other houses we saw, and people on the street. Her curiosity was never sharper. I laughed about it, and she laughed, too. We were all getting better, I thought. Arden was right about everything. But when Sylvia mentioned her picture of the baby again and asked me what name it would have, I decided I had better be firmer about it. There was too much dreaming going on at Whitefern. It was something I remembered Momma saying from time to time.

"I am not pregnant yet, Sylvia. I don't know if I will be, and unless you adopt a baby, go to an orphanage and choose one, you can't get a baby. I'm afraid the stork doesn't really bring them." I smiled. "Understand?"

She shook her head. "Baby's coming," she insisted.

Rather than upset her after such a pleasant day of shopping, I decided to drop the subject.

But to my surprise, she wouldn't. As soon as we entered the house, she turned to me and said, "Baby's inside me. He's coming."

I grabbed her shoulder. "What? Sylvia, what did you say?"

She turned, her arms full of her packages. "Baby is coming."

I thought for a moment. When was the last time I had checked on her period? Although she was good at taking care of herself once a month, I usually followed up, especially if she complained about cramps. I realized that she hadn't complained about anything.

I hurried to her as she started away and grabbed her arm so hard to turn her that she dropped her boxes. "Oh, look at what you made me do."

"Forget that, Sylvia. Did you have your period? Did you take care of it?"

"No."

"No? What are you saying?" I stood there, thinking hard, as she picked up her boxes. "Sylvia?"

"I don't remember," she said. "But I don't care. I don't like it." She walked to the stairway. "We have to get dressed up," she said. "Come on, Audrina. You said we'd do my hair, too."

I nodded and watched her walk up the stairs.

Was my heart still beating?

"I'll be right up," I shouted to her, and hurried to the telephone.

To my surprise and delight, Arden picked up instead of Mrs. Crown. "Hey," he said. "My secretary is in the restroom," he added, as if that was important. "Did you get some nice things?"

"Arden . . ."

"I'm still here, Audrina. Yes?"

"I think . . . I'm afraid . . ."

"What?"

"Sylvia."

"What about her now?"

"She might be pregnant," I said. The words seemed to burn my lips. I couldn't swallow.

"Arden?"

"Why do you say that?"

"She missed periods. I forgot to check her, and she even said she had a baby in her."

"How would she know that?"

"I don't know."

"Next thing you'll tell me is she said your father told her," he said. "Lucky this is a slow day. I'll come home early, but please be sure this isn't something imagined. I'm mentally exhausted. With both of you," he added, and hung up.

From somewhere in the shadows of Whitefern, I could hear Vera's gleeful laugh.

Truth Is the Loneliest of All

"I hope this isn't a false alarm, Audrina. You tend to get very melodramatic about everything these days," Arden said the moment he entered the house. He ripped off his scarf and took off his coat angrily. I knew he was upset about having to come home early.

The two of us went into the living room to talk. Sylvia was upstairs. He poured himself a drink quickly, claiming he needed it to settle himself down. He had rushed out of the office and left others to answer important calls.

"I'm sorry, Arden. I thought you should know right away."

"It seems to me that all we do these days is move from one crisis to another. It makes my head spin."

He turned to me with his drink in hand and took a long swallow.

I was tired of saying everything was my fault, but it was. Why didn't I check on Sylvia earlier? Why didn't I tell Arden that I had the terrible suspicion something more might have happened between Sylvia and Mr. Price?

He looked a bit calmer after the whiskey settled in his stomach. "Now, as I understand it, Audrina, women can miss periods for reasons other than pregnancy," he said, sitting in his favorite chair, which had been Papa's favorite. He continued to sip his drink and looked at me, probably expecting me to be more optimistic, too. But I wasn't.

"She's missed two periods. After I called you, I went upstairs to talk to her. I asked her questions as directly and simply as I could."

"And?" He leaned forward. "Well? What did she tell you?"

"All she talks about is Papa telling her she can bring a baby to Whitefern. That he will help."

"He will help? How's he supposed to do that from the grave?"

"Nothing she says makes sense, but she did admit again that Mr. Price had touched her when she was completely naked."

"You don't make someone pregnant by touching her," he said, leaning back and finishing his drink.

"She never complained, but her breasts are somewhat swollen and tender. As far as I know, she has had no nausea, but that doesn't always occur. I don't count how many times she urinates, and she hasn't shown more fatigue than usual, but everyone reacts differently to being pregnant. While I was waiting for you, I read up on it as much as I could. So? What should we do?"

He stared at me a moment, his eyes taking on that now familiar mix of anger and determination. "For now, I'd like you to do nothing, Audrina," he said.

"Nothing?"

"Don't say anything more to her about it. She'll just get more confused, and who knows what will happen?"

"We should at least bring her to Dr. Prescott," I said. "He can give her a full examination and tell us exactly what's happening."

"Let's wait. If it's something else, we'll only have opened a can of worms."

"And if it's not something else?"

He stared at me so long that I thought he hadn't heard the question.

"I mean, if she is pregnant, Arden . . ."

He shrugged and relaxed again. "We wanted a baby," he said softly.

"What?"

"She's your sister," he said, his gaze never wavering. "You have the same blood. It's almost the same as you having a baby."

"What?"

"Stop saying 'What?' I'm just thinking aloud."

"But it won't be our baby, Arden."

"You once suggested we adopt . . . not so long ago, in fact, didn't you?"

"Yes, but . . ."

"Well, at least you know the mother of this child. If it's a boy, he could look more like your father."

"But everyone would know."

"They don't have to know," he said. He put his empty glass down. "This is a house that has an easy time keeping secrets. What's another?"

"How do we keep this one? Eventually, she'll need real medical attention."

He smiled. "First, do you agree with me that if she is pregnant, the baby is at least half an Adare? The baby's half you?"

"It's not half me—it's half Sylvia. But yes, it does have our family blood."

"And certainly belongs here more than some strange orphan, then, right?"

"Yes, but I was thinking more about Sylvia, actually. She could never be a real mother, and people who find out about the child will assume the child is like her, with her disadvantages. He or she would have a difficult time in public school. I can't imagine other people permitting their children to play with Sylvia's."

"Let's not worry about that yet," he said. "Let's wait to confirm that this is true beyond a doubt, Audrina. I have a way of confirming it one way or another without risking any embarrassment."

"What way?"

"I know someone who will definitely keep any secret involving us, whether the secret was born in Whitefern or not."

"Who?"

"Her name is Helen Matthews. She's a retired maternity nurse. We have her retirement portfolio. It's not a very big one, but it's something. I know she could use the money, and she's very reliable. She would keep a confidence if I asked her to."

"How do you know that?"

"Let's just say I know a secret pertaining to her."

"What secret?"

"If I told you, it wouldn't be a secret, and she'd have no reason to believe I'd be reliable, trustworthy, thus she would have no reason to keep our confidence. But believe me, she does, and she will."

"How did she come to be one of my father's clients?"

"She wasn't. She became one of mine. I approached her one day and persuaded her to transfer her funds into our brokerage. That's all beside the point," he said, waving his hand at me as if he was chasing off a fly. "The point is, she was a practicing maternity nurse for more than thirty years and on many occasions delivered babies all by herself. I wouldn't exactly call her a midwife, either. She's more educated. She almost became a doctor."

"She lives in our village?"

"Not far, on the outskirts. She did once, but when her husband died and her son moved off to marry and live in New York City, she got herself a smaller home."

"But she's not a doctor, Arden. Sylvia would need real medical attention."

"Stop saying that," he snapped back at me. "I assure you that she can do whatever Dr. Prescott can do. And she has the wherewithal to do it all at my request. Can't you trust me on this? Don't you have any faith in me at all as the head of this household? Am I forever going to walk six paces behind in your father's shadow, a shadow you insist on casting over everything involving this house and us? How do you think this makes me feel?"

"It's not that. Honest it isn't, Arden. I feel so . . . overwhelmed and so stupid," I said.

He smirked, shook his head, and took a deep breath. "Audrina, Audrina, Audrina, what would you have done if you realized it earlier? Would you have taken her for an abortion?"

I looked up at him. The thought had crossed my mind.

"Of course, I thought of it, too, but regardless of the situation, the child is still your father's grandchild, is it not?"

"But . . ."

"But nothing. It's too late to sit around and ponder. Let's get a confirmation of your suspicions, and then we'll make a decision, a decision best for us all, not just Sylvia," he added. "Okay?"

"Matthews. That name is familiar."

"Her son attended Whitefern High School, but he was a grade ahead of me. Well? I'd like to get things arranged today, Audrina. I do have a business to run."

"Well, if you think she's capable . . ."

"I don't think it. I know it. Didn't you listen to anything I said?"

"All right. Then do what you think best, Arden. I feel too overwhelmed to think straight."

"Exactly." He stood and started for his office. "Where is she now?"

"She's up in her room getting herself ready for dinner at the restaurant tonight."

"You sure you'll be up for it now?" he asked.

"Oh, yes. I don't want to disappoint her. Or myself," I added.

He smiled. "Nor should you, nor should any of us. I'll make arrangements with Mrs. Matthews and come up to shower, shave, and dress. I'll think of something to celebrate," he said. He turned to start away.

"We'll wait for Mrs. Matthews to examine her, but in my heart, I feel Sylvia was right," I said.

"What?" He turned back. "About what? She didn't diagnose herself, did she? You haven't educated her that well."

"No, but if you'll remember, she was the one who predicted that there was a baby coming," I said.

He shrugged. "You're a tribe of witches. What can I say?" He laughed and walked on.

If Sylvia had even the slightest suspicion that I was worried about her now, she didn't show it or maybe even care. She was too excited about going to a restaurant for dinner. She flitted about, gazing at herself in the mirror every ten seconds, checking her hair and her makeup. I continually had to assure her that she looked pretty enough to go out. Finally, I decided to share some of Momma's jewelry with her, something I rarely wore myself.

She was stunned when I opened the case with the rectangular diamonds in a necklace and matching earrings.

"You can wear this tonight, Sylvia."

"Me?"

I plucked the necklace out and put it on her. She sat gazing at herself in the mirror. It lay just at the peak of her cleavage. She touched it, her eyes wide with more feminine pride than I ever thought her capable of having. Then I showed her how to put on the earrings. She looked at me to see if I approved.

"It all looks beautiful on you, Sylvia. Momma would have been very proud."

"But what will you wear?"

"I have something Arden bought me four years ago. Don't worry."

She turned to look at herself again and ran her fingers over the diamonds.

For a few minutes, at least, I thought maybe I could, for the evening, put aside my fears and anxiety and really enjoy myself. Helping her choose what to wear, sitting beside her at her vanity table, and doing my own makeup, I did feel as I had dreamed I would with my younger sister, two young women giggling and flirting with their images in a mirror.

Aunt Ellsbeth, Vera, and even Papa would surely be sitting up in their graves, astounded that I had brought her so far from the disabled little girl who had been brought to Whitefern and left for us all to treat as a burden. Of course, she was still a far bigger responsibility than a young woman half her age would be. Pregnancy would be terrifying for her. No matter how many times I explained things to her, she would be confused. I hoped this Mrs. Matthews would be sensitive to all that. I made a mental note to be sure Arden impressed her with just how special this patient would be.

Arden was dressed to the nines, as Papa would say.

He had never looked more handsome and successful in his charcoal-black suit and silver tie. And when Sylvia and I descended the stairs, he raved about how beautiful we were. Sylvia actually flushed with embarrassment when he winked at me and gave her a kiss before hooking his arm with hers and then with mine.

"I'll be the envy of every man there," he declared. He walked us out and then surprised me by saying, "Why don't you two sit in the back? I'll be like your chauffeur tonight."

He followed that with a look suggesting that I should stay close to Sylvia and keep her comfortable and confident. He held open the door for us, and we got into the car.

"I have the Whitefern girls," he declared. "No man could ask for more."

There was probably no one better at ignoring and avoiding unhappy thoughts than Arden. Look at how well he had done with all that had happened to me. The way he was behaving right now made it seem like everything we had discussed earlier was simply a misunderstanding. I was afraid to interfere with his joviality by asking after Mrs. Matthews, how the phone call had gone. It would wait until later, when we were alone.

After all, I had yet to tell Sylvia that I thought she was pregnant. It was probably better to wait until Mrs. Matthews confirmed it, and then the explanations would begin. How dark that tunnel through which we would pass looked to me now. *Blot it out for the moment, or you won't enjoy a second of the evening*, I told myself. I turned to my sister, who sat so still with a smile frozen on her face. The excitement in her eyes made them glisten in the glow of passing car lights. She continually touched the diamonds, maybe to be sure they were still there and she hadn't imagined them.

I realized that for Sylvia, dressing up with makeup and jewelry and going out to dinner was like going to the moon. I was more excited for her than I was for myself. Arden had chosen one of the fancier restaurants just outside of Whitefern. He explained that he often came here to take very wealthy clients to lunch or sometimes dinner. They certainly knew him well enough at the restaurant. The maitre d' fawned over him and took us to what Arden said was the best table. He sat between Sylvia and me. When I gazed around the beautiful room, with its landscapes and mirrored wall sconces, the bulbs looking more like candles, and I saw how most of the other guests were gazing our way, I couldn't help but feel the optimism Arden cherished and sought.

"Darkness seeks those who keep their candles of hope unlit," Momma once told me. I had to brighten mine.

Arden ordered a bottle of champagne. Everyone was watching when the waiter popped it open. Sylvia laughed as some of it bubbled over, but it was poured quickly into our glasses, and then Arden raised his. Sylvia looked at me to copy everything I was doing.

"To the future of Whitefern," Arden said. "May it finally become the grand home it was meant to be."

Sylvia giggled at the clink of glasses and carefully sipped hers while watching how I sipped mine.

"Should I order a bottle of wine?" Arden asked.

"I think this is all the alcohol we should have right now," I replied, nodding at Sylvia.

"Okay. I'll get my favorite red by the glass. Tonight I want to have the filet mignon." He winked. "Maybe Sylvia should have that, too."

I ordered it for her, so I had to order it for myself, even though I had nowhere near the appetite to finish half of it.

All the table manners I had taught Sylvia over the years had their first real test this particular night, because she didn't have the comfort and security her own home provided. Whenever anyone nearby laughed, she looked quickly to see if she had done something wrong. What made me laugh was the way she inspected the salad.

"They don't cut the carrots right," she said. "Some pieces are bigger than others."

"It's okay, Sylvia," I said. "They don't have someone with your artistic talent doing it, but it will taste the same."

She looked at me skeptically. Maybe it would taste the same to me, I realized, but not to her. She did like the filet mignon and especially enjoyed the chocolate soufflé we had for dessert.

While we ate, some men stopped by to say hello to Arden. He introduced us, and Sylvia recited the "Pleased to meet you" I had practiced often with her. I could see all the men were attracted to her, but she was oblivious to the looks of admiration and desire in their eyes.

Before one particular man approached us, Arden informed me that he was one of the top five investors in our brokerage firm. He looked to be in his mid-sixties, with a tanned face and beautiful blue eyes. I thought he was close to Papa's height. I recalled his name, Charles Billings, and I remembered him now from Papa's funeral. He was one of the few who had attended the church service, but he hadn't come to the house later.

"Now, how do you deserve two beautiful women, Arden, while most men here are lucky to have one?" he asked, feigning annoyance.

Sylvia's eyes widened. She looked at me to see how I was going to react.

"Thank you, Mr. Billings," I said, before Arden introduced us. "This is my sister, Sylvia."

"I can see the resemblance. You lucky dog," he told Arden.

"I married well," Arden said, sounding a little peeved at the way I had taken control.

"In more ways than one," Mr. Billings said. "Tough week in the market. I hope we see a little bull in the coming days."

"We will," Arden said, as if he had control of the stocks and bonds.

"So, what are you celebrating?" Mr. Billings asked, nodding at the champagne bottle in the bucket.

Arden looked at me for a moment with an expression

on his face that I rarely saw these days. He looked like he was fighting not to burst with pride.

"We are almost one hundred percent sure," he began, and turned to Mr. Billings, "that my wife is pregnant."

Every muscle in my body seemed to collapse with shock. I had to put my glass of water down quickly, or I thought I would drop it.

"Well, congratulations," Mr. Billings said. "Making money is great, but making a family is divine."

"Exactly," Arden said. "Thank you."

I watched Mr. Billings walk away and saw him start to tell his wife and everyone at his table what Arden had just said. Sylvia had her attention completely on the chocolate soufflé now and apparently hadn't heard a word. I stared at Arden, my eyes full of questions.

He just shook his head. "Don't look so worried, Audrina."

"Worried? Why did you say that?"

He smiled and finished his wine. Then he looked at the bottle of champagne. "A little left." He poured it into his glass and drank it.

"Arden, answer me."

"Relax, Audrina. I have a brilliant plan."

I said nothing. After he paid the bill and we started to leave, he paused at Mr. Billings's table, and Mr. Billings introduced his wife and his two friends.

"I'm so happy for you," Mrs. Billings told us.

"Me, too," Sylvia said. I hadn't noticed, but she had some chocolate soufflé on her lips. "I love chocolate."

No one spoke, Sylvia's words hanging in the air.

"Thank you, Flora," Arden said to Mrs. Billings, before turning to Mr. Billings. "Here's to a bull market."

"Amen to that," Mr. Billings said, and we walked out.

The valet brought our car around, and we got in.

"Did you enjoy your dinner, ladies?" Arden asked as we drove off.

"They could have cut the carrots better," Sylvia said.

Arden laughed loudly.

I said nothing until we had gotten home and I had Sylvia get out of her clothes and prepare for bed. Then I went to our bedroom, where he was already in bed, browsing through one of his business magazines. He looked up sharply when I entered.

"Everything is set with Mrs. Matthews. She'll be here tomorrow. I'll take a break and come home, but you had better prepare Sylvia for her."

"What were you saying at the restaurant? What is this plan you have?" I asked.

He put down his magazine and put his hands behind his head.

"Everything you said about how Sylvia's child would be treated is true, and everything you said about how difficult it would be for her to be any sort of mother is even more true. Now, no one knows that Sylvia might be pregnant. Hardly anyone knows her, while most who know us, this family, know how she is."

"And?"

"So why not have people believe the baby coming is your baby, our baby?"

"My baby?"

I knew what he wanted, but the idea of my simulating pregnancy was daunting. What if someone found out I was pretending? The embarrassment would be frightening, but it was a way to protect Sylvia. Maybe I had to risk it.

"How do we do that, Arden?" I started to take off my dress.

"Simple. We have you go through the pregnancy just as Sylvia is going through it. If anything," he added, sitting forward, "it might make it easier on her to have you mimicking whatever happens to her and whatever she has to do."

"But people will see me and—"

He put his hand up. "I have that figured out, Audrina. After about four or five months, we'll keep people from seeing you." He shrugged. "We can have something made for you to wear that makes you look pregnant. Maybe we'll deliberately let some of the weekly groundskeepers, or someone else who comes onto the property, get a look at you and be able to tell people you're pregnant."

"What about Mr. Ralph? He will see Sylvia. He's in and out of the house often to fix things."

"Mr. Ralph will do and say whatever I tell him. He sees nothing and says nothing. He's always been that way. You know that."

"And Sylvia?"

"We've kept her pretty much sheltered here. We'll

just make it more intense when the time is right. We'll keep her up in her room. You can tell her she has to stay in bed, or Mrs. Matthews will tell her."

I stood there in my bra and panties, looking at him and thinking about his plan. "This Mrs. Matthews, she'll know the truth."

"She'll just have to keep two secrets," he said, smiling. "As I've said many times, what's another secret or two at Whitefern?"

"That's a lot of trust to place in a stranger, Arden."

"It's not a matter of trust. It's a tradeoff. Don't worry about it. I have it all under control."

He picked up his magazine, glanced at it, and then lowered it again. "The best part of this, Audrina, is that you will be a mother after all. But," he said cautiously, "let's wait for Mrs. Matthews to confirm that Sylvia's pregnant."

He started to read his magazine as if I had agreed to everything. It wasn't that easy for me. For one thing, I would be pretending to be something I wasn't again. I'd have to act a part, like in a play. It was still painful to remember how I'd been convinced that I was a second Audrina. Even when I'd believed it, I had wanted so much to be myself. For another thing, this would be as much as admitting that my becoming pregnant and having my own child was truly a dead idea. It would never happen.

I felt his eyes on me as I crossed the room to the bathroom to prepare for bed.

"I hope you enjoyed our dinner otherwise," he said when I reappeared in my nightgown. "I thought

Sylvia did very well, too. That's all thanks to you. You both did look beautiful."

"I enjoyed it, yes."

"Well, if there is a baby, when he or she is old enough, we'll go out a lot more. I've always envied fathers taking their wives and children out for Sunday brunch. Just think. We can really be a family . . . finally." And as if that explained everything, he put out his lamp and lay down.

"You told Mrs. Matthews about Sylvia, right?" I asked. "She understands that she's special and needs special treatment?"

He turned. "Of course I did, Audrina. You've got to stop worrying. As I said, I have it all under control now. You will have to trust me."

After a moment of thinking, I said, "That horrible man. He shouldn't get away with this."

"Don't start that again. If we accuse him of something, we'll ruin our plan. For now, just let it go. We have more important things to occupy our attention. And if you cross-examine Sylvia about it, about how it happened, when it happened, where it happened, any of it, you'll make things worse. I know her well enough after all these years to predict she'll feel guilty and terrible and sit around crying all the time. A bad thing happened. It's done, over with. Now we have to be sure nothing else terrible occurs, like a miscarriage. You probably remember Vera's vividly enough to know what that could mean for Sylvia."

"Papa would have taken out his Civil War pistol and driven over to the Prices' and shot him," I said.

"You mean like he shot the boys who raped you?" Arden asked.

It was a cold and cruel thing to say, but I understood why he was saying it. I was implying that he wasn't doing the manly thing for Sylvia.

"Clever people handle things like this in a way that doesn't bring more pain and trouble to themselves," he continued. He looked away as if he was remembering something. "Stop thinking about it, or you'll never fall asleep."

He turned toward me again, and although there was just a glimmer of light from the moon peeking between trees, I could see his wry smile.

"Think about being a mother instead," he said.

If he meant that as a comfort, he was wrong. That kept me from falling asleep even more.

Living a Lie

Arden had said that Mrs. Matthews was scheduled to come to Whitefern at around eleven in the morning. Right after we had cleaned up our breakfast dishes and put everything away, I had Sylvia sit on the settee in the living room, and I began an explanation to prepare her for a stranger coming to our home to examine her. The way she smiled at me was eerie. It was almost as if she knew exactly what I was going to say, and, contrary to what I might think, that made her happy.

"Something is going on inside you, Sylvia," I began. "Arden and I think you might be pregnant."

She nodded. There was certainly no shock, surprise, or fear on her face. This was unexpected. Perhaps she didn't understand and was simply trying to please me.

"Do you understand what I'm telling you, Sylvia? When I say we think you might be pregnant, we mean there might be a baby forming inside you."

"Yes, I know," she said. Then she smiled and said, "Papa told me, and he said the baby would be forming in you, too, Audrina."

For a moment, I was speechless. If I ever said anything clever or prophetic when I was little, Momma would always smile, tenderly brush my hair, and say, "Out of the mouths of babes . . ." I felt like saying that to Sylvia. Even if she had somehow overheard the things Arden had said, his plan in particular, she would never be able to comprehend it and embrace it. However, I couldn't imagine her coming up with this idea herself. Her even suggesting such a thing gave me a chill. Out of habit, I looked at Papa's chair. So often when I was teaching something to Sylvia, he would sit there and half-listen, occasionally smiling at how hard I pursued something with her until she had grasped it. I could easily imagine him sitting there now, with a similar smile on his face, encouraging me to go on.

"This is a house that welcomes ghosts," Aunt Ellsbeth had once told Vera and me. She'd hugged herself when she'd said it, and both of us had looked around, expecting to see some spirit whisk past us.

"When did Papa say this to you, Sylvia?" I asked now. It was like following someone you knew was lost, traveling down roads that led nowhere, but I had to question her.

"One time when I was in the rocking chair," she said.

"What time? When?"

"I don't know the time, Audrina. I didn't look at a clock." She looked like she was going to cry because she was disappointing me. "I don't remember."

"Okay, okay. Forget about that. There is a woman coming to see you this morning. Her name is Mrs.

Matthews. She's like a doctor. She helps deliver babies when it's time for them to come out. She will make sure you are pregnant and that you are doing okay, and then she will help us with everything that has to be done. I'll be with you all the time."

"You have to be. She has to make sure everything is all right with you, too," Sylvia said.

I closed my eyes. She was fixated on this idea. Perhaps, though, Arden was right. It would make things easier for her, and for us taking care of her, if she thought it was true and I mimicked everything happening to her.

"Right. Me, too. She'll be like Dr. Prescott, okay?"

She nodded, continuing to smile.

I still wasn't sure she understood the significance of what I was telling her. How detailed and scientific should I get? For most women, being pregnant wasn't exactly a picnic. There was expected discomfort. Sylvia, who liked to rush around the house and practically fly up the stairs, would find it a terrible burden, especially when she was four or five months along, and when she was seven or eight months . . . I simply couldn't imagine it. It wasn't only what she would look like and how confused she would be. There were dangers, too, not only to the baby but also to the mother.

However, I decided not to say too much more before Mrs. Matthews arrived. Arden's advice that morning as we dressed to go down to breakfast was to take it day by day and not obsess about it. He was the one who had warned, "We don't want to panic Sylvia or frighten her about all this. That could turn out worse."

"I know that, Arden," I'd told him. "Will Mrs. Matthews know that?"

"She's been well informed about Sylvia," he had assured me. "She is quite capable. We'll be lucky to have her. She'll make this far easier than you could imagine."

Nevertheless, I was on pins and needles until the doorbell rang. I had told Sylvia to go up to her room, change into her nightgown, and wait. She would be examined there. I wanted a few minutes alone with Mrs. Matthews before she saw Sylvia and before Arden got home, too.

When I opened the door, I found a lean woman, as tall as Arden, with dark gray hair trimmed sharply halfway down her long neck. She had a hard face, her cheeks flat, with skin so white it was almost transparent. Inky blue veins could be seen in her temples. I thought you wouldn't need an X-ray to discover if she had fractured a cheekbone. Her nose was small but a bit pointed, and her pale pink lips were as thin as string. Her eyes were coal-black with tiny gray spots. She wore a navy-blue coat over a nurse's uniform and carried a satchel that looked exactly like Dr. Prescott's, clutching it in her long fingers so tightly I could see the veins in the top of her hand. It was as if she was afraid she'd drop it or have it snatched away.

"Mrs. Matthews?" I asked. I knew it was a silly question. Who else would be at our door precisely at eleven? But I didn't want to just say hello.

"That's who I am," she said. She nodded her head

and stepped forward as a way of saying, *Please step back and let me in.*

It was a gray, cold early-February day. I retreated quickly, and she entered and paused to gaze at the house, her head bobbing from nine o'clock to twelve o'clock to three o'clock.

"It's as big as I expected," she said. "Quite cluttered. Family heirlooms, most of it, I imagine."

"Everything has some memory for us, yes," I said.

She looked at me, nodded, looked at the house again, and then turned back to me. "You are Mrs. Lowe, then?"

Did she think I was a maid?

"Yes, ma'am. Audrina Lowe, Arden's wife."

She studied me as if I really was the one who was pregnant. "I remember you when you were a little girl. You've grown into an attractive woman."

"Thank you."

"I recall your mother was quite beautiful."

"Yes, she was."

"That's a tragedy we don't want repeated," she said, the corners of her mouth drawn in.

"I hope not," I said. "The very thought terrifies me."

"As it should anyone. Well, let's get to it. Where's your sister?"

"She's in her room. I'll take you there. You understand what she's like?"

"Mentally retarded. I would hate to count how many girls like that I've delivered or assisted in delivering. Nature gave them the ability to produce offspring but left them unprotected when it comes to sexual matters, not that some of the smartest girls don't get into trouble. I've had plenty of them, too. Whenever I see that, I believe there very likely is a vengeful God."

"I wouldn't categorize her as mentally retarded. She's slow to understand things, but that's because she was underdeveloped when she was born prematurely and—"

"Call her what you want. I know what to expect."

"She's very, very sensitive, Mrs. Matthews. She has the body of a woman but the emotional development of a little girl."

She turned to me, the corners of her mouth drawn in again as she pressed her upper lip over the lower one before speaking. "I think I've been doing this long enough to know how to handle a pregnant girl regardless of her mental and emotional age. The physical aspects aren't different. Shall we get on with it? According to Mr. Lowe, you're not even certain she's pregnant, and it could be that this is all idle chatter."

"I am sure of it, I'm afraid," I said. "I don't have medical training like you do, but there are things a woman can sense."

She raised her eyebrows. "We'll soon see."

I nodded and led the way to the stairs. After I started up, I realized she wasn't following. She had paused at the bottom and stood looking up. "Something wrong?" I asked.

"Any bedrooms downstairs?"

"There are two in the rear of the house, but neither one has been used for ages, decades, really. They were meant for servants, and we've never even thought of them as part of the house. They don't have fireplaces and haven't even been cleaned for ages. Why?"

"I don't fancy climbing up and down the stairs between the kitchen and her room as many times as I might have to. If she is indeed pregnant, at one point I'll be attending to your sister closely, and it will be easier if she is down here. It's also wise to avoid any possibilities of falling when you're pregnant, and I think we both know that stairways can be deadly. If she's pregnant, you'll put her in one of the rear bedrooms," she declared with the tone of a fait accompli.

"But . . . they don't even have heat. The central heating my father had installed didn't provide for them."

"You'll get portable heaters. Really, this is not a world-shattering problem."

"It will be for Sylvia. She is very comfortable in her room. She's been there ever since she was brought home from the hospital. It's not easy for her to adjust to changes."

She made a *humph* sound. "Imagine the changes that come over you when you get pregnant. She'll have a lot to adjust to. This should be the least of it." She started up after me, glaring at me when I didn't move.

"What about her going up to her studio to do her art?" I asked.

"Are you serious? Send her up another flight of stairs for a hobby?"

"It's not a hobby for her. It's very important to her."

She sighed deeply and shook her head. "Bring her art supplies down to her room."

"But—"

"Am I to see her or not?"

"I'm sorry," I said, and continued up quickly. I led her to Sylvia's bedroom. When we entered, Sylvia was at her vanity table. She had brushed her hair and tied it with a red ribbon. Now she was putting on lipstick, too.

"What is she doing?" Mrs. Matthews asked. "We're not taking pictures for a maternity magazine."

"Sylvia, don't you remember I said Mrs. Matthews was coming to examine you this morning?"

"Oh, yes, Audrina." She smiled. "I just wanted to look nice for her."

Mrs. Matthews's thin, mostly gray eyebrows knitted, and then she stepped further into the room. "Hello, Sylvia," she said. "I'm Helen Matthews. I'm here to see what's going on with you."

"We're having a baby," Sylvia said.

"Perhaps," Mrs. Matthews said, not picking up on the "we." "Let's check you out. Just lie down on your bed, please. Nothing will hurt, I promise."

"It hurts when the baby comes out, but it doesn't last long. Papa told me that."

"Hopefully that's so," Mrs. Matthews said. She looked at me and almost, I thought, smiled.

I stood back to watch her. Sylvia watched her, too, her eyes wide with interest after Mrs. Matthews had put on plastic gloves. Sylvia's face was full of surprise, but she did not utter a sound when Mrs. Matthews had her bend her legs and spread them.

"Can you see the baby?" Sylvia asked. I brought my hand up to cover my smile.

Her innocent trust never ceased to amaze me. It was probably the main reason Papa had made me swear I would always look after her. But I hadn't done that very well, I reminded myself.

"Not yet," Mrs. Matthews said. When she stepped back, she took off her gloves and turned to me. "We can confirm it with a urine sample, but I would say she's a good six weeks along."

"Six weeks? You're sure."

"I said we'd confirm it with a urine sample, but yes, I'm sure. I've seen more wombs than Henry the Eighth," she added, which was a line I imagined she had used often.

"Hello!" We heard Arden shout from below. He had come in and was heading up the steps.

"I'll see to the urine test," Mrs. Matthews said. She turned to Sylvia. "Let's go into the bathroom, Sylvia. We have one more thing to do today."

I stepped out into the hallway as Arden turned toward Sylvia's room.

"Well?" he asked.

"She's confident it's a yes. Six weeks, probably, which makes it right when Mr. Price was giving her art lessons. She's conducting a urine test to confirm it."

He nodded, not looking as upset as I felt or as I'd imagined he would be. "Well, then, there's nothing to do but go forward with our plan."

"Your plan," I said. He looked at me sharply. "But

a plan, yes. I understand. It's just that now that it's all true, I feel a bit numb."

"You'll get over it," he said. He walked past me to the bathroom and stood in the doorway, looking in. "Hi, Helen," he said. "When you're finished here, Audrina will show you to my office downstairs, and we'll discuss the arrangements. Come quickly, as I have to get back to my office."

From the way he spoke to her, the tone of his voice, I concluded he'd been telling the truth; he did have some secret he could hold over her. Did he have such confidence in her that he didn't have to wait for a confirmation? How did he know so much about her abilities? All sorts of suspicions burst like fireworks in my mind.

He walked past me without another word and hurried down the stairs. I heard Sylvia return to her room and went there. She was sitting comfortably on the bed, her hands in her lap. She didn't look at all disturbed or upset, so I had to conclude that Mrs. Matthews did know how to turn on good bedside manner when it was necessary. But that didn't give me full confidence in how she would handle Sylvia. After all, Mr. Price's assurance that he knew how to handle special education students was what had brought us here.

"You don't have to do it right away," Mrs. Matthews said, "but prepare that bedroom downstairs. The test confirms it." She closed up her satchel methodically. "I'll look into prenatal vitamins. Of course,

I'm assuming you and Mr. Lowe want to keep the baby."

"Yes," I said. I knew I sounded weak and indecisive, but she chose to ignore it.

As she started out, Sylvia called to her, and the prickly woman turned back.

"Don't you have to do it to Audrina, too?" my sister asked. "Audrina has to pee on that little stick."

Mrs. Matthews looked at me, squeezing her nose and pursing her lips as if a whiff of something rotten had flown under her nostrils.

"She'll do it in my bedroom, Sylvia," I said. Mrs. Matthews shook her head and stepped out. "I've got to show Mrs. Matthews something first. I'll be right back."

"Pray tell, what was that about?" Mrs. Matthews asked.

"My husband will explain it, Mrs. Matthews. Right this way," I said, and started down the stairs.

She followed me, and when we arrived at Arden's office, he looked up from his desk.

"Mrs. Matthews wants to know why Sylvia thinks I'm pregnant, too, Arden."

"Thank you, Audrina," he said. He stood up and came around his desk to the door. "Why don't you go back to see if everything is all right with Sylvia while I speak with Mrs. Matthews and explain it all." He smiled with his all-too-familiar self-confidence.

I looked at her and nodded. The moment I stepped back, Arden closed the door.

Secrets had a natural life here, I thought as I went back upstairs. They were born and nurtured like precious flowers. They never died in revelation, either. They stuck to our walls and our lives.

"While I was peeing, I told Mrs. Matthews I had drawn and painted the baby," Sylvia said, as soon as I returned to her room. She was lying on her bed, staring up at the ceiling.

"Did you?"

"Yes, and told her that's why I knew the baby was coming. I told her it might be a boy, too."

"Was she surprised?"

"No. She said boys are harder. What's that mean?"

"Harder to bring up, I imagine."

"Because they get dirty and get into fights?"

"Among other things, yes," I said. "Let's get you dressed. Today we're supposed to clean the pantry, remember?"

"No."

"Well, we are. You go there and start taking everything out the way we did a few months ago."

"Is there going to be a mouse again?" she asked, sitting up and making a scrunched-up face.

"I hope not."

"Maybe there'll be one dead in the trap. Don't worry. I'm not afraid of it."

"I know you're not, Sylvia, but remember not to touch it. They can carry diseases, and you can't get sick now."

"I can't?"

"I mean you shouldn't. Not when you're pregnant."

"Then you can't get sick, either?"

"Right. Let's go."

When we went downstairs, she went off to the pantry, and I returned to Arden's office. Mrs. Matthews was already gone, and he was on the phone. He put his hand up, finished his call, and turned to me.

"It's all set," he said.

"What's all set?"

"What I described we would do, Audrina. She's fully aboard. She understood completely and will play along with your being pregnant, and Sylvia, as far as the world outside is to know, is not." He sat back, smiling. "She's even going to come up with a sort of girdle apparatus that you can wear to show the months as time goes by."

"I wish I knew why you were so confident in her, Arden."

"You'll have to trust me." He stood. "Now, I have to go back to the office."

"She wants me to move Sylvia into one of the rear bedrooms downstairs."

He nodded. "Yes. She mentioned that."

"They'll need portable heaters and more light, and we'll have to bring her art supplies down. She won't like it."

"Don't worry. We'll clean up both of those rooms and make them comfortable."

"Both? Why both?"

"What Sylvia has to do you'll have to do, right? She'll put up with it if you are doing it, too. We'll have to prepare one of the rooms for Mrs. Matthews. She'll move in after a while, Audrina. It will be like having a private-duty nurse around the clock. Don't worry about it," he said. He kissed me quickly on the cheek and started to leave.

"But why would we have a private-duty maternity nurse, Arden?" I asked, chasing after him.

He paused. "Because you will be said to have problems with the pregnancy, and that's why you can't leave the house. See? It's a perfect plan." He smiled and continued out.

I stood there thinking. I recalled one of Momma and Aunt Ellsbeth's Tuesday teatimes in which Momma, playing Aunt Mercy Marie, had pointed her finger accusingly at Aunt Ellsbeth and shouted with venom, "Lies are like rats. You give them a home, and they will devour it and everyone in it."

"Why?" Vera had asked. She always loved to sit on the floor and watch them go at each other, taking turns to be Aunt Mercy Marie.

Momma had turned to her, her eyes narrowed. "Because one lie begets another, and that begets another, and woe be to anyone who swims in that swamp."

Vera hadn't been afraid of anyone or anything, even Papa. She'd giggled.

Momma had turned to Aunt Ellsbeth and, pointing to Vera, said, "See?"

I hadn't been sure what she meant by that, but in time, I understood. Aunt Ellsbeth's whole life with Vera was born from a lie.

Now I went to join Sylvia to try to keep her busy and not thinking about what lay ahead—for both of us.

The next day, Mrs. Matthews brought Sylvia her prenatal vitamins and a bottle full of the same pills for me, telling me it couldn't hurt me to take vitamins. She checked Sylvia's vitals, blood pressure, and temperature and, with Sylvia watching, did the same for me.

"She has better blood pressure than you do," Mrs. Matthews muttered.

How could she not expect that? Sylvia was totally relaxed and trusting; I was the one who was tense and nervous. No matter what Arden had agreed to with Mrs. Matthews, I was still embarrassed by the deception.

"As I understand it, your sister performs many household duties?" Mrs. Matthews asked.

"She helps out, yes."

"At one point, we'll want to restrict her activities. I encourage walking, but you have a special circumstance here, so you'll have to restrict that after a while to inside only."

The full impact of all this subterfuge hit me, and for a few moments, I was stunned. Too often, I remembered how restricted I had been when I was growing up. Papa wouldn't let me go to school for years, and I practically never left the house, except for church and visits to "my" grave in the cemetery.

"My goodness," Mrs. Matthews said, seeing the expression on my face. "You've not been sentenced to life imprisonment. Frankly, I think your husband has come up with a very clever plan. Just think of all the nastiness you'll avoid. Believe me, people are unforgiving and eager to pounce when they have an opportunity to take joy in someone else's misery. I've seen plenty of that," she added, and closed her satchel.

"Yes, so have I," I said.

"Then you understand." She smiled, if I could call it that. Her skin seemed to fold in at her cheeks, and her thin lips stretched so that I could see tiny ripples in them. Her smile was more like a flashbulb going off, an instant of light and gone. "I've put my telephone number on the refrigerator. Call me if there is the slightest problem. You want to watch for unexpected bleeding, shortness of breath, sudden dizziness, or any swelling and pain in her calf muscles."

I didn't think Sylvia was listening. She seemed absorbed in one of my new fashion magazines. But without looking up, she asked, "Audrina, too?"

We both looked at her and simultaneously said, "Yes."

I glanced at Mrs. Matthews, realizing I had a co-conspirator.

"I'll stop by every two days for the time being and then more frequently," she said. She nodded at Sylvia and left.

"She's very nice," Sylvia said. "You were right, Audrina. She told me she gave birth to a boy."

"I can't imagine what his life was like," I muttered, and went into the Roman Revival salon to ponder the journey we were embarking on, as short as it might seem. There were months to go, and I painfully recalled how slowly time would pass when I was confined. I hated the thought that I might once again be sitting by a window, gazing out, and dreaming of going off to be with other girls and boys my age, something that should have been so natural and easy to do.

Every day now, I tried to forget all that by working harder in the house. In the weeks that followed, I prepared the two unused bedrooms in the rear. I wanted to give their walls a fresh coat of paint, but Mrs. Matthews thought the odor would disturb Sylvia. Arden brought home the portable heaters and hooked them up. He moved some lamps and even rolled one of our bedroom rugs up and carried it with Mr. Ralph to the bedroom he'd decided I would be using. I wanted him to put it in Sylvia's, but he insisted, claiming that I was the one who was making the greater sacrifice.

Although Mr. Ralph was as trusted a servant as anyone could have, he naturally was curious about why we were preparing the rooms. I heard Arden explain that I was pregnant and the maternity nurse had insisted on my not having to go up and down the stairs. There could be a lot of medical attention needed.

"Sylvia," he said, "is so dependent on Audrina, as you know. She imitates everything she does."

The explanation satisfied Mr. Ralph. Arden whispered something to him that caused him to laugh. I nodded to myself, thinking that Arden really was good at handling people. He could be charming and convincing when he had to be. In more and more ways, he reminded me of Papa. They were both comfortable with lies.

For now, he had nothing more to explain. Sylvia

wasn't showing, of course. That didn't happen until she was in her fourth month, and it was then that Mrs. Matthews brought the customized girdle for me to wear in public. Sylvia didn't have to move downstairs yet, and I was still permitted to leave the house to do basic shopping, but Sylvia was not. I had to do it while she was taking a nap or involved in her art up in the cupola. Enough people saw me and believed that I was pregnant. Arden would brag about who had been deceived and how well our plan was working.

The following week, Sylvia began complaining about lower back pain, and one day, she had some blood spotting on her panties. I called Mrs. Matthews, who came over quickly and examined her. She said Sylvia was all right, but she decided that the time had come for her to move in with us. To make Sylvia happy, I complained about lower back pain, too. Maybe it was my imagination, but I thought I actually felt it.

It wasn't until Mrs. Matthews physically moved into the house that the reality of what would happen struck me. Every moment of our day and all our waking hours at night, there would be a stranger present. The privacy we had enjoyed, even the privacy associated with our family memories, would be invaded. I was, of course, afraid of what would come out of Sylvia's mouth. Mrs. Matthews was to be there at our dinners, breakfasts, and lunches. She would hear everything Arden would tell us about the business, or as much as he would want to share. There would be real privacy only in our bedroom or if I met with him in his office. I kept telling myself that it would only be for a few months.

But if anyone knew that months could seem like years at Whitefern, it was I.

As soon as Mrs. Matthews brought her things, she ordered that Sylvia be moved downstairs immediately, which meant that I would move, too. During all the time those rooms were being prepared, Sylvia had never asked me why. When I had to tell her now that Mrs. Matthews was here and insisted that Sylvia sleep in one of those rooms, she looked as frightened as she had when she was a little girl of five or six. She retreated from me, nearly backing herself against the wall behind her bed.

"I can't go downstairs to sleep," she said, shaking her head. "No, Papa won't like that."

"Papa would want you to be safe," I said, and explained again why Mrs. Matthews required it.

Sylvia clutched the bedpost.

Would Mrs. Matthews and I have to tear her away from it and force her downstairs? I couldn't do that.

"I have to stay here, Audrina."

"It's only for a little while, Sylvia. It will be okay. I promise. Remember, I'll be sleeping downstairs, too. I'll be in the room next to yours."

She shook her head even harder. "I can't be downstairs at night."

"Why can't you, Sylvia?"

"I have to talk to Papa. I have to be in the rocking chair," she said.

"You're still going there? When do you go there?"

"When you're asleep."

It stunned me for a moment. Had Arden ever heard her doing that again?

"I won't sleep downstairs," she repeated, raising her voice. "I won't!"

"What's going on here?" Mrs. Matthews asked, entering quickly when she heard Sylvia shouting.

"I told you she wasn't going to like sleeping downstairs. Why can't I bring her things? I don't mind going up and down the stairs, and . . ."

"It's not simply bringing her things. I thought you understood," she snapped at me, then turned to my sister. "Now, you will go downstairs, Sylvia, and that's that."

Sylvia was close to crying.

"This can't be good for a pregnant woman," I said.

"Woman? Don't you mean child?" Mrs. Matthews said. "I don't have time for this nonsense. There are things to do."

"Okay, okay. I tell you what, Sylvia. I'll have Arden bring the rocking chair down and put it in your room for now. Okay?"

"Rocking chair?" Mrs. Matthews said. "This is all about a rocking chair?"

Sylvia thought for a moment, relaxed, and then nodded.

"Well, now that the nonsense has ended, let's get on with it," Mrs. Matthews said. "Let's move the things we need downstairs." She went to Sylvia's armoire to choose what she would be wearing.

"Audrina's things, too," Sylvia said.

Mrs. Matthews looked at me. I thought she smiled, although with her you could never be sure it wasn't a smirk of disgust. "Yes, Audrina's, too," she said. And then she really did smile when she added, "Maybe she will rock in the chair, too."

Sylvia widened her eyes. "Papa would like that," she said.

"Well, then, it's settled." Mrs. Matthews laughed. "We'll be able to sing 'Rock-a-bye Baby' and mean it."

Losing Track of Who I Am

❧⎯⎯❧

"Did you know that Sylvia was still going to the rocking chair at night?" I asked Arden as soon as he had come home and I could be alone with him in our bedroom.

He paused as he changed out of his business suit and stood there thinking. "You know, there were times when I woke to the sound of her shuffling along, I think, but frankly, I was too tired to get up and chase her back to her room. Audrina, I've told you many times to get rid of that chair and everything in that room. Why do you ask?"

"She would agree to go into the downstairs bedroom only if we brought the rocking chair to the room. I told her you would."

"You told her I would? Half of the problem here is that you feed this insanity," he said.

"That's not fair, Arden. Sylvia is delicate."

"Don't blame it on Sylvia. You're still afraid to throw out that chair and empty that room. You're the one keeping the ghosts alive here, Audrina, not Sylvia."

I looked down, tears bubbling like boiling milk. I thought I heard footsteps in the hallway. Mrs. Matthews had moved into her room, which was only a little way down and across from ours. The old wooden floors creaked and complained whenever anyone walked around up here. Was she eavesdropping? How much did she know about us? How much did she want to know? There were more than ghosts watching and listening to us now. It was embarrassing to have arguments in front of a stranger. How did people in big homes with servants keep their privacy?

"Okay, okay," Arden said. "I'll bring down the rocking chair. It's not light, you know."

"I can help."

"I'll manage," he said. "Or I'll ask Mrs. Matthews to help."

"Why her and not me?"

"You're pregnant, Audrina, remember?"

"What?"

"You've got to convince yourself, or you won't act properly in front of people. And it would set a very bad example for Sylvia if she saw you carrying something heavy while she's been told not to do that. When you're taking special care of yourself, you're taking special care of her. I thought you understood that."

"I do. I just forget sometimes. You can't blame me, Arden. I'm not really pregnant."

"Well, we're doing this for Sylvia as much as for us," he said.

"I know, I know."

"Shouldn't you be moving what you need to your

room?" he asked as he started to put on more casual clothes.

"I'm just as unhappy as Sylvia is about doing this. I don't know why Mrs. Matthews is so insistent about her being downstairs. She acts like going up and down the stairs is the same as climbing a mountain. She's not elderly."

"The woman knows what she's doing, and making the right decisions is what we're paying her to do. She's been hired to make sure this all works out well for us."

"I would have hoped you would be more unhappy about my moving out of our bedroom, Arden."

What really bothered me was that our space for any sort of privacy would be even more limited once we didn't share the bedroom, but he thought I was referring only to sex. He smiled. "Don't worry. I'll keep you company until you're tired enough to sleep. I'd do more, but we have to be careful. We don't want to get a pregnant woman pregnant."

He laughed, and before I could protest that I wasn't referring to that or say that he could use birth control, he went into the bathroom and closed the door. For as long as we had been together, he hadn't used any protection. We were always supposedly trying to have a child. I didn't want to emphasize that now, because it wasn't the point I was trying to make.

Frustrated, I started choosing the clothes I would bring downstairs, and when he came out of the bathroom, I went in and gathered my toiletries without saying another word. I had to have as much in my downstairs bedroom as Sylvia did, or she would wonder why I didn't. At times, she seemed more intense about my mimicking her pregnancy than Arden, Mrs. Matthews, or I were. As it was, we were taking the prenatal vitamins together and being examined together. We were now eating the same foods, too. Mrs. Matthews explained that she didn't want us gaining too much weight. Of course, she was saying this for Sylvia and not for me, but the way she looked at me when she spoke gave me the eerie feeling she really meant it for both of us. It was as if she was so focused on her work that she forgot or ignored that I wasn't really pregnant.

"It's a tricky balance sometimes, because you have to eat enough for two, and in the case of twins, three," she continued to explain at dinner. "But I'm relying on the most up-to-date nutritional information for pregnant women."

Arden smiled and complimented Mrs. Matthews on how thoroughly she went about her work. He thought it was wonderful. He thought almost anything she did or said was wonderful. Again, I wondered how he knew so much about her abilities. What gave him so much confidence in her medical abilities, or was it simply that she was someone who would keep a secret? I would have thought that was the main reason he had any interest at all, if it wasn't for how much concern he sincerely showed for Sylvia's well-being. Whenever he could, he would cross-examine me like a nervous father.

"Are you making sure Sylvia's following Mrs.

Matthews's orders, Audrina? Are you helping to keep Sylvia calm? Are you letting her do too much when Mrs. Matthews isn't around?"

I constantly reassured him about Sylvia, but he was just as anxious about how well I was mimicking her pregnancy so that Sylvia would be happy. As time went by, he was more intense and nervous about it. If I questioned him about that, he would explode in a rant about his reputation. Any exposure would destroy our ruse.

"I can't even imagine how I would explain it," he said.

He couldn't have had a better co-conspirator than Mrs. Matthews. I had to admit that. She'd had someone she trusted create the girdle-like apparatus I wore under my clothes. It had a large zippered pocket into which we stuffed large wads of wool that Arden brought home. As Sylvia expanded, so did I. Mrs. Matthews took great pains to be sure we were the same size.

At first, I felt terribly foolish wearing it. Early on, it was almost as burdensome as a real pregnancy. I'd forget and reach for something or bend down to pick something up and practically topple. I questioned Arden and Mrs. Matthews about it, pointing out that no other part of me reflected my simulated pregnancy.

"That's why you should eat on the side," Arden suggested. "Don't follow Mrs. Matthews's diet designed for Sylvia. Gain some weight."

"That would work," Mrs. Matthews seconded.

"What? I don't want to gain unnecessary weight."

"It's not unnecessary," Arden said. "You just made a good point about your appearance. We want people to believe you're pregnant, don't we?"

"But—"

"I'll buy some high-calorie foods for you to eat," Mrs. Matthews said, nodding. "You know, cakes and cookies and ice cream."

"Is that a healthy thing to do?" I asked. "Force myself to gain weight?"

She shrugged. "You'll go on a diet as soon as Sylvia gives birth. It will make sense then that you lose weight, although I must say, I've known many mothers who didn't. There are women, you know, who won't have children because they are afraid they will lose their precious beautiful figures."

She smiled at Arden, who smiled back as if they shared her medical histories and he knew exactly the women to whom she was referring.

What if they didn't have a beautiful figure to begin with, like you? I wanted to fire back. She could be so infuriating sometimes—actually, most of the time. The part I was playing to enable Arden's plan to work sometimes made me feel foolish, but of course I understood why we were doing it. When I waddled around and sympathized with Sylvia, who really was beginning to feel the weight and slow down, complaining about her lower back pain, with me echoing about mine, I could see Arden and Mrs. Matthews off to the side watching us, smiling and whispering something that made the two of them laugh.

Sylvia was starting her seventh month, and Mrs.

Matthews really began to restrict her activities. Arden had brought down her easel and her art supplies, but she wasn't doing much with them now. The new sheet on her easel remained untouched.

"Why don't you draw something new?" I asked her finally.

She looked at the easel and shook her head. "Papa wanted me to do my art in the cupola, Audrina. I need to be in the cupola."

I had the feeling she was about to tell me that it was only there that he could tell her what to draw and when to draw it. Mrs. Matthews came around just then, and I decided not to discuss it. Without her artwork, however, Sylvia's days were longer, and she looked so lost. When she just naturally, out of habit and routine, began to clean the kitchen or attempt to vacuum the carpets, Mrs. Matthews would lunge at her and take away dust cloths and cleaning sprays and practically tear the vacuum cleaner handle out of her hands, chastising her for disobeying orders.

She complained to me. "I told you she isn't to do these things now. I can't be following her around every moment of the day. You're supposed to be part of this."

"I'm sorry," I said. "She's bored."

"Don't you have any jigsaw puzzles? It might take her months to finish one, and by then, she could go back to being your maid."

"She's not my maid; she's never been our maid. This is her house, too," I snapped back. "She takes pride in what it looks like."

Mrs. Matthews looked at me without any sign of

emotion. Any complaints directed at her were like water off a duck's back. After all, Arden had put us in a situation where even the thought of firing her was impossible.

When I was a little girl, Papa had impressed on me how important it was to keep our secrets. "When you trust someone with a secret, Audrina," he had said, "you make them your master. They can always threaten you with revealing it. Be careful about that."

Of course, he'd been talking about all the secrets involving me, but it was still very true now.

"I don't want you lifting things or pushing things now, Sylvia," Mrs. Matthews told her. Her angry tone brought tears to my sister's eyes, so I had to intercede quickly and explain that I couldn't do those things, either.

Mrs. Matthews apparently thought housework was beneath her. She wouldn't even wash a glass, much less a dish. I was permitted to do that, but only behind Sylvia's back. The house was beginning to run away with itself. Half the time, we weren't even making the beds.

I complained about it to Arden, but he said, "For a while, we'll have to put up with it, Audrina. All of us have to make sacrifices. We certainly can't hire a temporary maid and have some stranger in our home witnessing all this."

"I'd be embarrassed to have anyone see how far behind we are with the upkeep of Whitefern."

"It'll be fine," he insisted. "I have no intention of having guests until this is over. Just leave it all be."

It was easy for him to say that. He wasn't haunted

day and night by images of Aunt Ellsbeth outraged at how Whitefern was being treated. She would explode over muddy feet on a carpet or food left on a counter in the kitchen, and if our beds weren't made, she would have Vera and I make them twice just to teach us that we should care more.

Mrs. Matthews's rules and orders left me feeling armless, but what could I do but try to amuse Sylvia, who looked lost most of the time?

Consequently, I spent most of my time watching television with Sylvia, something we hadn't done that much of because I had to explain so much about what was happening that I couldn't keep up with the program anyway.

Growing tired of the chore one day, I went looking through my old things and found a jigsaw puzzle rated for children ages nine to twelve. I began it with Sylvia, and when she fit a piece in, she was very pleased with herself. Mrs. Matthews saw us doing it and nodded with that bony-looking smile of hers. This was a woman who lived to be right, I thought. I couldn't help feeling that she enjoyed wielding power over us, especially me. Sometimes when she told me to do something or criticized me for doing something, I sensed a little vengefulness, bitterness.

Was there something about her that I was missing? Did she dislike my family for some reason? I felt at such a disadvantage. I knew only what Arden had told me about her, and there was still that secret that she feared would be revealed, the secret he held over her head like a flaming sword.

When she wasn't tending to Sylvia, Mrs. Matthews would leave the house to look after her own needs. As far as I knew, she never contacted her son while she was living at Whitefern, and she never spoke about other relatives. What about friends? I wondered. Wouldn't they be asking her questions about us? About why she was living here now?

When I asked Arden about that, he said, "Don't worry about it. She can be trusted to say the right things anyway."

She was doing all our shopping now, buying what she preferred to eat and drink. After I complained to Arden about this one night in his home office, he told me to accompany her the next day when she went to the supermarket.

"You can choose what you want, if it fits the nutritional principles Mrs. Matthews has set out for Sylvia. Besides, it's a good idea for you to go with her to the supermarket this week."

"Why?"

"It's time people saw you two together and understood that I've hired her to give you special attention."

"But no pregnant woman takes a nurse along to buy groceries, Arden."

"You do, because you've had some problems, Audrina," he snapped back. "Where's that brilliant mind of yours? We're claiming now that you can't drive. Don't forget that. She or I have to drive you anywhere, as far as people in this town are to know. Remember, in a few weeks, you will never set foot out of this house," he warned. "I have to develop a believable story for our employees and clients. Otherwise, everything we're doing will be for nothing, and you'll feel like a fool."

"I feel like a fool now."

"Don't start, Audrina, not now when we're so close to the end."

I sighed, resistance smothered, self-pride practically drowned. "I'll go with her, but we can't leave Sylvia alone, especially now."

"I'll babysit," he said.

"You will?"

"Yes. We both have to make sacrifices. I'm just as much a part of this, Audrina. I've told you time and time again that I'm risking my reputation, too. I could look like an idiot if the truth leaked out. And what do you think the impact would be on our business, the faith our clients have on us? Remember, Audrina, a brokerage firm's lifeblood is trust and faith."

"Everything always seems to snake its way back to business with you, Arden. You remember people's birthdays and anniversaries just so they'll continue to invest with you. You take them out to dinners and lunches to, as Papa would say, lick their boots. You even took a client out on our anniversary last year!"

"Your father? You bring up your father? He did everything I'm doing. He's the one who taught me how to do it, why it was important to the company. He set the example for me."

"Do you have to be like him in every way? You weren't always like this, Arden. Or were you?"

He smiled.

"What's so funny?"

"You're acting just the way Mrs. Matthews told me most of her pregnant patients behave, emotionally. They're very moody. Anything can set them off like firecrackers."

"I'm not really pregnant, Arden! I'm not being moody!"

He held his smile.

It was exasperating me more. I was having the shortness of breath Mrs. Matthews had predicted a pregnant Sylvia might experience.

"I know you're not really pregnant, Audrina," he said softly, "but maybe it's like a cold or something. It's catching. Sylvia's different, so you're different."

"Of course she's different. Her life has been upended," I said, my voice straining. "She's confused about her body. She can't do what she's been used to doing. She's not sleeping in her own room. Yes, she's different. She was raped! And that man is getting away with it."

He lost his smile. "All right, Audrina. Don't shout. You're getting yourself unnecessarily overwrought. What do you want?"

I fumed inside, but I couldn't explain it simply. I was sure Mrs. Matthews was outside his office listening. Was I going to bring up my childhood, what it was like to be so constrained, trapped, after I had been raped?

"I don't know," I said finally. "Maybe just to get this over with."

"Exactly. It isn't much longer now, and the outcome

will please you. We'll have protected Sylvia, and there'll be a baby in our house, a child to raise, someone to inherit all we have. Whitefern won't go to strangers," he said calmly. Then he walked over to me, hugged me, and kissed me on my forehead and cheek. "Mrs. Matthews says it's all going well now. You're doing your part. As soon as we're able to, as soon as Sylvia gives birth and the baby can travel, we'll all take a holiday, okay?"

I nodded, gazing down at the floor, my heart still thumping with the frustration I felt.

"I need to finish something here, and then I'll come out and sit with you and Sylvia."

"And Mrs. Matthews," I reminded him, the bitterness undisguised.

He nodded. "Yes, and Mrs. Matthews."

"Promise me something, Arden. Will you promise me something?"

"I'll try. What is it?"

"When this is all over, you'll tell me what secret you have of hers, what you hold over her. Will you?"

I saw the reluctance in his eyes, but he saw the need in mine. "Okay," he said at last. "You're right. By then, it might not matter to her. She'll be gone from our lives."

"Good."

I turned and started out. When I reached the mirror in the hallway, the full-length one in the mahogany frame, I glanced at myself and paused. I did look pregnant, but I felt idiotic. I was a walking, talking lie. What would I say when people in the supermarket stopped to ask how I was and if I had any idea if my baby would be a boy or a girl?

"It will be neither," I whispered. "It will be a hunk of wool."

I couldn't help laughing. I was still laughing when I entered the Roman Revival salon and saw Mrs. Matthews sitting with Sylvia and helping her do her jigsaw puzzle. They both looked up, surprised, which only caused me to laugh harder. Sylvia didn't need to know why I was laughing. She began to laugh, too. Mrs. Matthews looked from her to me, astonished. I was laughing so hard now that tears were streaming down my cheeks.

"I think," Mrs. Matthews said, "that you should go to your room and gather your wits."

"Gather my wits. Yes," I said, and hurried away.

I went to bed early that night. I was as exhausted as a real pregnant woman might be. It was getting very weird, I thought. There were times when I imagined a baby moving inside me, just the way it was moving inside Sylvia, surprising, frightening, and exciting her almost at the same time. As a matter of fact, it felt like it was kicking right now.

I fell asleep dreaming that the roles were reversed. It was Sylvia who was mimicking me. I was the one who was really pregnant. And Sylvia, who was truly still a child, wanted to be like me. She always wanted to be like me.

"Let her pretend," Arden told me in my dream. "What harm could it do?"

Sylvia was even lying in the bed beside me in the delivery room, screaming with pain.

And when I gave birth to a beautiful baby, Sylvia gave birth to the baby she had drawn with eyes on fire.

The image shocked me awake. I sat up, my heart pounding. I could hear the house creaking more down here. Upstairs, I didn't hear how the wind threaded through every crack. My dream raised my worry about Sylvia, so I got up and went to her room. The door was always left open.

When I didn't see her in her bed, I began to panic, but then I saw her in the rocking chair in the corner. She was asleep. I wondered if I should wake her and get her into her bed. I recalled how often I had fallen asleep in that chair, under Papa's orders to dream and capture the imaginary first Audrina's gifts. What was Sylvia dreaming about?

Let her dream, I thought, and returned to my bed. It took me almost until morning to fall asleep again. I was afraid of returning to the nightmare that had woken me.

That morning, Arden delayed going to work so he would be home while Mrs. Matthews and I went shopping. I was almost too tired to go along, but I forced myself to do it. Ironically, if I ever complained about being tired or having a pain, both Mrs. Matthews and Arden acted as though it was expected. After all, I was supposed to be pregnant. They were both sure to do this whenever Sylvia was present.

"Try a heating pad," Mrs. Matthews might tell me. "I don't like giving medication to pregnant women."

I glanced at Sylvia and saw how that pleased her, because Mrs. Matthews surely had told her something similar. It wasn't only my movements and activities that were restricted. I even had my thoughts confined. When did I pretend to cross the line into and out of reality? How could I be defiant? I was gagged and handcuffed, trapped and imprisoned, even more than I had been as a young girl who was forbidden to tempt the evil spirits that had ravished my supposed namesake. As a result, I kept my complaints to myself and even began doing jigsaw puzzles.

Now, eager to get out of the house, I hurriedly dressed and joined Mrs. Matthews at the front door. She held her hand on the knob and looked at me as if she was deciding then and there whether to let me out.

"There are things to remember now, Audrina. You're out in public. Do not walk quickly. You're in your seventh month. No fast moves in the supermarket. For our purposes, it would be best if you looked somewhat uncomfortable. Occasionally, put your hand on your lower back. Arden and I have discussed all this," she added. "If there are many people at the market, we might decide to cut the shopping short because you're having problems. Any questions?"

I stood stunned and speechless. Then I turned around and saw that Arden had heard it all.

He nodded and smiled. "Don't mess things up now, Audrina," he warned. "Listen closely, and do exactly what Mrs. Matthews tells you to do."

"Ready?" she asked.

I nodded, and she opened the door.

"Watch yourself on the steps," Arden called from behind us. I glanced back at him. He had a wide, impish smile on his face. If I could only enjoy this as much as he apparently was, I thought. I closed the door and followed Mrs. Matthews to her car, a blue station wagon that looked like she had driven it for a decade.

It was the sort of summer day Sylvia would love, I thought as I looked at the burst of color, the soft green, olive, and emerald leaves. Wildflowers were everywhere, and the squirrels were as lively as ever, doing amazing gymnastic feats on the tree branches. I remembered how much pleasure Sylvia got from sitting and watching them for hours, one or two coming very close to her until she'd raise her hand or start moving in their direction. When she was an infant, she would crawl around on the grass, and if she found a dandelion, she would immediately put it in her mouth.

Soon, I thought, she would be able to be outside and enjoy nature again.

"Your sister is doing very well," Mrs. Matthews said as we drove along the road to Whitefern village. "I am not anticipating any difficulties with the delivery."

"I don't want her to be in too much pain."

She looked at me and raised her thin eyebrows. "Some pain is good," she said. "It's the body's way of giving us instruction. Like what to avoid."

She sounded too much like Aunt Ellsbeth. "What do you mean?"

"The pain of a burn, the sting of a bee. Pain protects us, too."

"Well, it wasn't her fault she was burned and stung."

"No, but I doubt she'll be as easy to abuse after this," she said.

I turned away and stared at the side of the road, where trees ran into trees. Houses didn't appear for miles, our nearest neighbor living twelve miles from Whitefern. I never thought much about them or any of the families farther along the way. Once, according to my mother and Aunt Ellsbeth, the Whiteferns had been the most notable family in the Tidewater section of Virginia, giving the country senators and even vice presidents. But over time, we had fallen out of favor, not just with the villagers but also with everyone in the surrounding suburbs. We were no longer as honored or, in Aunt Ellsbeth's words, "even respected."

Whitefern village, where the supermarket was located, was fifteen miles from our house. It was also where I had gone to school. I had not kept in contact with any of my schoolmates. None had ever paid a visit to my home. But I did have fond memories of my teachers.

Heads turned our way when we got out of Mrs. Matthews's car and started for the supermarket.

"Walk slower," she ordered under her breath. "Don't make it seem so easy."

I thought back to what my mother had been like when she was pregnant with Sylvia and tried to emulate her stride, putting my hand on my lower back from time to time after we got a cart and began to go down the aisles. If I chose something I liked, Mrs. Matthews would give me a sideways glance and sometimes shake her head no. I felt like a little girl with no power to choose anything.

Rounding the turn toward the meat counter, we saw Mrs. Haider, the retired principal of Whitefern High School. Mrs. Matthews didn't think anything of it. In fact, she looked like she didn't even want to say hello to her, but I stopped immediately.

"Oh, Audrina, how are you?" Mrs. Haider asked, acting as if I'd startled her. Mrs. Matthews paused and looked back at me, her eyes full of warnings. "I heard you were pregnant."

"I'm getting along, but it's been a little difficult."

"Oh?"

"Do you know Mrs. Matthews?" I asked, feeling awkward now, with her just standing there and Mrs. Haider wondering why.

"Yes, I believe so. You had a son who attended Whitefern. Philip, I believe."

"Yes," Mrs. Matthews said.

"And how is he doing?"

"Staying out of trouble," she replied. It wasn't an answer, and Mrs. Haider didn't smile or react in any way. "He's working for my brother at his paper mill in Richmond," Mrs. Matthews added.

"Not married?"

"No," she said briskly. "Audrina, we don't want to keep you on your feet longer than necessary . . ."

"Mrs. Matthews is a maternity nurse," I explained.

"Yes, I know, but I thought you were retired," Mrs. Haider said to her. She was not a woman who was easily intimidated, probably hardened by her many years as a school administrator.

"I am, but I've come out of retirement to assist Mrs. Lowe. Her husband persuaded me," Mrs. Matthews said. "She's having a difficult pregnancy. In fact, I'd rather she didn't come out of the house to do shopping, but I gave in this once." She smiled with icy lips.

Mrs. Haider nodded. "I'm sorry you're having difficulties, Audrina. I do hope it all works out well for you. How is Sylvia?" she asked, still ignoring Mrs. Matthews, who was exhibiting her impatience by pushing and pulling on the cart.

"She's well, thank you."

"I'm sorry Mr. Price took sick and couldn't continue with her art lessons," she said.

"Took sick?"

"Oh, didn't you know? I would have thought you would."

Mrs. Matthews raised her eyebrows, her face reflecting annoyance now.

This was the hardest part for me, pretending that I cared and not revealing the terrible things Mr. Price had done. I practically choked on the words. "I knew it was getting harder for him. He seemed very tired, but I thought in time . . ."

"Yes, well, I'm surprised you don't know. He had a stroke. It's left him paralyzed on his right side, and for an artist who draws with his right hand, that's devastating. Perhaps you can give the Prices a call. They'd appreciate it."

"She has to be concerned about herself right now," Mrs. Matthews said sharply. "Perhaps after the baby is born."

"Yes, when are you due?"

"A little more than six weeks," Mrs. Matthews answered for me.

"Do you know if it will be a boy or a girl?"

I shook my head. I really was having trouble breathing now.

Mrs. Haider laughed. Why was she laughing? "Well," she said, glancing at Mrs. Matthews, "my grandmother used to swear that if a pregnant woman's face turns red while you're speaking to her, she is definitely having a girl. I can't wait to see if she was right. Good luck." She continued on her way.

I looked at Mrs. Matthews.

She was smiling, and not coldly. "You really do look sick to your stomach, Audrina. I think we do have to cut the shopping short." Gleefully, she hurried along.

Ancient Voices,
Forbidden Dreams

"Do exactly what I tell you," Mrs. Matthews said when we reached the front of the store after having done all our shopping twenty minutes later. "Now, lean on the cart as if to catch your breath."

As soon as I did, she hollered, "Can I get some help here?"

She was loud enough for nearly everyone in the supermarket to hear. Customers stopped and turned our way. The busy cashiers paused, and the store manager came running.

"What's wrong?" he asked, looking like he might burst into tears or throw up his breakfast. He was a short, stocky man, with thinning dark brown hair and round eyes that seemed sunken in his pudgy face like dark cherries in soft vanilla ice cream.

"Mrs. Lowe isn't feeling well. She has a very delicate pregnancy. Open a register for us." When he hesitated, she added, raising her voice, "Do you want a terrible scene played out on the floor here?"

He leaped to open the register himself and signaled for a packer, who rushed over.

The manager's assistant came over, too. He was taller and younger, with the slim physique of a tennis player. "Can I help?" he asked Mrs. Matthews.

She thought a moment, glanced at me, and then told him to take me out to her car very carefully while she finished with the groceries.

"Walk slowly," she added when he offered his hand.

His name tag read "Marv Russel, Assistant Manager." He had a boyish face and cerulean-blue eyes, and his light brown hair was cut in a short, military style. He looked more frightened than I was supposed to be, but when I took his hand, he let go and decided instead to put his arm around my shoulders. We started out. "Where's your car?" he asked, seeming afraid to look at me.

"It's that blue station wagon," I said, nodding at it.

"When are you giving birth? I hope not any minute. I once saw a woman go into labor in a movie theater. I think I came close to fainting. My girlfriend thought it was quite funny." I could hear the trembling in his voice.

"Don't faint now," I warned.

He smiled. "I won't."

"A little more than six weeks," I replied to his question, making sure to agree with what Mrs. Matthews had told Mrs. Haider. Conspirators have to dot their *i*'s and cross their *t*'s when they're telling a contrived story.

"How far do you have to go?" he asked when we reached the car.

"Fifteen miles. I live in the Whitefern mansion."

He shook his head. That had no meaning for him. "My family and I moved here recently. I don't know the area that well yet," he said apologetically.

"Do you go to college?" I asked.

He laughed. "I guess I'll never look older. I graduated three years ago. I majored in business administration. Should we rest a moment?"

"Just a moment," I said. I really did want to catch my breath, but I was also feeling bad about what I was doing to his nerves. He would surely spend the rest of the day describing me and what had happened. And it was all a lie.

"How long have you lived here?" he asked.

"All my life. My family is one of the oldest ones in the Tidewater area."

"Oh. It's nice here," he said, searching for things to say.

"Very. Are you still going with the girl from the movie theater?"

"No. She dropped me for the captain of the football team, but I have a nice girlfriend here. We're talking about marriage."

"Talking about it?"

"Planning," he said, smiling.

"Get her into the car!" we heard Mrs. Matthews shout. "I want her sitting."

"Right away," he called back, and leaped into action, taking me to the car, opening the door, and helping me in. He breathed a sigh of relief the moment I was out of his hands. "Good luck with your delivery, and stay out of movie theaters," he joked.

"I haven't been to one in years," I said.

He looked surprised at my admitting that and then stepped back as Mrs. Matthews shoved her cart of groceries toward the car as if she was delivering a missile. He rushed forward to catch it and then helped her unload and pack the car. She opened her purse to give him a tip, but he refused and backed away.

"Good luck," he called to me, and hurried back to the safety of his supermarket.

"Very good," Mrs. Matthews said when she got in. "Your husband will be pleased about how you behaved."

"How I behaved?"

She made it sound like I was a child on an outing. "You know what I mean. That principal was watching us the whole time. I'm sure she'll gossip."

"She doesn't gossip," I said.

"How would you know?"

"I just know. From knowing her in the past," I added.

"We'll see. Whatever, it's fine now. There were many others who will talk about it."

"What do you know about Mr. Price?" I asked. She was silent. "And Sylvia?" I added firmly.

"I know what your husband told me. How he and you handle this is your business. I don't have to know everything." She paused and then said, "I know enough."

I bet you do, I thought. *I bet you've had your ear to the door of Arden's office whenever I was in there.* I asked her, "Did you know he had a stroke?"

"No. Why would I want to know? It would be very unwise to show any interest in him right now, Audrina. You are such an innocent." She shook her head as if that was a sign of failure.

"Wouldn't people just think you were being considerate, compassionate, if you asked about him?" Maybe I was innocent, but why would her questioning about him cause any suspicions?

"Why have them think anything at all?" she countered. "Besides, his welfare especially is the least of our concerns. We should stay focused on the project."

"Project."

"Whatever you want to call it—fake pregnancy, switch, whatever. Choose the words you want. Anyway, after this, you'll have no trouble staying inside until Sylvia gives birth and even a little while afterward. People who saw you today or those who hear about you will question me whenever I'm out and about. I'm going to tell them you're confined to bed now. In fact, I'd be happier if Sylvia was."

I didn't like her tone, the way she was ordering me about, taking charge of everything, even Arden's and my lives. "I'll discuss it with Arden," I said.

"I've already done that. He agrees, of course. Concentrate on your sister, not yourself," she said.

"That's what I'm doing," I practically shouted back at her.

Anyone else would have realized she had insulted

me by suggesting otherwise, but not our Mrs. Matthews. She simply shrugged and drove on, not even batting an eyelash. How had she ever become a nurse, I wondered, someone who had to have extra sensitivity and compassion for others?

"You weren't a nurse in a prison, were you?" I asked, still frustrated.

"What?" She actually smiled, a real smile toying with a laugh. "Why did you ask that?"

"You seem to have the right temperament for it," I said.

Her smile quickly evaporated. "There'll come a time when you'll look back at all this and be very grateful that I had the right temperament," she said, not hiding her crossness.

Had I finally chipped the walls of that cocoon in which she dwelled? I was sure she would tell Arden. They seemed to share a lot more with each other than they shared with me these days.

Mr. Ralph was waiting for us at the steps of Whitefern. He rushed forward, as well as he could rush, to help bring in the groceries.

"Go rest," Mrs. Matthews told me. "It's obviously been an emotional morning for you."

Without comment, I went into the house. Arden, obviously anxious to leave, was dressed for work and standing like a relay runner about to hand me the baton.

"She's in her room now, resting," he said. "How did it go?"

"You'll get a full report from your chief of staff,"

I replied, and walked past him quickly to go see how Sylvia was doing.

She was lying with her eyes open but looking up at the ceiling like someone in a daze.

"Sylvia," I said, sitting on the bed and taking her hand. "Are you okay?"

She looked at me without expression and then suddenly realized it was I. "Audrina, Papa spoke to me here this morning. I kept sitting in the chair, waiting, and he didn't speak, but today he spoke."

"And what did he say?"

"He said I should stay in my room now and wait. The baby will be coming. He said I have to be extra careful. You'll have to stay in your room, too," she added.

I looked back at the doorway. How odd, I thought, that the whispering Sylvia imagined coordinated so well with the orders Mrs. Matthews gave. It was a fleeting thought, but it lingered for the rest of the afternoon, until I asked Mrs. Matthews if she had said anything to Sylvia about being confined to her room.

"I might have mentioned that the day would come when she would be. Why?"

"She thinks she has to do that now."

"Perfect. It makes my job so much easier when the patient anticipates my orders and carries them out." She flashed her usual cold smile and went into Sylvia's room.

When the phone rang, I was anticipating Arden to be calling to tell me why he couldn't be at dinner again tonight, but I was surprised and even frightened to hear Dr. Prescott's voice.

"Audrina? Dr. Prescott here," he said. "I heard the craziest story today," he continued. "One of my patients, Ceil Rubin, told me she saw you at the supermarket and that you were quite pregnant, as she put it. She mentioned that Helen Matthews was with you and there was some sort of emergency scene at the cash registers. What's this about?"

This was something neither Arden nor I had anticipated. We certainly should have, I thought. Dr. Prescott was our family doctor. Of course, he would be interested in anything involving us. My brain scrambled for the right answers. I could mess up everything, all that we had worked for these past months. I wasn't concerned as much about my efforts going for naught as I was concerned about what would happen to Sylvia. We would fail to prevent all that would follow, all that we knew would be unpleasant. Arden would be enraged for sure.

Why? I asked myself, imagining the question he would ask. Why would we not have immediately called Dr. Prescott if I was indeed pregnant?

"I'm sorry, Dr. Prescott."

"Sorry? Are you pregnant, Audrina?"

"Yes, I am," I said.

He was silent for a moment. I waited, afraid to utter another word. "Why didn't you come to me?" he asked finally.

"Arden hired Mrs. Matthews to look after me. She's full-time here now."

"Pregnant. Well, I am happy to hear it. I know that's what you and Arden wanted. I'm just surprised when you consider the odds."

"Maybe it was something that was meant to be," I offered.

"Yes, apparently so. Well, I don't mean to sound upset or anything. I'm quite pleased." He paused. It was coming. "But really, I am surprised you didn't come to see me."

"Arden was upset with the results you got from the testing and the prediction you made for us," I said. "He wanted us to handle it this way, but as soon as the baby is born, I intend to bring him or her to you to examine and care for all the time."

"Pleased to be of service," he said, but his voice was heavy with hurt. "What happened at the supermarket?"

"Oh, just a little spotting. It turned out to be nothing. I'm doing fine," I said. "I'm going to take it a lot easier for the remaining time."

"Spotting? How far along are you?"

"I'm a little more than six weeks away," I said.

"And Mrs. Matthews told you that, gave you the approximate date of delivery?"

"Yes."

"Very well. I'm aware of who she is and how vast her experience is. I'm sure your father would have been very excited about it. Good luck, and call me if I can be of any help."

"Thank you. Thank you for calling, Dr. Prescott," I said.

He hung up without saying good-bye. I held the receiver for a few moments, my heart still pounding. Dr. Prescott's voice had been full of skepticism. I didn't think he would make the leap to Sylvia immediately, but he was certainly suspicious. And I was feeling very guilty. I knew how Papa would have disapproved of our not using Dr. Prescott, but then again, how could we? It would surely be unethical, even illegal, for a doctor to do what Mrs. Matthews was doing for us.

I hung up and called Arden.

"What is it now?" he asked as soon as he got on the phone.

I told him about Dr. Prescott's call. "He was full of disbelief," I added when he was silent. "What if he starts talking to people, asking more questions?"

"He won't. A doctor's relationship with his patient is private. I could sue him if he told anyone about the tests he gave us. Don't worry about that."

"I can't help but worry. I can't imagine what we would look like in this community if the truth came out."

"You don't have to tell me that. But I said not to worry," he snapped. Then he changed his tone. "I received a call already from one of our clients whose wife happened to see you in the supermarket. They're swallowing it all out there, hook, line, and sinker. Mrs. Matthews is ingenious. Trust in her. Now, I have to get back to work. I'll soon have a child's welfare to consider, his or her education, other needs. Lots more money must be made."

"Arden, did you know that Mr. Price had a stroke? He's paralyzed on one side and can no longer do his artwork."

"No, but that's truly poetic justice," he said. "Oh," he added quickly before hanging up, "I won't be at dinner tonight. I'm taking the Allans to dinner. You were supposed to come along, but they'll understand. Another opportunity to solidify our story," he said. "Take care of Sylvia. And yourself, of course." He laughed and hung up.

When I turned around, Mrs. Matthews was standing there. "It would help the situation now if you would retire to your room. I'll bring you your dinner tonight," she said.

"What?"

"Your sister keeps asking about you. We don't want her unnecessarily disturbed. A pregnant woman's emotional health is just as important as her physical health. Calmness is the word of the month."

For a moment, I stood staring at her. I was becoming a prisoner in every sense of the word. "How would she know if I was in that room or not?"

"She could call for you and you wouldn't be there to hear her. Then she would want to get up to find you. I don't know why we're arguing about it. I would hope that you would be the most cooperative of all."

"I'm not arguing."

"Good, then do it."

It was easy for her to say. When I was confined to our house and grounds during my youth, I'd at least had my mother, Aunt Ellsbeth, Vera, despite her jealousies, and, of course, Papa to keep me company. My real entertainment came from watching all of them interact. How I looked forward to the Tuesday teas, when Aunt Ellsbeth and Momma resurrected Aunt Mercy Marie. It was major entertainment. Sometimes Vera would be nice, and we would play a game together, and I did feel like her ally when her mother punished her or scolded her for something she did wrong.

The point was that during my confinement, there were other people, their laughter bringing smiles to my face. I was even fascinated by the arguing. Now there was mostly silence in my confinement. The things I would hear were mostly the memories of old voices. I feared the flood of nightmares, forbidden dreams invading both my waking hours and my sleep. I assumed that Mrs. Matthews had no idea why I was so reluctant to cooperate. Arden could paint broad strokes of my youth for her, but he was not aware of the myriad details that I had tried to bury in the empty grave of my false self.

"Well?" Mrs. Matthews said, holding the spoon with which she was preparing our dinner. I imagined it to be a ring of jailer's keys.

"Don't you need help with dinner?"

"From now on, I'll do it by myself. I'll even wash the dishes myself," she added, and smiled her cold smile, as if that was going to make me feel better. "And yes, I'll do more to keep up the house. I know how concerned you are, but frankly, sometimes you act as if Whitefern is a national treasure, a museum. Most of what I see here would have no special meaning for anyone other than yourself."

"Which is reason enough to protect it," I snapped back. "It's a sacred obligation to care for all that your family held dear. Don't you have any heirlooms? Have you inherited nothing from your parents and grand-parents that you cherish?"

"I live for the here and now. We have museums for everything else. Besides, what I have and how I live are not the issue here. We have a job to do, and that's all that matters. You, of all three of us, should feel this the most. When this is over, it's you who will have to carry the deception forward. You'll have to be a real mother to this child, and don't forget, you'll have to convince your child that you are his or her mother, too." She paused and nodded, as though what she said made a great deal of sense. Then she added, "Consider all this as nothing more than practice for that day—preparation."

This time, she smiled with such self-satisfaction I felt sick to my stomach. Maybe I should go to bed, I thought. The episode in the supermarket, Dr. Prescott's call, Arden's glee, and now this witch of a woman's obvious enjoyment at wielding power over me all sent a dark sword of helplessness through my very soul. I wobbled for a moment as the room seemed to spin.

"Are you all right?" she asked, suddenly very concerned. After all, if something happened to me, what would she say? How would she explain what went on here, too?

It occurred to me that she was taking just as much of a risk as Arden and I were. How could she explain her behavior? She was retired from any regular work, but what sort of reputation would she have then? She might have to move away. Any friends she had, and I had trouble imagining that she had any, would certainly take a step away from her. Why, it would be like running a gauntlet to go shopping in this community because of all the looks and whispers behind her back.

"I am tired. This," I said, placing my two hands over the bundle of wool that I had to wear, even sleep in, just in case Sylvia saw me during the night, "is becoming a real burden."

"Imagine what a burden it is for truly pregnant women. Imagine what Sylvia is enduring," she said, the slight note of sympathy I thought I had heard gone. "Go lie down."

She stepped aside, and I walked out and to Sylvia's room. She was sitting up at the side of her bed, her legs dangling. She was scribbling on a pad in her lap.

"Sylvia, what are you drawing?"

"I'm writing a name," she said.

"A name?"

"When Papa told me to stay in my room, he told me a name," she said. "A name for the baby."

"He did?"

She nodded. "He whispered it in my ear and told me to practice writing it."

"But you can't pick a name until you know if the baby is a boy or a girl."

"It's a girl's name," she said.

"Okay. What is the name?"

"A-d-e-l-l-e," she spelled.

"Adelle? Adelle is my middle name," I said. She had heard it, of course, but as far as I knew, she had never said it or indicated that she remembered it. Arden and Papa often said it in her presence. If she was in a room when it was mentioned, she was usually distracted with some toy, a doll, even a piece of cardboard she had formed into something only she understood. She didn't listen to anyone but herself. In any case, I had no idea how she knew to spell it correctly.

This seemed like another thing she had plucked out of thin air. In my mind, the words of my parents, my aunt Ellsbeth, even Vera, swirled in and out of all the rooms in Whitefern. There was no silence here. Echoes never faded away. Cries, laughter, and screams of delight and pain rode in the belly of shadows. When night came and the lights were turned off, they were especially free to move about and circle me, invading my dreams.

Did Sylvia hear all this, too?

"As I said, Adelle is a girl's name, Sylvia. The baby might be a boy. We'll have to choose a boy's name, too. Did you get any ideas for that?"

She shook her head. "Girl," she insisted. "Remember? Papa told me her name. So it has to be a girl."

For now, she was so happy about it that I thought there was no point in discussing it further. "Okay. I'm going to lie down for a while. Mrs. Matthews will be bringing us our dinners."

"Because we have to stay quiet," Sylvia recited, nodding her head.

"Yes. I'll be right next door if you need me."

"Mrs. Matthews says I don't need you. I need only her."

"Did she? Well, she knows everything. I know only all the rest," I said, recalling a joke Papa had enjoyed. It was something Mark Twain had said.

I went over to her and kissed her on the forehead, the way I always did.

"She might be the nurse," I said, "and she can take care of you right now, but I'm the only one who can give you love, Sylvia. You will always need me."

She didn't react. She was absorbed in writing the name Adelle in different ways with flourishes of script.

Actually, that would be the perfect name, I thought, if I was going to be the child's mother. Maybe Papa really was whispering to her. Who was I, as someone who often heard whispers, to doubt it?

I fell asleep minutes after I lay down and woke up when I heard Mrs. Matthews come in carrying a tray.

"Are you really going to treat me like an invalid, too?" I asked. "It's double work for you."

"It's what your husband is paying me to do, what we all decided we had to do for Sylvia," she said. "He's very keen on everything going right. Don't worry. I'm being paid well. Besides," she continued, laying the tray on my lap, "the more you simulate pregnancy, the easier it will be to convince yourself that the baby is indeed your baby. It's good psychology." She smiled like she really cared. But then she added, "After all, you had good practice for something like this. A trained impersonator brought up to impersonate herself. Who could do better?" She laughed and left the room.

I felt the venom travel though my veins as I looked after her. I hoped that Arden really possessed a secret that would tear her heart in two if it was revealed.

Maybe someday I would do just that.

Almost reluctantly, I began to eat. The food was nowhere as well seasoned as when I made it, but I did have to eat, pregnant or not.

Mrs. Matthews came for the tray and dishes, nodding in approval at how much I had eaten. I looked at her as if I thought she had gone mad. She grimaced and left quickly. Even though I had slept, I was groggy again and dozed on and off.

Hours later, the sound of Arden's laughter woke me. I had started to get up to go out and see him when he appeared in the doorway.

"Good, you're awake," he said.

He was going in and out of focus. I scrubbed my cheeks with my palms and took a deep breath. "This is ridiculous. I'm not staying in this room."

"Don't do anything to mess up things now, Audrina. We are so close I can taste it. Mrs. Matthews says Sylvia had what she considered labor pains about an hour ago."

"Labor pains? But she predicted at least six more weeks."

He shrugged. "Did you forget? Sylvia herself was born premature. It could happen again."

"But complications like that would make things more difficult for us."

"Mrs. Matthews is aware of that and is giving Sylvia extra care."

"How is she now?"

"Sleeping," he said. "Comfortably."

I stood. "I want to go out and sit in the salon."

"What if she wakes and calls for you? We can't expect Mrs. Matthews to man the lookout here twenty-four hours a day. Now's the time for you to really pitch in and help. I certainly can't do it."

"But—"

"Audrina, you just made mention of it. If something happened to Sylvia now and she had to go to a hospital, there would be hell to pay, especially since Dr. Prescott called and seemed full of suspicion. We've got to take extra care of her for all our sakes. For better or worse, we started this. Now we have to carry it out to completion. I stress *we*," he added.

I sat back on my bed, weighed down by his words.

"I had a very successful day today, and tonight at dinner, I garnered another million dollars in investments. We're on a roll, and the birth of the baby will be the crowning moment." He stepped forward and kissed me on the forehead, the way I kissed Sylvia all the time. "Get some rest," he said.

"Rest? I slept all afternoon."

"You do look tired. I know this is a burden on you. Stay well, my love. I need my little mother and wife." He kissed me again on the forehead and walked out.

I lay back.

The bundle of wool on my stomach had never felt heavier, nor had any of my regrets and fears.

It was easy to fall asleep again.

After all, right now, sleep was my only escape.

Trapped in Your Own Web

During the days that followed, Sylvia's recurrent pains began to worry me, and judging by the look on Mrs. Matthews's face whenever she examined her, they were increasingly concerning to her, too. I tried to be of more help, but ever since the day we'd gone to the supermarket, I had found myself with diminished energy. I dozed on and off. I would start reading a book and after only three or four pages find myself drifting off the page. I would wake up with the book in my lap, opened to the same page, totally unaware of how much time had passed. Often, it was hours.

I made no effort to interfere with Mrs. Matthews's plans. She continued to bring us our meals, and I did nothing to help clean up. I did no household chores and wondered who was making Arden's bed and changing his linen. He never did. What's more, Arden seemed to be busier than ever with the business. According to what he told me, there were some issues with the stock market that were taking up extra time. By the time I was up and around in the morning, he was always already gone, and there were many nights when he didn't come home for dinner. I would fall asleep before he did come home, so days went by during the next month when I didn't see him at all.

"Investors are very nervous about the economy," he explained one night when he did stop by and I complained. "You have no idea how many rich people I am babysitting, comforting, and assuring. If this isn't all handled right, we could lose a lot at exactly the wrong time in our lives, Audrina. You'll have to excuse my absences. I'm running from one to the other and applying soothing balm."

"What's happening in the economy to put all this pressure on you?"

"Oh, it's too complicated to explain."

"I'm not stupid about economics, Arden. My father made sure that I was aware of what made it better or worse."

I was anticipating the debate again about signing papers and negating what Papa had done in his will, but Arden didn't bring it up. He hadn't for months, and I fell into the idea that it had lost importance for him. We were, after all, a married couple. Why would I hurt him, especially if we had a child to raise?

"I know you're quite intelligent about it, Audrina, but why have you lie around here worrying about those things, too? You need to be a real assistant for Mrs. Matthews."

"Assistant!" The mere exertion of extra effort to cry out made my head pound. "How am I any assistant to her? She does everything now. Every time I start to wander around the house, she sends me back, telling me Sylvia was asking for me. I haven't washed any clothes or changed any bedding, much less vacuumed a rug. The house is running away with itself, I'm sure."

"It's fine, Audrina. She does what has to be done, and I'm paying her more for that. So don't worry. If you do, I'll only worry about you, too." He looked sincere.

"I don't mean to complain about it. I'm happy I have the time to sit with Sylvia, of course. She's very uncomfortable."

"And crying a lot, I understand. You underestimate your contribution. Mrs. Matthews tells me it would be ten times worse if you weren't right there comforting Sylvia. Just keep up what you're doing."

I looked down and shook my head. Tears were coming into my eyes.

"What? What else is wrong?" he snapped, not hiding his impatience.

"Something's not right with me, Arden. I know you can't take me to see Dr. Prescott or have him come here, but I am so unenergetic these days. Half the time, I don't even try to get up out of bed. I don't care about what I'm wearing. I've been in this bathrobe for days, I think. That's another thing, Arden. I've been having trouble remembering things, even things I think I did the day before. I know you haven't been around that much these past weeks, but surely you see a difference in me. Surely you do!" Now my tears were free to streak down my cheeks. "Look at my hair," I cried, tugging on the loose, wiry strands. "I can't recall when

I last cared to put on lipstick. I'm turning into some sort of hag, something you accused me of once."

He rushed over to sit next to me on the bed and put his arm around me. "Oh, Audrina, don't cry. It breaks my heart to see you so sad when we are on the verge of bringing new happiness to Whitefern. The wonderful sounds of a newborn baby's cry and laughter will drive away the shadows and dark memories from every corner of every room. We have lived under the cloud of sadness far too long. Both of us losing our parents too soon and your struggle with your twisted past would be far too much for most to bear. We have such strength. You have such strength. Together we'll conquer it all, Audrina. Don't cry."

I sucked back my tears and nodded. "But I'm not feeling as well as I should, Arden. Something's wrong."

"I know," he said, standing again. "Mrs. Matthews told me."

"What? When?"

"Recently."

"What did she tell you?"

"She said you are suffering from intense anxiety. She said she has seen it many times, especially with pregnant women, so she is as familiar with the symptoms as any doctor and knows just how to treat you."

"Treat me? What do you mean?"

"First, you do agree that you have been extraordinarily anxious recently, especially after that last trip to the supermarket, right?"

"I suppose so, but—"

"Well, as we've discussed time and time again, Audrina, we can't take the chance of anything happening to either you or Sylvia right now, and we can't expose either of you to the outside world. Up to now, we've been very successful convincing people that you're under special care as you draw within the last days of your pregnancy. A day doesn't go by when I don't have at least six or seven calls asking after your health. Why, even Mr. Johnson has bought it hook, line, and sinker. That's why we've put all the legal business on hold. You should be proud of yourself. You're making this possible. Just think how wonderful you'll feel with the baby in your arms, the four of us on some Sunday outing. That day is coming, Audrina, and it's coming soon."

"What did you mean when you said Mrs. Matthews knows just how to treat my anxiety?" I wasn't going to let him change the subject.

He smiled down at me. Both he and Papa always accused me of being a bulldog whenever I bit into something. "You've got to appreciate how lucky we are to have Mrs. Matthews for all this, Audrina. Imagine, someone with her medical knowledge willing to do just as we ask and not only that but do it with enthusiasm and dedication. Why, all this has become almost as important to her as it is to us."

I stared up at him, holding my expression, still waiting for my answer.

He saw that and walked to the door, peered out, and walked back to the bed. "We don't want to insult her, Audrina. That's the first thing and maybe the most important."

"Insult her?"

"Challenge her instructions or her wisdom when it comes to you and Sylvia."

"Me and Sylvia? Arden, get it through your head . . . I'm not really pregnant. I don't need a maternity nurse's tender loving care."

He laughed. "Of course you're not. I didn't say otherwise. But what I'm talking about, what Mrs. Matthews is talking about, has nothing to do with whether you're pregnant. It has to do with your anxiety. She says she has seen women as anxious as you are do rather bizarre things. Some show it with aggressive acts, sometimes hurting themselves as much as others."

"She thinks I would hurt Sylvia?"

"Oh, no. She's worried you might hurt yourself in some way, and then everything would be lost. She's only trying to make sure that doesn't happen, Audrina. It's not for long."

"What's not for long? What is she doing?"

"She's been giving you some tranquilizers to keep you calm," he confessed. "With my approval, of course. They're similar to the pills you took once before, remember?"

"Tranquilizers?" That made no sense. I took no pills. "When? How have I been taking tranquilizers?"

"She thought it would be easier to include them in your dinner. It's a very common prescription she has actually gotten for herself from time to time. It's why you sleep so well at night."

I stared at him in disbelief. "You let her do this to me without telling me?"

"It was for your own good, our own good. I'm only telling you this so you won't think there is anything seriously wrong with you, and you won't insist on going to see some doctor or rush out and do that yourself. It would be far too dangerous now."

"I'm being drugged," I thought aloud.

"Not drugged, treated. I'll speak to her about reducing the dosage, perhaps, but you should want this, too. You don't want to let your anxiety ruin things," he said firmly.

"I should have been told, have had everything explained to me," I said. "I'm not a child, and I'm not crazy. Arden, how could you let her do this to me?"

"Audrina, Audrina," he said, shaking his head as if I was a child. "Mrs. Matthews says that one of the things about people who suffer anxiety is self-denial. You have to admit that you wouldn't have accepted the diagnosis so quickly, and who knows where that would have led? And now, to really tell you the truth and add to all of this, I've been taking some of the same medicine myself. I'm not taking as much as you are, but you don't have to function throughout the day like I do. Have you any idea what it has been like for me to try to concentrate on intricate financial moves while worrying about what was happening at home and if our plan would explode in our faces? I've had great trouble sleeping. You haven't noticed?"

I shook my head.

"I know I put on a very good act for you, Audrina. I seem so strong and in control of everything, but there have been days when I was teetering on the edge of disaster. Maybe you can appreciate that now and not be so judgmental." He looked down and paced for a few moments like someone in deep thought. Then he stopped and looked up quickly. "Listen," he continued when I didn't say the words he wanted to hear—that I forgave him and Mrs. Matthews and that I understood. "I knew I needed some help to get through it, and I'm not ashamed to admit it. If someone with my ego can say that, you certainly can."

I sat up and rolled the blanket off me. "It just seems so deceitful for it to be done to me this way, Arden."

"Sometimes, as we are proving in spades, as your father would say, deceit is good. What we're doing is quite a bit more than a little white lie, I know, but look at all the good that will come of it. When it was necessary, you lied. You lied to Dr. Prescott. You lied to Mrs. Haider. You lied to everyone who saw you in the supermarket. Frankly, not a day goes by when you don't have to lie to Sylvia about something."

"And I don't feel good about any of it." I sat at the edge of the bed but still felt a little dizzy.

"But you did it because you knew it was necessary," he insisted. "So Mrs. Matthews did what she thought was necessary to protect you, Sylvia, and me, as well as herself. I admit that, but don't be angry at her and do anything that would jeopardize what we're doing, not now, not at this critical moment."

"I feel . . ."

"What?"

"Like I've lost all control of my life."

He nodded and approached me to put his hand on my shoulder. "For a while, you have, and so have I, but it will be over, and we'll have more control of our lives than ever. I'll speak with Mrs. Matthews about reducing your medicine to the amount I take. If I can take it, you can," he added, nearly growling at me like a wolf.

"I don't want to sleep all the time and lack the energy to care about myself," I said, shaking.

His hand flew off my shoulder like a frightened bird. "You won't. I don't, do I? But you'll remain calm enough for us to get through this. I'll go speak to her about it right now."

I heard him meet her outside Sylvia's room, and I rose and went to the door. They were speaking so loudly that I didn't have to listen in the hallway. Sylvia's room was right next to mine.

"Why did you tell her?" I heard Mrs. Matthews say.

"She complained about her lack of energy and wanted to see a doctor. She's a strong-willed person. You told me so yourself. It's better to be honest now. She understands why it was necessary, but you should reduce the dosage to what you've given me."

"Very well. I'm only doing what I think is required to get through this," she complained. "I don't want to be criticized for doing my job properly. I won't stand for that."

"Don't worry. She appreciates that as much as I do," he told her.

I retreated to my bed and sat waiting.

He returned. "Okay, it's all set. You will barely notice the dosage, and you'll get through this just like I will." He stepped closer and put his hands on my shoulders. "I can't stress it enough. It's very, very important now, Audrina, that you don't upset her. All we would need is for her to quit on us."

"She won't quit that fast, Arden. She would have a hard time explaining what she's done here."

"Nowhere near as hard a time as we would have and nowhere near as much to lose. Do you understand? Do you?"

"Yes," I said, feeling like my arm had been twisted.

"Good. All right. I've got to get back to some important things. Sit with Sylvia for a while. She was crying when I was in there just now. Try to think only of her."

I looked up sharply. "I don't understand why you've said that and you say it now. When have I ever thought of myself before I've thought of Sylvia's welfare?"

"I'm just trying to keep everything in perspective. It's what a good broker does, and most everything in life is in some way or another just another investment," he replied, smiling. "Another thing your good old Papa taught me."

He kissed me quickly on the cheek this time and left.

I sat there, stunned, angry, and, of course, very frustrated. I wanted to shout but knew that I couldn't. I wanted to tear the blob of wool from my stomach, tear it into shreds, and see myself as I really was again, but I knew I couldn't. I wanted to go find Mrs. Matthews and fire her on the spot, but I knew I couldn't. I felt like I was in a straitjacket and wanted to rip it off. I got up instead and went to sit with Sylvia. Mrs. Matthews wasn't in the room.

Sylvia groaned deeply and looked at me. "It hurts again, Audrina," she said. "Does it hurt you, too?"

"Yes." I hated to see her grimacing with pain. It did hurt me, too. I wasn't lying.

I put my hand on her stomach. I could feel the baby kicking and smiled in wonder.

"The baby's moving inside you, Sylvia. Feel it?"

Her stomach hardened but only for a few seconds. "Baby's coming," she said, nodding.

"Yes, soon."

"Fix her pillows behind her, and sit her up," Mrs. Matthews ordered from the doorway as she entered with Sylvia's dinner. "She hasn't been eating well. I want her to finish all of this tonight."

I did as she asked. As soon as Mrs. Matthews put the tray in front of Sylvia, Sylvia looked at me. "Audrina has to eat, too," she said.

I looked at Mrs. Matthews.

"Pull the chair up to the bed. Maybe she'll eat better with you eating beside her. I'll fetch your dinner."

"I don't want to fall asleep too quickly tonight," I said pointedly.

She looked at me, her eyes narrowing. "You won't. And you'll be doing a lot more now." She nodded at Sylvia. "There will be a lot more for both of us to do."

"How close is she?"

"I doubt we'll finish the week," she said. "Make sure she drinks all the water," she added, and left to get my food.

Sylvia was very uncomfortable. She pleaded to be permitted to lie back, but I did what Mrs. Matthews prescribed and kept her eating and drinking. She was a little more cooperative when Mrs. Matthews brought me my tray and I began to eat. I ate slowly, suspiciously, wondering if Mrs. Matthews had indeed done what Arden had asked her to do and reduced the dosage of whatever she had given me. Perhaps she wasn't putting anything in my food now. I couldn't detect it, but then again, I never did.

She returned to see how much had been eaten and nodded with approval. She took Sylvia's tray.

"I can bring mine," I said, starting to rise.

"Just stay there and keep her company. That's more important. Now you can understand why I wanted her brought down to this bedroom. I can't imagine running up and down those stairs. I hope you can appreciate everything I've asked you to do and everything I have done."

"As you've said often, Mrs. Matthews, you're being well paid," I replied with a cold tone of realism.

Her face looked even tighter than it habitually was. I thought the skin would tear at her jawbone. Then she turned and left. She didn't return for my tray for quite a while. I put it at the foot of Sylvia's bed and helped her get as comfortable as she could be. Memories of my mother during the week before she was rushed to the hospital returned. She'd been in such agony sometimes, but the furthest thing from my mind had been the thought that she would die in childbirth. Every time Sylvia moaned, I was whipped back to that day Papa returned and Aunt Ellsbeth forced him to tell me the dreadful news. I'd thought my heart had been torn from my chest.

I reminded myself now that if something so terrible was to happen to Sylvia, I would blame no one but myself. I had dropped my protective shield around her. I had provided the opportunity for this to happen. Papa would scream from his grave. Everything, everything possible, had to be done to ensure that Sylvia would not face a fate similar to Momma's. For this reason above all others, I had to placate Mrs. Matthews and appreciate all that she was doing. I shivered at the thought that something I might say or do would drive her out of Whitefern and leave us panicking over Sylvia's final moments.

When she returned, I handed her my tray. She saw the look of obedience on my face and softened her eyes into her confident smile of self-satisfaction that only someone with her ego would enjoy. I avoided looking at her and sat down again quickly.

"She's at the point where she can't sleep well," Mrs. Matthews said. "Do your best to get her to doze as much as possible. We don't give pregnant women drugs they don't absolutely need."

"Okay."

"Tell her a story, or sing to her." She shook her head. "A child giving birth to a child."

At least for the moment, she appeared to really feel

sorry for Sylvia. Perhaps I was wrong to judge her so harshly, I thought. She was simply a woman with a personality that didn't warm your heart. Maybe it was her way to get through the day, through each crisis, for her work was not work I would enjoy. Few would enjoy it. As Papa used to say, you had to have thick skin if you were going to walk among the bees.

"How old was the youngest woman you helped deliver?" I asked. I was curious, but I also wanted to be sure she thought I appreciated her and her experience.

"Woman? Hardly a woman. She was eleven," she said. "Very bloody delivery and very painful."

"Did she die?"

"No. Not in the sense you mean, but what sort of a life do you think came after that?"

"Sylvia will have a good life," I said. "I promise you that."

"As good as she might have, I expect."

"Better than she might have," I insisted. "Better."

We looked at each other. Her face did soften. There was a surge of warmth in her eyes. I looked at Sylvia. We did need to save all our compassion for her. There was enough tension without my creating any between Mrs. Matthews and myself, especially in Sylvia's presence.

"Well, I will say one thing for you, Audrina. You have an extraordinary capacity for love."

I sat back, amazed. A real compliment? From her?

"But then again," she added, "it's when we're most desperate to please others that we're in the most danger of hurting ourselves."

"Who taught you that?"

"Life," she said, and left the room.

I turned back to Sylvia and smiled. I saw no way I could hurt myself by pleasing her, not now. She looked at me curiously when I put my hand on her stomach again. Then she turned to reach toward me and put her hand on my mound of wool. I watched her face. Would she realize now that what I was doing was a bald-faced lie? Would that frighten her? Would it make her feel silly and alone?

She smiled. "She kicked," she said, and lay back. "Baby's coming."

I sat holding her hand and realized that the saying of my father's that Arden had reminded me of was true: deception was sometimes good, especially if the end result brought happiness to someone who desperately needed it, someone as fragile as my Sylvia.

She finally fell asleep. I sat quietly watching her breathe and seeing how her lips moved slightly. Somewhere in her dreams, she was talking. Was she talking to Papa? I envied her for her dreams. They were a way out of the web we were all caught in right now, at least for a few hours.

I didn't think I had been given more tranquilizers, but I did doze off. I woke when I realized Mrs. Matthews was standing beside me.

"Go to bed," she said. "I'll stand by with her. I've decided you're strong enough to contend with what is happening, and I will need your help. So get some rest, and be ready for what lies ahead."

"Her stomach gets hard for a few seconds, and she cries."

"This isn't false labor. I think she might be delivering earlier than anticipated."

"Oh," I said, the worry ringing in me like a bell.

She smiled, not coldly, not warmly, just a bland smile. "Look at it this way. It will be over sooner than we thought."

Birth, a Step toward Truth

Sylvia went into real, full-blown labor three days later. It happened late in the morning. She was screaming and crying so hard I could barely move to follow Mrs. Matthews's commands after Sylvia's water broke.

"I didn't pee!" Sylvia cried. "I didn't pee!"

"It's not pee," Mrs. Matthews said, and turned to me. "Clean it up," she ordered.

I started out for the mop and then stopped. "I should call Arden," I said.

She turned and looked at me with such disdain that I could feel the blood rushing into my face. "You want to call your husband? Will you be screaming and crying like she is but over the phone when his secretary answers?"

"Of course not."

"Then pray tell me how you intend to convey the situation we are now in. It is supposed to be happening to you."

"Oh!" I moaned. Of course, she was right. Dislike her as much as I did, I still had to give her credit for keeping her cool and never losing sight of what we had to do.

"But he should know," I offered weakly. Sylvia was crying so hard. It made me shudder.

"Clean this up. I will call him when I get a moment here. Your husband and I planned for how to handle this."

"Why wasn't I part of that planning?"

"Do you want to have a long discussion about it, or do you want me to care for your sister?"

"Okay," I said.

I ran out for the mop, and while she got Sylvia back into the bed, I cleaned the floor. I put the mop and pail aside. Sylvia looked like she was having trouble breathing. Her eyes rolled with the panic she was feeling.

"Is she all right?"

"Of course she's all right. Keep this cool washcloth on her forehead, and hold her hand. The first birth for any woman is always the most difficult. Her next one will be easier."

"Next one?"

"You never know," she said, and went to call Arden, leaving me alone with Sylvia. Now I was sorry I had even mentioned calling Arden. Sylvia was clawing at my wool belly, begging me to stop the pain.

"It will get better as soon as the baby comes," I said, and repeated it like a chant. I had read about deliveries and seen them acted out in movies, but nothing had prepared me for this. Sylvia's screams were so loud I was sure people working on the grounds out-side would hear. I had no idea what else to do. I went to the door to look down the hall for Mrs. Matthews, but she was nowhere in sight.

"Papa!" Sylvia screamed. "Papa!"

I returned to her side and took her hand again while I dabbed her forehead with the cool cloth. What if her heart stopped? I thought. Momma had given birth too soon and died. History was repeating itself. If she died, I wouldn't care about our precious reputa-tion. I'd call the police and have Mr. Price arrested, stroke or no stroke, I vowed.

As casually as she would have entered Sylvia's room weeks ago, Mrs. Matthews returned.

"She's in too much pain," I said. "Isn't there any-thing else we can do?"

"We? No. There's nothing else to do but let nature take its course."

She took Sylvia's blood pressure and then suddenly seized her shoulders and shook her so hard Sylvia stopped screaming.

"Now, you listen to me, Sylvia. The baby is com-ing. Here's what I want you to do," she said, and began to give her instructions. She already had the bed changed into what looked like a hospital bed now, with something protecting the mattress. Beside it was a pan in case Sylvia threw up. Mrs. Matthews had moved a table and all the medical supplies she needed, turning the room into a delivery room. I felt help-less standing by and watching her as she told Sylvia to push. Sylvia's eyes were still wide open and wild with fear and confusion. Her face was flushed, her forehead beaded with sweat. I continued to dab it with the washcloth. She looked at me with such pleading. I had always been there to help her, to wash her cuts and bruises, to hold her and make her feel better again, but there was nothing I could do for her now that would ease the pain.

"Why is the baby hurting me, Audrina?"

I looked to Mrs. Matthews. "It's supposed to hurt," she said sharply. "Just do what I tell you, and it will stop when the baby comes out."

Sylvia looked at me to see if I believed it. I smiled and nodded to reassure her, and for a few moments at least, she calmed.

"What did Arden say?" I asked, my heart racing with the anxiety and tension Mrs. Matthews had predicted I would experience.

"He's on his way," she said, sounding annoyed that she had to reply.

Sylvia started to scream and cry again. Mrs. Matthews gazed at her with a wry smile on her lips, reminding me of my aunt Ellsbeth, who had seemed to enjoy Vera's pain before her miscarriage. Agony was the perfect and just punishment for a woman who transgressed. I thought Aunt Ellsbeth saw herself as the voice of an angry God, enraged at the violation of one of his commandments. But Sylvia hadn't transgressed. She had been transgressed against. Yes, God had punished Mr. Price by giving him a stroke, but now, if anything, Aunt Ellsbeth's angry God should show mercy and reduce Sylvia's pain to almost nothing.

"She's not trying," Mrs. Matthews suddenly said. There was a little panic in her face. "I don't like this. It's almost as if she is deliberately holding the baby hostage in her birth canal."

"She can't do that, can she?"

Mrs. Matthews turned to me with the strangest look in her eyes. For a moment, I thought she had gone mad. It was as if Sylvia's failure to do everything exactly as she wanted reflected badly on her. "There's something else going on here," she said.

"What?"

"Take off your skirt and panties, and lie beside her," she ordered.

"What?"

"Don't you see what's happening? She's constantly watching you. She keeps waiting for you to scream in agony."

I looked at Sylvia, who was staring at me now. "But—"

"You have to give birth, too," Mrs. Matthews declared.

"Give birth, too?"

It was one thing to placate Sylvia and keep her calm all these months, to go along with her belief that I had to be as pregnant as she was and that Papa had declared it in one of those mysterious rocking-chair dreams, but to actually act out a delivery beside her . . .

The look on Mrs. Matthews's face was frightening and maddening. For a few moments, I wondered if she didn't believe Sylvia's dreams, too.

"But I can't—"

"Do it!" she cried. "It will be your baby, won't it? Deliver it!"

My heart was pounding, just as I imagined Sylvia's was. I looked at the space beside her, looked at Mrs. Matthews, who was poised and waiting, and then took off my skirt and panties and slipped onto the bed. Sylvia grasped my hand immediately. Mrs. Matthews nodded with satisfaction and then, shockingly, lifted my legs, spread them, and looked between them. I felt her fingers on the insides of my thighs.

She is mad, I thought, *as mad as a hatter*.

I looked at Sylvia. For a moment, though, she suddenly seemed to have no pain. She smiled at me and then turned to Mrs. Matthews and began to follow her orders. When she groaned, Mrs. Matthews looked at me expectantly, and I groaned, too. When Sylvia cried in pain, I did. It was a duet of agony.

"Push!" Mrs. Matthews cried. "Push! I can see the baby's head."

Suddenly, seconds felt like minutes. I felt my cheeks and realized I was breaking into a sweat. My heart was pounding. I took deep breaths. Did I feel pain? Maybe I was going mad myself, but I realized I was actually pushing. All I had read about giving birth ran through my mind. This was how it went; this was what to do. Finally, Sylvia and I let out a last, almost primeval scream, and then Mrs. Matthews lifted the baby, with the umbilical cord still attached, and placed the newborn girl, crying and covered in blood, on my stomach—not Sylvia's. Mrs. Matthews expertly cut and tied the umbilical cord. I couldn't move. Sylvia was just as quiet, watching.

"I need to suction out her mouth and nose a bit," Mrs. Matthews said.

Both Sylvia and I watched her bring the baby to the table she had set up beside the bed. After she did the suctioning, she weighed her.

"Six pounds four ounces. Being born early didn't do any harm."

She began to wash her. I was frozen, unable to move, until we heard the baby cry again.

"Adelle," Sylvia said.

Mrs. Matthews brought the baby back to me. "Newborn babies' bodies don't have the ability to control their temperature well. We want to keep her warm and dry."

She continued to dry her while the baby was lying on me. Then she put the blanket around her carefully, leaving some of her exposed skin against me.

"Your body will warm her, and this is the first opportunity to bond with your baby," she explained.

"Is everything all right with her?"

"I'll do a full Apgar assessment shortly, but I think she's just fine. Right now, I need to do some stitching on Sylvia. There are some nasty tears."

"What's an Apgar assessment?"

She looked at me, disgusted. "You clearly didn't read the pamphlet I left for you. I will judge the baby's color, check her heart rate, reflexes, muscle tone, and respiratory function. I don't just pull them out and leave for dinner," she added, and turned back to Sylvia.

I gazed at the baby. The little hair she had was similar to Sylvia's and mine. And she looked like she had Sylvia's eyes.

"What's happened?" Arden cried, rushing to the bedroom door about ten minutes later.

"Happened. A baby happened. You missed it," Mrs. Matthews said dryly, and kept working on Sylvia.

I looked up at him and smiled. "A girl, Arden. Sylvia wants her to be named Adelle."

He walked in slowly, his face full of more excitement than I had ever seen him express about anything. He was flushed from rushing, but he was so pleased that it brought tears to my eyes. He looked at me and at the baby and back at me, as if I really had just delivered her. We had pretended this for so long that we had begun to believe it. When you wanted to believe something so much, it would happen, at least in your own mind, I thought.

Arden stood gazing down at Adelle with an expression of pure joy. I couldn't say anything to contradict the way he was treating me. He would be no different if I had actually delivered her.

"Adelle is a perfect name, now that I see her, yes," he said. He smiled. "And now a surprise for you, Audrina. The nursery is ready."

"Nursery?"

"Of course. While you were down here, I redid that room. I worked on it myself at night."

"He did," Mrs. Matthews confirmed with a nod and a look of both amazement and approval. "The man lived on four hours of sleep the last week or so, because I suspected this early birth might happen."

"What room?" I asked. I knew the answer and feared hearing it, but I had to ask.

"Well, the other Audrina's room. I put new wallpaper on the walls, put down a new rug, repainted the window frames, and changed the light fixtures," he rattled off proudly. "I've been studying how to do it for months, and I had some good tradesmen give me advice. I even put together her first playpen. There's a bassinet, too, which I'll bring here."

"You did all that? Yourself?"

"We couldn't bring anyone into the house while all this was happening, as you know, so I had to rise to the task. Your father would have been quite surprised and impressed, don't you think? He didn't have faith that I could change a lightbulb."

"What did you do with everything that was in there?" I asked.

"I put it all in the basement for you to go through. Maybe now you'll throw out some of it, if not all of it. Including this damnable rocking chair."

The baby whimpered more loudly. Mrs. Matthews paused and looked at her. "Our next task," she said, "is getting Sylvia used to breastfeeding. Healthy newborns tend to be alert right after they're born. It's a good time to begin breastfeeding."

Sylvia looked very tired. She was fighting to keep her eyes open. The emotional tension had worn me out, too.

"We should move the baby over near her," I said. "Get the baby used to her."

"I thought we could avoid that," Arden said to Mrs. Matthews. "You and I did discuss it."

"I didn't say we couldn't, although I don't think it will matter much for Sylvia. Breastfeeding is a better, healthier option for the child. So many of my former-beauty-queen mothers were afraid their breasts would scar or shrivel. We have everything needed in the kitchen if you choose otherwise. I can tend to it right after this," she said.

"I think we'd prefer that," Arden said. "Right, Audrina? That way, Sylvia will be less confused. We want her to get used to thinking of Adelle as your baby and not hers."

"But we want Adelle to be as healthy as she can be, Arden."

"She'll be healthy," Mrs. Matthews said, straightening up and turning back to the baby. "Most mothers who want to breastfeed want to establish a stronger bond with their child. Obviously, that's not the case here. I'll take her now and do the evaluation and then set up the first feeding, which you can do, Audrina, perhaps in your room. Just place her on the bed with you."

"Good," Arden said quickly. "Audrina?"

"Yes, of course," I said.

"You can expect that Sylvia's breasts will leak and ache," Mrs. Matthews said. "She'll survive it, but I can imagine, having spent all this time with her, that she will be quite frightened and confused. I'll do what I can, but none of this will be my business soon."

"I'd rather we do it the way I want," Arden said. "Audrina will feed the baby." He was firm about it.

"Do as you wish," Mrs. Matthews said, sounding not so much angry as indifferent that her advice wasn't being followed. She took the baby to the table to begin her exam.

I looked at Sylvia. Her eyes were open, but she looked like she was in a daze.

"Sylvia?" I said. She didn't turn to me, nor did she speak. "Is she still in pain?" I asked.

"Some, but it will pass. I'll give her something soon," Mrs. Matthews said. "There's only one of me here."

"But are you sure she's all right? Sylvia? She's not hearing me."

Mrs. Matthews glanced at her. "A little shock. It'll pass," she said.

I sat up and kissed Sylvia's cheek. "Are you all right, Sylvia?" I patted her hand gently and kissed her again. "Sylvia?"

She didn't answer.

"Are you sure she's all right?"

"I'm sure," Mrs. Matthews said without turning back. "Leave her to rest."

"Do what Mrs. Matthews says," Arden ordered. "We hired her to handle this, Audrina."

I got up slowly and dressed, my eyes still on Sylvia, waiting for her to look at me or speak, even cry. She did nothing.

"Audrina!" Arden said sharply.

I followed him to my room. As soon as we entered, he turned to me, his face full of excitement, his eyes wide.

"We did it!" he said, holding his hands up in fists. "We did it!"

He looked like he was going to burst and waited for me to react similarly, but I sat silently on my bed, feeling like I was the one in shock, not Sylvia. What Mrs. Matthews had put me through had had an extraordinary effect on me. It would be ludicrous to say that I felt like I had truly given birth, but the mimicking had certainly given me more than simply a sense of it.

"Aren't you happy?" Arden asked when I didn't respond to his joyful outburst. "What's wrong with you?" he demanded.

"I feel so strange, like a woman who has gone through false labor and discovered there was no baby inside her."

"But there *is* a baby, damn it, get that through your head. We've prepared months and months for this."

"I know, I know, Arden. It's just one thing to plan for it and another to have it happen."

"Yeah, well, it happened, so start reading those books I brought you about being a proper mother. Mrs. Matthews recommended all of them. It's all on you from here on out as far as taking care of the baby goes."

"Adelle," I said. I wanted him to reconfirm that he would accept the name that Sylvia had suggested.

"Right, Adelle. Now, Mrs. Matthews will stay on

for a few weeks. The story is that you had a tough delivery, and she's here to help until you're strong enough."

"I'm worried about Sylvia."

"Well, stop worrying. It's all going to be fine. We've escaped the embarrassment and the damage to our name and our business. After Mrs. Matthews leaves, we'll begin inviting people over to see the baby and you. We'll have a party or something."

I nodded, but still not with the enthusiasm he wanted. I saw the unhappy look on his face hardening.

"Listen," he said, taking a softer approach. "We'll be moving you both upstairs now. You'll see how beautiful the nursery is, and you'll be too busy to think of anything else. I'm sure you'll feel a lot better then. As soon as we can take the baby out, we'll go shopping to get you new clothes. That's what new mothers do. And we'll go shopping to get the baby things, too. And yes, we'll bring Sylvia along when she's well enough and no one can tell what she's been through, and we'll buy her things, too. Okay? Okay?" he repeated when I didn't answer.

"Okay," I replied.

"All right." He brushed back his hair and fixed his tie. "I'm going to return to work and announce the baby's birth. Everyone's waiting on pins and needles at the office. I've got a box of cigars in my car that I bought months ago in anticipation. See you later for our private celebration dinner. Get yourself together, Audrina. I'm looking forward to wonderful days ahead for us all."

He walked over to kiss me on the cheek and then left. I went to the window and looked out. Mr. Ralph was trimming a tree. If I closed my eyes and imagined it, I could be back years and years ago, when I had stood by windows of Whitefern and looked out at a world I feared without realizing why. I was doing the same thing now.

I shouldn't be, I thought. After all, Arden was right. His plan was ending up just the way he wanted it to. Everything we had done was working, although it still would be strange having Sylvia think of the baby as more mine than hers. Maybe it would be enough to have her think it was ours. People who heard her say or think that aloud would surely smile and shake their heads, believing it was all part of her being a child in a woman's body. There would be nothing strange about it to them, only to me.

A little later, under Mrs. Matthews's supervision, I gave Adelle her first feeding. Despite how she had been conceived, I thought Adelle was beautiful. It was impossible to predict what her features would be like months, even years, from now, but at this moment, I thought there were very strong resemblances to Sylvia and, therefore, to me or the Adares. As soon as the baby had gone to sleep on my bed, I rose to check on Sylvia.

She was lying with her eyes open, just as before, but clearly not seeing anything. Mrs. Matthews came up beside me, looked at her, and moved to the bed and began to check her blood pressure. She listened to her heart with a stethoscope and then looked at me. "She'll be all right. Just sit here and talk to her," she ordered.

"Are you sure? Maybe she needs more medical attention. I wouldn't want anything to happen to her just because we were afraid of revealing the truth now. Really. I'm worried."

"Calm down," she snapped. "Just read her a story or something."

When she left, I sat next to Sylvia and began to talk to her.

"Our baby has been born, Sylvia. You have to help care for her, you know. You can't sleep too long. We need you. I know it was painful, but when you see her and see how beautiful she is, you will agree that it was worth it."

She blinked, but nothing else in her face moved.

"Someday soon, you'll be playing with her, Sylvia. You'll show her things, how to do things. And when she can walk, you'll take her into the woods and show her the squirrels. But you have to be strong, Sylvia. You have to be healthy and well."

I took her hand and held it. This couldn't be right. This couldn't be just a little thing. She wasn't moving or trying to speak. I lowered my head and closed my eyes. *Papa*, I thought. *Papa, help us.*

I looked at the rocking chair.

"I'm going to tell Papa about the baby, Sylvia, but he'll want you to tell him, too."

I went to the chair. It had been years since I had sat in it. It actually terrified me a little. When I sat, memories came rushing back—the visions, the voices, everything I had ever seen or heard when I closed my eyes and rocked. I glanced back at Sylvia. She looked like she had turned a little toward me. I took a deep breath, like I would if I was going to jump into the pond, and then I put my arms on the arms of the chair, closed my eyes, and rocked.

I saw Papa's angry face. The words I feared resonated.

You were supposed to protect her, Audrina. You promised.

I started to cry, crying like a little girl again. I couldn't have Papa mad at me. I couldn't.

"I'm sorry, Papa. I'm sorry," I moaned.

"Papa?" I heard, and opened my eyes. Sylvia was sitting up. "Did you hear Papa?"

"Yes." I nodded. "He's waiting for you, Sylvia, for you."

She started to get out of the bed.

Mrs. Matthews, as if she had been listening just outside the door, appeared. "You stay in that bed," she ordered, pointing with her long right forefinger at Sylvia. "I'll tell you when you can get up."

Sylvia froze.

"But it helped her," I said. "The rocking chair."

"I told you that her lethargy wouldn't last. You don't have to go through some stupid magic. She'll be fine. Now, go keep your eyes on the baby. I'll handle Sylvia. Go on!" she ordered, so sharply I winced and then got up.

"Papa," Sylvia said.

"Lie down," Mrs. Matthews commanded. "I won't have you tear those stitches and bleed all over the place. Go on. Do as I say."

Sylvia lay back reluctantly, her eyes on the chair.

Mrs. Matthews glared at me. "You'd have her up rocking in that chair with those stitches still fresh? I can see I'll be here for a while yet. Go on. Go to your room."

I wanted so much to shout back at her, but we were still trapped, trapped by the secrets. I glanced at Sylvia and then went and stood beside the bassinet, watching Adelle breathe and occasionally whimper like a puppy. Could I do it? Could I make her my baby? Could I stop thinking about who her father was and how she had been conceived? Of course, it was wrong, even stupid, to blame the baby, but it wasn't easily ignored.

I sat on my bed softly beside Adelle and picked up one of the pamphlets about caring for an infant. Hours later, Arden returned, beaming as brightly as he had before, if not more. He rattled on and on about all the congratulations he had received, the clients who had called, and how wonderful it had made him feel.

"Maybe I should have been there," I said, my voice full of bitterness.

"Now, how could you do that, Audrina? Really? If you're going to be a mother, think like an adult," he said, and looked at the baby. "Of course, like your father, I wanted a son," he said, "but for now, she will do."

"For now?"

"Maybe simulating a birth has helped make you fertile. We'll try for a son. One can hope. Of course, we can't get right to it." He smiled. "Women who give birth don't conceive days after."

What was he thinking? Women who give birth don't conceive days after? Sometimes he sounded like someone who had been through this many times. Once again, I wondered about his college years. How many secrets had he buried?

"How's Sylvia?" he asked.

"You'll have to go see for yourself. I was dismissed," I said.

"Dismissed?"

I turned back to the baby. He left and later returned to tell me Sylvia was doing well. She had even eaten something.

"A day or so of rest, and everything will be fine," he said. "I've ordered our celebration dinner. Mrs. Crown made all the arrangements. We're having lobster. You, of course, will do nothing. Mrs. Matthews is setting the table. I've bought a bottle of the best champagne. So just rest for now. Later we will move everything upstairs, and you'll be back in our bedroom, and Sylvia will be back in hers. Mrs. Matthews says we can move her later, too."

"I wouldn't go up without her."

He started out and stopped, turning back. "I'll bring the rocking chair back up if you like, but we'll put it in Sylvia's room for now. I imagine that will make her feel better. When Mrs. Matthews leaves, we can move it into the guest room or out of the house completely. Up to you," he said. "Okay?"

"Okay," I said. It would make Sylvia happy right now.

He smiled and left.

Adelle was still asleep. I lay back, keeping very close to her, and closed my eyes. I dozed off but woke when Mrs. Matthews entered. She didn't realize I was awake. I opened my eyes slightly and saw her check Adelle and then wrap her comfortably in the blanket. She picked her up and held her, smiling at her. Could this woman feel motherly? She had helped deliver so many children, I imagined, but I was certain she had never been as involved as she had been in Adelle's birth.

The moment she saw that I was awake, she stopped smiling.

"We've brought the bassinet down to be at the dining-room table," she said. "For tonight's celebratory dinner. It's what your husband asked."

"What about Sylvia?"

"It's best she remain in bed for a while longer. I'll bring her some dinner later. She's sleeping now. I gave her something to help her sleep and ease any pain."

"Okay."

She looked at me strangely for a moment. "I'm sorry you couldn't have your own child properly, but I assure you, this is a blessing in disguise. Your husband is a very smart man." She started out with Adelle in her arms. Then she stopped and looked at me. "You might want to put on something special and do your hair."

"Why is that important to you?" I asked.

"It's not important to me, but I know that the part you're playing has really just begun. My free advice is for you to get right into it."

"Somehow I doubt that advice is free," I said.

Her smug expression faded.

I wanted to be defiant, just to go out as I was, but I realized she was not wrong. The baby had been born. Sylvia would be fine. The world would know only what Arden had revealed, and we would go on, maybe even as the family Arden imagined.

After all, what other choice was there?

Our secrets begot secrets. They spun around us, tightening their grip on Whitefern.

Arden didn't realize it, I thought, but in the end, we might be in a stronger trap, and those shadows that draped themselves in every possible corner would only grow darker. They would be there for Adelle, just as they always would be there for me.

Unless, of course, I found a way for us to escape ourselves.

Pathway to the Light

There were moments during our celebratory dinner when I felt more like an observer than a participant. Arden and Mrs. Matthews talked to each other as if I wasn't even there. She had set the table, but not as nicely as I or Sylvia would. She used paper napkins, something Arden would normally criticize, and she didn't have separate forks for salad. Arden had told her to bring in some glasses for champagne, and she forgot other glasses for water. Following what I believed were her orders, Arden had placed the bassinet next to my chair. She had put Adelle in it. I started for the kitchen when the food arrived from the restaurant, but Arden told me just to sit.

"Mrs. Matthews will handle it all," he said. "Tonight you have to be a woman who just delivered a baby."

"But I didn't, Arden. I obviously can do what has to be done."

"Audrina, if you don't act like the child's mother, no one will believe you are," he said. "It has to come naturally to you. We're over the crisis, but we can still make serious mistakes. Besides, haven't you always wanted a child?"

"Yes, of course."

"Then why fight it? Enjoy it. Be the mother you've always wanted to be." He leaned toward me to whisper. "Besides, with what I'm paying her, we should let her work."

"How long will she be here?"

"Not long now. Everything will return to the way it was. Not to normal, exactly. We have a child to care for now. And you have some work to do with Sylvia, I'm sure. She'll be quite confused. I don't want her out in public too fast, although I'm sure you can ascribe anything she says to her lack of intelligence."

Before I could speak, Mrs. Matthews entered with a tray on which were three dishes crowded with food. She looked very pleased with the dinner we were about to enjoy. We had beautiful lobster tails, salad, and french fries. I had started to reach for mine when she put the tray in the center of the table, but she seized it first and brought it to me.

"Our new mother has to be treated a little specially tonight," she said. I saw the sardonic look in her eyes.

"Thank you," I replied, as if I thought she was being kind.

Arden popped the champagne and poured glassfuls for the three of us. Then he raised his and waited for me to raise mine.

"To a successful pregnancy and delivery, bringing a new child to Whitefern. Thank you for your professional care, Mrs. Matthews. To your expertise. And finally, to our new daughter, Adelle Lowe."

We clinked our glasses and drank. Adelle whimpered as if she had heard and understood it all. I couldn't help being uncomfortable, now that it had happened and Sylvia's child was to be mine. It felt very deceitful, and I wondered if it always would. Arden insisted that joy was flooding over us. In his smile, I could see that, at least for now, I had to put all my fears and dark thoughts aside. Perhaps he was right. The new days of light and happiness had arrived with the child. I didn't feel like being grateful to Mrs. Matthews, but I had to admit to myself that without her, this would not have been accomplished. A healthy child was born, Sylvia was safe, and we had not suffered a bit of embarrassment.

As we ate, Arden looked like a young boy again, his pride so bright that he seemed to glow. Rarely at any dinner since this had begun had he been as talkative as he was tonight, and he ate as if it was his first meal in weeks. I saw that even Mrs. Matthews was impressed with his glee. He rattled on and on about the changes he would now make at Whitefern, changes that were important to what he called a new family. He wanted to brighten up the house as much as he could.

"We need to repaint walls, sell off some of those old, dark paintings, and finally put in some real lighting."

"I couldn't agree more," Mrs. Matthews said. "When I first entered this house, I thought I was in a funeral parlor!"

"Precisely. That's going to change," he replied. Apparently, he had already had some important discussions with decorators and had scheduled one to visit us next week.

"Good," Mrs. Matthews said.

I looked at her. She was behaving as though she was going to be living here forever.

"Of course, nothing will be decided until Audrina confirms it," Arden said. "A husband can't make a home happy unless his wife is happy in it."

"Very true," Mrs. Matthews said. Like Arden, she was suddenly more talkative than ever. "I wish my husband had realized that."

I perked up. She never talked about her family. "What happened to him?" I asked.

"He was an alcoholic and eventually destroyed his liver. He died twelve years ago."

I wondered to myself if living with her had driven him to become an alcoholic. "I'm sorry to hear that," I said. "I wondered why you never mention much about your own family."

"Yes, well, it doesn't do us any good to belabor the dreadful past events in our lives. Look to the future. Now you have one," she added. "Be grateful, and let that gratitude drown any sadness."

"That's not always as easy as it sounds."

"It's as easy as you want it to be," she insisted. "Dwelling on disappointments and tragedies will steal away your chance for future happiness."

She always made statements that sounded like declarations from a higher power.

"Hear, hear," Arden said, and poured her and himself more champagne. "You want any more?" he asked me.

"No, thank you."

As if he was at one of his business dinners, Arden began to talk about the economy and how he would like to adjust Mrs. Matthews's portfolio.

I didn't eat half as much as they did, and when I was content with what I had eaten, I thought that one of us should go check on Sylvia. "She might have woken up and would be frightened," I suggested.

"I doubt it," Mrs. Matthews said. "I gave her enough to sleep well for a few more hours at least. She needs to sleep now. If you're restless, why don't you clear the table?"

Arden nodded in agreement. So just like that, I was back to my household duties, I thought. She looked so confident, so pleased with her power over me.

I felt my spine harden and sat back. "Would a woman who had just given birth get right back to her household duties?" I asked.

She raised her eyebrows.

I looked at Arden. "I'm simply trying to behave like a woman who just had a baby. I should get to the point where I do so without thinking, don't you agree?" I was so saccharine-sweet that I almost turned my own stomach.

"She has a point, Helen," Arden said. "Perhaps you can see to some coffee for us, too, when you clear the table. I'd like to have some with brandy tonight."

She didn't flush red, exactly, but I could see the

fury in her eyes. She rose and began to clear off the table. At that moment, I really appreciated Arden. He smiled at me, and I thought that maybe now that this was all coming to an end, we could return to being the husband and wife we had set out to be. We'd return to feeling the affection we'd had for each other when we first met, a time that felt so very long ago.

Adelle woke and began to cry. For a moment, I panicked, but then I lifted her carefully and rocked her.

"That's not what she wants," Mrs. Matthews said as she returned from the kitchen. "It's time for another feeding. Get used to it. You won't be sleeping too many hours in a row for quite a while."

"Well, you can surely help for a few weeks, can't you, Helen?" Arden asked. I listened carefully to his tone of voice. Whenever he asked her to do something now, there was an underlying threat.

"I can help a little, but if she becomes too dependent on me, it won't do you any good when I leave."

"When will you leave?" I asked, perhaps a bit too harshly.

"As soon as I can," she said. "Don't worry about that. Come with me to the kitchen. I'll fix the baby's bottle, and you can watch and know how to do it after this." She looked at Arden. "Maybe you can pitch in, Mr. Lowe, and help clear the rest of the table. I will prepare some coffee, too, as you requested."

He laughed. "Me? Clear off a table? I haven't lifted a dish off a table since—"

"Since now," she said.

I almost laughed out loud at the way the smile flew

off his face. He looked at mine and then, not hiding his displeasure, began to pick up dishes and glasses.

Later, he drank too much brandy and nearly fell asleep on the settee. I reminded him of what we had to do to get Adelle and me upstairs this evening.

"Why don't we wait?" he asked.

"You promised me, Arden. It hasn't been pleasant sleeping in those rooms, either for me or for Sylvia."

He groaned and got up.

While Adelle was sleeping, I brought up some of my clothing and then went to the first Audrina's room to see the nursery he had created. I was impressed, but not seeing the familiar toys and furniture stunned me at first. Even after I had learned the truth and Papa had faced up to the deceptions he had created, he had not wanted to disturb the room. I think there was a point where he had convinced himself that there really was a first Audrina. He had wanted her so much, as he had enjoyed her. In a way, changing the sacred rocking-chair room was like burying another part of him.

Arden came up behind me. "Well?" he asked. "You're not going to start complaining about not having those dusty things in here, are you?"

"No, Arden. You did a beautiful job. I am proud of you."

"Good," he said. "Let's finish moving everything up. I have a big day tomorrow. I've decided that I'm not moving that rocking chair up tonight. It's late, and it's heavy."

"Okay, Arden," I said. I was too tired to argue about anything.

Shortly after, Mrs. Matthews decided we could help Sylvia back up to her room. She was groggy, but the pain seemed tolerable. The two of us practically carried her up the stairs and got her into her bed.

"I'll look in on her periodically," Mrs. Matthews said. "You look after the baby. You know now how to prepare her bottle, so you'll be the one to go up and down the stairs."

Adelle was set up beside our bed on my side. The first time she cried, Arden woke with a start and groaned. "I should have left you downstairs until she sleeps through the night," he said. "I have to have my sleep. It's important that I'm alert at the brokerage, and I get up so early."

"I'm sorry, Arden." I thought for a moment and then said, "Maybe for a while, it would be better if I slept with Sylvia and the baby slept in her room with us."

"Yes," he said instantly, jumping on the suggestion. "While you get the bottle prepared, I'll move the bassinet and Adelle in there. Brilliant."

As I headed for the stairs, Mrs. Matthews stepped out of her room in her robe and slippers. "What's the problem?" she asked.

I told her our plan and what had caused the changes.

"My husband was the same way when our son was born," she said. "I've never doubted that men are the weaker sex. Go on. I'll help him."

She headed for our bedroom, and I went down to the kitchen.

I guessed it would be true, I thought. It would be

as if Adelle was both Sylvia's and mine, rather than just mine. I fed her in Sylvia's room, and she fell asleep again.

I felt exhausted, too, and was happy to lower my head to the pillow. I fell asleep in minutes, and when the sun burst in, I was shocked at how long I had slept. My first thoughts were of Sylvia. I got up quickly to get the day started. She'd barely noticed I was there. She looked dazed.

"How are you, Sylvia?" I asked, and her eyes lit with a happy glow.

"Our baby Adelle," she said, sitting up.

Mrs. Matthews appeared in the doorway, dressed. "Is everything all right?"

"Yes."

"Good. Maybe I'll be leaving sooner than we thought," she said. She looked at Adelle, still sleeping. Then she took Sylvia's blood pressure and her temperature while I got up and dressed.

"How is she?" I asked.

"She's doing fine. You'll bring up her breakfast this morning, but tomorrow I want her downstairs for all her meals. She can do a little walking later."

"Watch Adelle," I told Sylvia.

She nodded excitedly. Then I followed Mrs. Matthews down to the kitchen. Arden had apparently left more than an hour ago.

"I can make Sylvia's breakfast," I said.

Mrs. Matthews paused and smiled. "You can do everything, Audrina, but for now, concentrate on the baby only."

I wasn't in the mood to argue. I told myself this wouldn't go on much longer anyway. *You were patient and tolerant up to now. Hang on a little longer, Audrina Lowe.*

Sylvia grew stronger with every passing day. Oddly, the memory of what she had gone through seemed to drift, replaced with what she believed I had gone through. Mrs. Matthews was right about Sylvia's swollen breasts. The leakage frightened her, and she felt the pressure and discomfort for nearly ten days after the delivery. Mrs. Matthews bought a better bra for her to wear during this time and had her use some ice packs.

Mrs. Matthews was out and about more now. I took on my usual household duties, and as Sylvia grew stronger and felt better, she returned to some of her chores as if she had never stopped doing them. Most of the time, the two of us cared for Adelle and talked about every slight change we saw in her.

Arden often called during the day to be sure all was going well. He had dinner with clients only twice during the ten days after Adelle's birth. His interest in the baby amazed me. It seemed he couldn't wait to get home to see her and be sure all was well. Never once did he mention what had happened to Sylvia. I thought this was wonderful of him. He now cared more about her, talked to her more, and enjoyed how much she enjoyed Adelle. He even willingly had Mr. Ralph help him bring the rocking chair up to Sylvia's room.

"It's all turned out for the best," he said one night.

"We have seized disaster from the jaws of the devil himself. I'm very proud of you, Audrina. We could never have done this without your full cooperation and determination. I imagine even your father would be proud of us, don't you?"

"No. He would never forgive me for what I let happen, Arden. I don't think I can ever fully forgive myself. I can live with this, but I don't believe that I've compensated enough for my mistake."

"Oh, stuff that guilt, Audrina. You and your family have this tendency to hold on to every mistake any of you make forever and ever. Depressing and self-defeating. Listen to the advice Mrs. Matthews gave you."

The next morning, when I got up and went to prepare Adelle's bottle, I found Mrs. Matthews dressed and wearing her coat. Her small suitcase was at her feet. She was having a cup of coffee. At dinner, she had said nothing about leaving.

"Are you going?" I asked. I held my breath in anticipation.

"My work here is finished. Your sister is well, and you seem quite capable of caring for the baby."

"Does Arden know you're leaving?"

"Of course," she said, and put her cup in the sink. She flashed a smile and picked up her suitcase. "You are not fond of listening to my advice," she said, standing right in front of me now, like a grade-school teacher in front of a student. "But I'll give it to you anyway. Don't dwell on what happened here. Don't ask too many questions about it. Tell yourself nothing unusual occurred. A baby was born at home. It happens more often than people think it does. I have worked for families who had errant teenage daughters and kept their pregnancies secret. The girls even gave birth and returned to school a day or two later. The families gave the babies to church orphanages or such. Sometimes, couples who are having trouble having their own child adopt the baby. You live here in this mansion, fortified against the real world, and have no idea what really goes on out there. My advice is to keep it that way. You, my dear Audrina, are one of those women who are more comfortable with fantasy than reality. Your husband understands that. You're lucky. Other women like you have husbands who are far more intolerant when it comes to their refusal to face hard and ugly things. It's immature, of course, but as long as you're not out there involved in the day-to-day struggles most of us face, you'll do fine living in your own world. I wish you luck."

"You have no idea who I am," I said, shocked at her audacity.

She smiled. "Then maybe that's for the best. Your husband knows how to reach me if there are any problems."

"We'll be taking Adelle to see Dr. Prescott now. He'll handle any problems we might encounter."

"What a relief," she said, and started for the front door. I followed and watched her stop, turn, and look at the house again. "I do hope your husband follows through and gets you out of the past," she said. Then she opened the door and left.

For a moment, it was like she had taken all the air in the house out with her. Then I felt myself relax. I took a deep breath and, with renewed energy, began the new day. The odd thing, actually amusing to me, was that Sylvia didn't seem to notice Mrs. Matthews was gone. Perhaps she thought she had left to shop for us, but even later in the day, she never inquired about her whereabouts, and I said nothing to bring her to mind.

I couldn't forget her, of course, not as easily as Sylvia apparently did. Once again, I found myself envious of my disadvantaged sister. It brought a smile, which brought another and another. Later, we sat outside on the rear patio with Adelle wrapped comfortably in my arms. Sylvia laughed at the squirrels and the rabbits and pointed to them for Adelle to see and appreciate.

"When will she talk and walk?" Sylvia asked me.

"Sooner than you think, I'm sure, but not for a while, Sylvia. I remember when you first did, and I remember you crawling around out here."

"I don't," she said.

"That's all right. Everything you did, Adelle will do, and that might remind you."

She stood there smiling at the baby and me.

"What?"

"We're lucky," she said. I knew she was simply repeating something Arden or I might have said, but she said it as if she understood everything we had done together and everything that had happened. There wasn't an iota of disappointment or regret in her voice or in her smile. I wondered if she even thought now of Mr. Price.

"Yes, Sylvia," I said. "We *are* lucky."

We went in to prepare dinner. Whenever we did this now, we brought Adelle in with us. Sometimes she slept through the whole process, but often I caught her awake, listening and watching. The sounds surely made her curious, I thought. She was going to be a bright child. She would have the advantage of people not assuming she was slow-witted. Right now, with the three of us there and all of us well, I thought I was the happiest I had been in a very long time.

As soon as Arden arrived, I told him Mrs. Matthews had left. He nodded.

"Why didn't you mention it to me last night?" I asked. "I came down while she was having coffee and found her in her coat, with her suitcase packed."

"I thought it best not to say anything until she actually left. There was the slight possibility that she might stay another day," he said. For the first time in a long time, I sensed that he was lying.

"Dinner's ready," I said. The faster I forgot that woman, the better off I'd be, I thought, but there was one more thing to be discussed about her.

I waited until we had eaten and Adelle was sleeping again. Sylvia was in the kitchen finishing the dishes. Arden had gone into the Roman Revival salon and sat on the settee, smoking his pipe and reading one of his business magazines. He looked up when I entered but kept reading. I sat across from him and waited. Finally, he lowered the magazine.

"What's up?" he asked.

"She's gone. You made a promise, Arden."

"Promise?"

"To tell me the great secret you knew about her, the thing you had to hold over her that would ensure that she would never reveal ours. I want to know it. If I had known while she was here, I might not have been so intimidated by her all the time."

"Intimidated? You did what had to be done, just like I did, Audrina. And no one forced either of us. We knew it was best for Sylvia and for Adelle. Don't start moaning and groaning about how horrible it was. It's over."

"Okay, it's over. So tell me."

He looked away and pressed his lips together. "It's not an easy thing for me to tell."

"I need to know," I insisted.

"You *need*," he said, nodding. "Okay, I'll make you a deal. Now that you are obviously going to be heavily involved with caring for Adelle, there is no possibility that you will have any time for our business affairs. This wild idea of yours about becoming a broker is surely to be put aside. I'd like those papers signed properly. You'll go with me to Mr. Johnson's office, and we'll do it together. He was put off by your not signing and doing the fingerprint when I first brought it all here. Now he won't accept anything but the proper procedure. After all that is done, I'll tell you what you're asking. Do we have a deal?"

"We don't need to make a deal, Arden. You made a promise to me. First, you keep your promise, and then we'll discuss those damn papers," I said. My words pounded into his ears like nails. I stared coldly at him, challenging him to move me even an inch.

He looked so astonished that I thought he was going to stop talking and start reading his magazine again, but he surprised me. "I'm not proud of what I'm about to tell you," he said. "And for that reason, it's very difficult for me. I don't like bringing up the ugliest event of the past, both for you and for me. Yes, it's obviously uglier and more painful for you, but it's still painful for me, and it will always be. Do you still insist on knowing?"

I would readily admit that I was frightened, but I needed to know regardless of what it would mean to me. "Yes."

"Mrs. Matthew's son, Philip, was one of the boys who attacked you in the woods. As you know, I saw them do it, and I was afraid to confront them. Later, they threatened me if I said a word, and I was afraid for my mother."

"Her son?"

"Yes. I told her, so she knew that I could identify him. I promised never to mention it if she did this for us and kept our secret. If I did go to the police, they would investigate and maybe get him to confess or reveal the names of the others, which I could have done. One or more would rat on her son. She knew that. It was enough to ensure that she would never speak about what really happened here."

His words seemed to lift me up and take me to the rocking chair. I heard the screams, my screams, and heard their horrible laughter. I saw myself running through the woods, crying hysterically, and saw my mother's face.

"Audrina," he said. "Audrina!"

I seemed to open eyes that were already open.

"See?" he said, putting a hand on my shoulder and shaking me slightly. "I knew I shouldn't have told you. What difference does it make now?" His words were like icicles dripping into my ears. I felt myself shudder and tremble. What difference did it make now? How could he ask that? Did he ever have even a tiny bit of real love for me?

"She knew her son had violated me, was one of them. You would think she would have been kinder, gentler, even remorseful, but she treated me like I was spoiled and guilty myself. I was only a little girl!" I raised my fists in the air and barely kept myself from pounding his chest. How could he make any bargains with such a woman?

"I know. A lot of things have made that woman bitter, but she's good at what she does."

"How did you know that so well, Arden?" I fired back at him. When he didn't speak, a thought that had been haunting me came to the surface. I practically yelled, "You've asked for her services before, haven't you? Well?"

"Nothing ever happened after we got married," he said.

"Are you forgetting about Vera?"

"I thought we'd never mention that. It's like nothing ever happened with her. That's what we agreed on."

"All right. So what are you talking about?" I was shaking inside. I wished I hadn't asked the questions but knew I'd had no choice. It was the story of my life, scraping away the lies that disguised the ugliness and pain feeding the shadows of Whitefern and darkening my heart.

"I was a bit wild in college. I think you knew that anyway, Audrina, but what I did then has nothing to do with our lives now. You heard her. Don't force me or yourself to drag up any more of the past, Audrina. Enough! It's over," he said firmly. He sat back and opened his magazine.

I stared at him for a few moments and then got up and walked out, feeling dazed. It was as if the floor had been torn away and I was hanging on by a thread.

Adelle had woken up and was crying for her bottle. Sylvia was rushing to get it ready. I watched her and stood back to see how she would do. She was gentle and loving. And for the first time in a very long time, I realized why we were closer than most sisters, despite her mental disabilities.

We had both been violated, and we both had to bury memories the way others might bury bodies.

Truth Will Not Die

Soon after Mrs. Matthews had left Whitefern, I had to shop for groceries. For the last month or so, she had done it alone. I wanted to take Sylvia and Adelle along for Adelle's first outing but wasn't sure if I should. I called Dr. Prescott and told him I would be bringing Adelle in for him to examine her and talk to me about what her care involved now, but I was really calling for his advice about taking her out.

"I'm looking forward to seeing her, Audrina. How are you doing?"

"I'm fine, Dr. Prescott. I was wondering if it's too early to take her out with me when I go shopping for groceries."

"What did Mrs. Matthews say?" he asked. It was easy to read between the lines and hear how hurt he was at not being the doctor to deliver Adelle. "I'm sure she performed an Apgar assessment, right?"

"Yes, right away. She said it was all very good. Mrs. Matthews is no longer looking after Adelle."

"No. I don't see why she would be. Well, I see no

problem with taking her out. We're having beautiful late-summer weather. I'm sure you'll take great care."

"I will. Thank you."

"Why don't we plan on my seeing you and the baby a week from today around two p.m. Is that okay?"

"That's good. Thank you, Dr. Prescott."

"Is Arden going to be okay with that?"

"Yes," I said. Again, it was easy to hear how hurt he was that we hadn't used him to deliver Adelle and oversee my supposed pregnancy. I hadn't spoken to Arden about going to Dr. Prescott so soon, but I was determined that I should.

I called Arden to tell him about the arrangements. He was so quiet that I thought he hadn't heard me because he was concentrating on something else. He'd often do that when I called, and I'd have to repeat myself.

"It's a week from today at two. You can come along if you want," I said.

"No, that's all right. I was just thinking. You have to be careful about letting him examine you, Audrina. I'm not sure what he could tell quickly. Helen and I did discuss the eventuality of your going to him and having Adelle under his care, of course, but your breasts aren't swollen like Sylvia's. If he gets suspicious and realizes what's gone on, it could lead to complications for us."

"I don't imagine he would announce it to the newspapers, Arden. There is an obligation to keep personal information between a patient and a doctor."

"Yes, but you're forgetting that a crime was committed here, Audrina. He might feel obligated to report Sylvia's pregnancy."

"Okay, okay. I won't go through any exam. I won't undress. I'll see that he just examines Adelle," I said.

"Be sure you do that."

"We're going to the supermarket. Anything special you might want?"

"No. Whatever you get is fine. Got to get back to work," he said.

I wanted Sylvia to help, so I sat with her in the living room and discussed what we were going to do and how she should behave when people approached us to look at Adelle.

"Don't mention Mrs. Matthews, Sylvia. Don't say anything about how Adelle was born, understand? This is only for us to know."

She nodded, but I was not confident that she understood. We packed what we needed for the baby and set out. Sylvia hovered over Adelle protectively during the drive. It brought a smile to my face. *We'll be fine*, I thought. *Everything will be fine from now on.*

It wasn't too busy at the market. Sylvia pushed the cart with Adelle comfortable in her infant seat set in the top part. We had dressed her in a little pink hat, pink socks, and a pink dress. It was one of the first outfits Arden and I had bought her. Strangers stopped to speak to us, but all they wanted to know was how old she was and what her name was. Sylvia answered them all. One elderly man jokingly asked what aisle the newborn babies were in. He said he wanted to buy one for himself.

Sylvia's eyes bulged. "Buy babies in the supermarket?" she asked.

The man laughed, saw that we weren't laughing, and quickly walked away. As we rounded a turn, I saw Mrs. Haider ahead of us, studying a box of rice. I wanted to back out and go to a different aisle to avoid her, but she looked up and waved. I had no choice.

"Oh, what a beautiful baby!" she cried after rushing over. "How happy you and Mr. Lowe must be. And this must be Sylvia?"

"Yes, my sister, Sylvia. Sylvia, this is Mrs. Haider. She was principal of the school when I was there."

"And long before that," Mrs. Haider said.

Sylvia held out her hand and smiled. "Pleased to meet you," she recited.

Mrs. Haider looked at me and nodded. "And I'm pleased to meet you and your niece, too."

"Niece?"

"I'll explain it to you later, Sylvia. I really haven't gone through all that yet," I told Mrs. Haider. "You understand."

"Yes, certainly. So how is your artwork, Sylvia? Are you still drawing and painting?"

"No," Sylvia said.

"Oh?"

"Too busy taking care of Adelle," she said.

Mrs. Haider laughed, and then her expression darkened. "It's too bad about Mr. Price."

"Yes, I know," I said, hiding my real feelings about that man and his stroke.

"Did you ever get a chance to see him or speak to Mrs. Price?" she asked.

"Get a chance? No. Why do you ask?"

"Oh, didn't you know? He passed away last month. Heart failure. Probably part of the stroke. Very sad. I always admired him, and he was very popular with the students." She paused. "I wondered why I didn't see you at the funeral. I just assumed you'd be there, but with your pregnancy and all, I'm sure you were quite occupied."

"Yes," I said. I didn't want to keep talking to Mrs. Haider about anything, particularly that man. Fortunately, Adelle began to squirm uncomfortably. "We'd better move along. Almost time for a feeding," I said.

"I'll do it," Sylvia announced. "We both do it."

"That's very good, Sylvia. I'm sure you're a wonderful and helpful aunt. I'll see you again soon, I hope. Good luck with the baby, Audrina. Beautiful child," she said, and walked away.

Sylvia looked very confused, but thankfully, Adelle was taking up all her attention now. For a few moments, I stood looking after Mrs. Haider as she pushed her cart away. I replayed what she had told me. Mr. Price was dead. I should be happy about it, and I was, but I couldn't show that, and the news had caught me by surprise. I was stunned. Why hadn't Arden mentioned Mr. Price's death? Surely, he would have known. I would have thought he'd come rushing with the news, saying how just it was that he had suffered. Maybe he thought it would have disturbed me, as it was disturbing me now, and decided not to mention it.

He was right. It would have reminded me of what I'd permitted to happen, practically right under my nose.

We finished our shopping and headed for home. Adelle was crying more and was very uncomfortable now. Just as we reached Whitefern, a car that had obviously been parked in front of the house began to pull away. It slowed as we approached and then stopped and backed up.

Mr. Ralph dropped what he was doing with a lawn mower and rushed to help us with the groceries. Sylvia wanted to carry Adelle.

"Put her in the bassinet, Sylvia," I said, keeping my eyes on the strange car.

"And warm the bottle," she recited.

Whoever was in the car just sat watching us. The afternoon sun threw a blinding glare on the car's windows, but I was able to see that the driver was a gray-haired woman. She watched us enter the house. How odd, I thought. Why would anyone come all the way out here and just sit in her car?

We hurried inside, and I began to put away the groceries while Sylvia tended to Adelle. Whatever problems she had taking care of herself didn't affect her care of the baby. I thought to myself that a mother's instincts were too strong to be discouraged. Sylvia read at the level of a seven- or eight-year-old, with a vocabulary barely more advanced. She had trouble with grade-school math, and her memory was like Swiss cheese, full of gaps, but she was as focused about the care of Adelle as any new mother would be.

When I had heard about Mr. Price's death, my anger

had been revived, and my satisfaction at how much
pain and suffering he experienced had been heightened.
But there was irony here, too. I was so happy for Sylvia
now. Adelle truly was giving her life meaning, more
perhaps than she was giving to Arden's and mine. Yes,
we'd be her parents. We would make all the major decisions for her from now until she was an adult herself,
but the bond between her and Sylvia would be forever
strong, although invisible to outsiders. In my heart of
hearts, I knew that Adelle would someday realize who
her real mother was.

Perhaps she would confront us and demand to
know the truth, especially as she grew and her features
resembled Sylvia's more than Arden's or mine. She
would go to sleep at night with the question on her
lips: *Who am I?* I was sure that Arden and I would
argue about it. I would want to tell her the truth, and
he would insist that I never do. "What difference does
it make now?" he would surely say.

How could I explain it so he would understand?
Could I really get him to see how difficult it had been
for me being told I was the second Audrina, never as
perfect as the first? How could I get him to feel what I
felt as I struggled to find my own identity while being
haunted by an angelic older sister whose name I possessed but whose perfection I would never realize? It
would certainly never be realized in my father's eyes,
the eyes that were most important to me.

I smiled as I watched Sylvia kiss and coo at Adelle.
She was fascinated by her tiny fingers and toes. I told
myself that I had to put aside my thoughts about what

had happened and especially not dwell on the revenge fulfilled with Mr. Price's death. I hated to give her any credit, but Mrs. Matthews had been right. I should not dwell on the dark past. I should dwell on the future.

The sound of the doorbell jerked me out of my musings. Whoever was in that parked car probably had decided it was time to call on us. I had no reason for it, but I began trembling. I didn't move until the doorbell sounded again and Sylvia noticed.

"Someone's here," she said.

"Just take care of Adelle, Sylvia. I'll go see."

She smiled gratefully. She didn't want her care of the baby to be interrupted.

Maybe it was another Jehovah's Witness or the like, I thought, and went to the front entrance. I opened the front door. It was the elderly woman I had seen in the parked car. She looked like she couldn't be much more than five feet tall. Her gray hair was thinning but curly and trimmed at the base of her neck. She wore a vintage-looking knee-length, embroidered, single-breasted denim dress with a pair of very worn leather shoes. On her right wrist was a multicolored beaded bracelet. Arden would say she looked as if she'd been put together in some thrift shop.

"Yes?" I said.

The woman's cheeks seemed to bubble at their crests, and she was wearing too much lipstick and rouge. Aunt Ellsbeth would have slammed the door.

"I'm Emmaline Price," she said. "Arthur's wife."

For a few seconds, I felt like Lot's wife when she looked back at Sodom and was turned into a pillar of salt. I was shot through with a stone-cold feeling that choked back my words.

Emmaline Price could see it in my face and began to speak quickly. "I know what you think of my husband, and I waited until the shadow of death left our home before coming to see you. I made him promises during his last days, and I beg you to let me come in and talk to you for a few minutes. I want nothing from you but possibly your understanding. His final days were full of such regret. I knew how heavy his heart was and how it would shatter under his sorrow. Please," she begged.

"I have no idea why you have come here. I don't know what you want from me," I finally said.

"Just your patience for a few minutes, please. When you make promises to someone you've loved with all your heart most of your life, you can't go on without keeping them. I'm sure you can understand that."

Yes, I could understand that, I thought. The promise I had made to Papa concerning Sylvia was a promise I did not keep, and this woman was at our front door precisely because I hadn't. But my rage turned quickly to empathy. I saw myself at the front door of wherever Papa had gone, pleading with him to give me a chance to explain.

Without replying, I stepped back to let her enter. She walked in quickly and waited for me.

"This way," I said, and took her to the Roman Revival salon, where I half-expected Aunt Mercy Marie's ghost to appear and begin shouting at her.

I indicated where she should sit, and I stood

watching her for a moment, deciding whether I should sit or simply look down at her with disdain. She looked at me with such desperation in her teary gray-blue eyes that I softened and sat on the settee.

"What is it you promised your husband, Mrs. Price? And how does that involve me?"

She looked up at the ceiling, took a deep breath, and began. "Arthur was not unlike most creative people—artists, writers, composers. They dream of being appreciated, succeeding in their field. They're told they have talent, and they struggle to make something of it. But Arthur was also a family man. When we first met and fell in love, we were immune to all the hardships. We had very little money. I did some odd jobs so Arthur could paint. He sold a few things but never made any real money. I know," she said, changing her tone a bit, "this is not very important or interesting to you, but I'm trying to explain enough so you will appreciate what I want to tell you."

I didn't speak. I didn't care if my silence made her uncomfortable. Her husband had brought a great deal of pain to this house and this family.

"Anyway," she said, squirming a bit, "Arthur decided to finish college and get his teaching certificate before we could think of having children and a home and all the things everyone who wants a family life wants."

"Mrs. Price," I began. I wanted to say, *I don't care. Please leave.*

But she sensed that and quickly went on. "Of course, he continued painting and trying to get noticed, but after a while, he was devoting much more of his energy to his teaching. He really enjoyed teaching. He loved young people, and they loved him. Arthur was one of the most popular teachers. I'm sure you know that. He was devoted to his students in ways most teachers are not."

"I can imagine," I said dryly. "In ways most teachers are not."

She ignored my sarcasm and went on. "He sold a few paintings, mostly to the parents of some of his students and a few to a dealer in Richmond, but he was never discouraged. Even after he retired, he worked hard at his art. When the children were younger, we traveled to see beautiful art everywhere. We went without a lot of things that other people thought were important so we could save our money for these trips. We've visited the Prado in Madrid, the Louvre, of course, the National Gallery in London, even the Hermitage in St. Petersburg."

"I still don't see—"

"What I'm trying to tell you is that Arthur was a lover of beauty anywhere he saw it. He could get inspired by a unique tree or the way an elderly man sat and stared while he thought about his life. He did a wonderful picture of that man, and a museum in Boston now has it. What I mean to say is that Arthur was a real artist, Mrs. Lowe, and not someone just amusing himself."

"What is your point, Mrs. Price?" I asked, moving to the edge of the settee, ready to stand in order to suggest that I wanted to end this conversation.

She leaned forward. "The point is that my husband really appreciated your sister's beauty, but from an artist's point of view."

"I'm sorry. I can't agree with you about that. What he did, how he touched her, was quite inappropriate." I stood and stared down at her. I didn't want this prolonged a moment more.

"He meant no harm. He was so upset over the misunderstanding," she said, dabbing at her eyes. "For days and days after your husband came to our home and screamed at him, he sat in the corner of his studio and stared at a blank canvas. He ate very little and was up often at night just walking around the house. I'm sure the stress brought about his stroke."

I took a step toward her. "My husband and I were even more upset, Mrs. Price. Do you know how my sister is, her condition, how she has been all her life?"

"I just know from what Arthur told me. I understand she's not what she should be mentally, but he said she was a very good student and very talented. He was simply taken by her innocent beauty. It overwhelmed him. He was driven to paint her. I can't tell you how many nights he described it all to me and cried and wished he could somehow get your forgiveness."

She clutched her hands together like someone about to offer a prayer. I stood there, impatient and tired. How could I care about forgiving him?

Sylvia came into the room with Adelle in her arms.

"Hello," she said, when she saw Emmaline Price. "This is Adelle."

"Your baby," Mrs. Price said to me. She stood up to get a closer look. "What a beautiful child."

"Did you feed her?" I asked Sylvia, ignoring our intruder.

"She ate a lot, Audrina."

"Good. Please put her in the bassinet now. She needs to sleep to grow, remember?"

"Yes." Sylvia paused, obviously wondering who this woman was and why I didn't do the proper thing and introduce her. This was something I had taught Sylvia she must always do.

"Go on, Sylvia. We'll have our lunch soon, too."

"Okay. I'll cut the tomatoes," she said, and after another quizzical glance at Mrs. Price, she left.

"She is a very beautiful young lady. I can see what drove Arthur to do what he did."

"Can you?" I fired back at her. My voice was so harsh she fell back into the chair. Now I stood, my temper flaring like Papa's would. "Your husband just appreciated my sister's beauty? That's all it was? An artist being inspired? That's all that went on here? Do you think I'm that stupid?" I caught my breath. "All right. You came to fulfill your promise to him. I appreciate your devotion to your husband, but this doesn't change anything, Mrs. Price. Your husband took advantage of my sister. He used art as an excuse to sexually abuse her. I'm afraid we're going to leave it at that. And you're lucky that's all we'll do."

My rage lit something in her. I could see how her body, which had been in a posture of pleading, changed. Her eyes brightened with fury. She stood, too. "I'm sorry there is no forgiveness in your soul for someone who suffered and has died. He was remorseful and sincerely in pain, a pain that killed him. His doctors confirmed that the stress was overwhelming. It took away his life when it caused his stroke. He was diminished, a shadow of who he was. Death had no struggle to take him. I'm sure he welcomed it."

She continued, "And for you, from the little I know of your family and the tragedies you've endured, to stand there and be so high and mighty . . . I feel sorrier for you now. I'm glad I came here to see who you really are. Now I can forgive Arthur for sure. The rumors about this Whitefern family have good reason." She started walking away.

Papa's rage exploded in me. "Stop!" I shouted.

She turned.

"You think I'm unsympathetic, selfish, cruel, and harsh? You blame my family? You defile my family's memory?" I stepped toward her. "Well, I'll tell you something that you don't know, that no one should know, and if you dare utter a syllable of it out there, I promise that I will destroy your husband's memory forever. And you along with it. That baby you just saw, that beautiful child in my sister's arms, that baby is her baby, not mine. Your husband *raped* my sister. How's that for artistic inspiration? Well? What do you say now? Who is the high and mighty and unforgiving one now?"

She shook her head.

"Go on, get out and leave us. We'll do fine bringing up your husband's child, a child who will never know anything about him until she can absorb such a horrible fact about herself. Maybe she'll visit you if you're still alive and make you face your husband's sin yourself. Maybe she'll visit your children and tell them they have a half sister."

She didn't move. Then she surprised me by moving back to the chair and sitting.

"Stunned?" I said. "I guess you didn't know the man you married, the man who was the father of your children, so well after all. It doesn't surprise me. He was quite good at deceiving me. Apparently, he was good at deceiving the whole community, too, especially the school community." Why was she still here?

She shook her head again. "He's not the father of my children," she said.

"What?" Now what was she confessing to? She dressed like a hippie. They probably lived with other hippies and had no morals. "I don't want to hear your confessions, Mrs. Price. Frankly, I couldn't be less interested in you. Please leave, or I'll call the police."

"All our children are adopted," she said softly.

"That's very nice, but—"

"No, you don't understand what I'm saying, Mrs. Lowe. Arthur was unable to get me or any woman pregnant. He contracted testicular cancer when he was in his early twenties. The radiation and chemotherapy stopped the cancer but led to infertility. He tested and tested and finally gave up. That's when we decided to adopt. My husband couldn't possibly be the father of your sister's child." She stood again. "If you want, I'll arrange for you to speak with Arthur's doctor. I can also send you copies of his tests and reports."

She waited for me to respond, but I couldn't. After a moment, she started out. She paused in the doorway, looked back at me, then said good-bye and left.

The door closing sounded more like a coffin being shut. I fell back onto the settee.

Sylvia returned to the living room and looked around. "Is the lady gone?"

"Yes, she's gone, Sylvia."

"I cut too many tomatoes."

"That's all right."

"Adelle's asleep," she said.

I nodded.

She looked at me, smiling, waiting for me to tell her to do something else.

A thought flashed into my mind. "Sylvia, Papa hasn't spoken to you since Adelle was born, right?"

She nodded.

"But you've been in the rocking chair; it's in your room. You haven't heard him whispering since I've been sleeping there with you?"

She shook her head. "No, Audrina. Papa has no more secrets."

I hugged myself when the chill rippled through my body. Then I put my hands over my ears.

They were all screaming at once, every ghost in the house.

Papa's Revenge

Later, when Arden called to tell me he was taking a client to dinner, I said "Hello," listened, and said "Good-bye." He didn't try to say more or ask me why I sounded like I did.

Sylvia was upstairs in the rocking chair with Adelle in her arms. We often went up there in the afternoons now. I had taught Sylvia one of the lullabies I remembered Momma singing to me. When Sylvia sang, she sounded like Momma, and sometimes I would find myself dozing off with Adelle. It made me happy. We often looked for ways to bring back something beautiful and tender from our past.

All through lunch, a lunch I didn't eat, I listened to Sylvia talk about Adelle. Since the baby's birth, a new fountain of words flowed from her lips. It was as if the traumatic delivery had jolted her ahead in years or awakened some sleeping undeveloped skills. Someone listening to her for the first time might easily assume that there was nothing abnormal about her, nothing at all.

It made it difficult for me to hate everything about

her pregnancy and certainly made it impossible to regret Adelle's birth. Look what had emerged from the darkest places in Whitefern. There sat Sylvia beside our beautiful child sleeping in her bassinet, both looking innocent and trustful. But I was once innocent and trustful, too. Something like that is sweet and pleasant to see, but in this world, it was like a door left open through which everything ugly, mean, and selfish could easily enter. It was why a loving parent must shut down her little boy or girl's childhood as soon as possible and paste those memories into albums to be remembered, though never restored.

Sylvia didn't notice how little I ate. She was too excited. She cleared the table, washed the dishes, and put everything away while I sat staring at the clock.

"Audrina," she said, "we forgot to get a baby carriage."

"What?"

She ran out and returned with a catalogue of infants' clothing and equipment. She put it on the table opened to pictures of strollers and carriages.

"Yes," I said. "We'll get one soon. She isn't ready yet, Sylvia."

"Soon," she said, nodding.

I left her and went outside for a while. I needed to be alone, and whenever I felt maudlin and even frightened, I would stroll around the grounds, in and around the woods, comforting myself with the singing of the birds and the sight of squirrels going through their bursts of gymnastics as though they were performing for me. When I was very young, I never went too far from the property. The house always held me, as if there was an invisible chain hooked to my waist.

As I paused and looked up at Whitefern, I recalled overhearing my father arguing with my aunt Ellsbeth about allowing me to leave Whitefern and go to college.

"You've managed to tie her hand and foot to Sylvia. It's not fair, what you're doing. I know you love her, so let her go to college. Set her free, Damian, before it's too late!" my aunt had cried, her voice full of desperation.

"Ellie," my father had replied, "what would happen to Audrina if she left here? She's too sensitive for the world out there. I'm sure she will never marry that boy, and he'll find that out once he tries something. No man wants a woman who can't respond, and I doubt she'll ever learn how."

Those words rang in my head, bonging like church bells. Had my father been right? Or had my aunt Ellsbeth been right to push for me to be free of Whitefern?

Was all that had happened decided the day I was born? Was Papa responsible for this now, molding me in a way that made it difficult to respond to a man, just as he had predicted? Could that justify what Arden had done, by any stretch of the imagination? Was I simply trying to find an answer that would make it possible for me to go on, blind and in denial?

There were no answers out here, no answers away from Whitefern. Whatever the answers were, they loomed inside, hovering in the corners with the secrets, waiting for me to pluck them like blackberries.

I belonged inside. Maybe I was too sensitive for the world out there, Arden's and Papa's world, in which deception and dishonesty were the currencies to buy your way to happiness. Regrets, morality, even simple compassion were obstacles, lead weights on your ankles that would only sink you in the sea of competition. Papa was right, and Arden was right. I didn't belong in that cutthroat world. As I saw too often, you couldn't leave it outside your home once you swam in it.

I went back into the house and walked up the stairs slowly. I felt like I was in a hypnotic daze. I could feel the past, with all its voices, closing in on me. It was as if I was falling back through time with every step. There was Vera smiling at me from the doorway of her room, the way she often did when something I had done made someone in the house upset or when something I asked for was denied. Her smile told me that her usually insatiable jealousy was satisfied.

There was Aunt Ellsbeth with some clothing I had not put away properly, holding it up like evidence in a murder trial. I could hear her voice cutting my ears. "Do you think your mother would be happy to see this?"

I touched the wall above my head to be sure I was not shorter, not a little girl again. Then I walked to Sylvia's room, my whole body as tight as a fist. For a while, I stood in the doorway. Watching Sylvia sing and rock intensified the rage building inside of me.

"Sylvia," I said, "I want you to put Adelle in the bassinet now."

She looked at the sleeping child and then did what I said.

"Come with me," I ordered.

She followed me downstairs and sat beside me on the sofa. I took her hands in mine. She wore her soft, innocent, and trusting smile, but she was a little frightened by my intense look. I could feel her fingers tremble.

"It is time for you to tell me a secret, Sylvia."

"Papa's secret?"

"Yes. Did he tell you to let Arden make the baby?"

I could see the wrestling going on in her mind.

"It's all right to tell now. Adelle has been born."

She nodded.

"It was Papa who told you that we would both be pregnant?"

"Papa said so." She looked like she was going to cry.

"It's all right, Sylvia. Don't worry. Papa talks to me, too."

She smiled. "I know," she said.

She wanted to go back upstairs and watch Adelle. She was never comfortable being too far from her. I poured myself some blackberry brandy and sat for a while. Sylvia came down to tell me that Adelle had woken up and that she was preparing her bottle. As if she could sense something different and important was going to happen but was afraid of it, she asked if she could take her dinner upstairs and eat alongside Adelle tonight.

I told her I thought that was a good idea. I had

no intention of eating anything myself. I drank some more brandy and looked at some old pictures. I dozed for a while, and when I woke, it was dark. The sun had gone down, and I hadn't yet put on any lights. I decided to turn on only the lamp by the sofa. It had a very weak bulb. Momma had liked it that way. She could sprawl out and fall asleep here. I thought the low illumination had comforted her. I recalled how her arm would slide off the edge, and when I was a little girl, I would crawl up to the sofa and hold her hand. Sometimes she'd wake up and smile at me, and sometimes she wouldn't wake even though I'd held her hand for quite a while.

I wished I could hold her hand now.

Hours later, I saw light from the headlights of Arden's car streak through the windows and trace along the walls before going dark. Soon after, I heard him open the front door and mutter about no one leaving a light on for him. When he first entered the salon, he didn't see me. He looked like he had drunk too much, as usual, and stood there acclimating himself to the subdued light. Finally, he noticed me and shuddered.

"Christ," he said. "You look like a ghost, and in this house, that's not an exaggeration."

"Do I? Maybe you're seeing Aunt Mercy Marie."

"Why are you sitting in the dark? And why didn't you leave lights on for me?"

"I feel like I've been in the dark for a long, long time in this house, Arden."

"Hmm," he said. "Well, you can blame your father for that."

"Apparently, I can blame him for a lot more."

"Huh?" He unbuttoned his jacket.

"We had a visitor today, Arden."

"What visitor? Did Dr. Prescott come here?"

"No, it wasn't Dr. Prescott, and it wasn't Mrs. Matthews."

"Well, who the hell was it? What's the mystery?"

"It was Mrs. Price."

"Price? Why the hell would she come here?"

"You never told me he had died."

"Yeah, well, good riddance." He saw the bottle of brandy on the coffee table. "Drinking? Good idea. A nightcap is in order," he said. "Another successful dinner to celebrate."

"Really." I watched him pour himself a glass.

He wobbled a bit and then drank half of it in one gulp. "Good stuff," he said. "So? Why did this Price woman come here?"

"She had promised her husband she would come to plead for forgiveness. She wanted to explain about him, to tell me how he was truly an artist and had only an artist's interest in Sylvia's beauty."

"Sure," Arden said, and finished his brandy. "Maybe she thought we might still press charges or something."

"She got me very angry, Arden. I wasn't going to forgive Mr. Price, and she was upset by how I treated her explanation. She said some nasty things about my family and our reputation in the community. I couldn't help myself."

"What . . ." He refocused on me and poured himself a little more brandy.

"She saw Adelle and Sylvia, and she thought Sylvia was beautiful and the baby was beautiful."

"So?"

"So then I told her we weren't only accusing her husband of groping my sister. We were accusing him of rape."

My words seemed to sober him instantly. "You told her what?"

"She was shocked and had to sit again."

"For Christ's sake, Audrina, she could go and tell someone, maybe a lawyer or someone, because she'd be afraid we'd press charges."

"Against a dead man?"

"Or discredit her in some way. How could you make such a mistake now? I don't care how angry she got you."

"What followed was very interesting, Arden. As it turns out, Mr. Price couldn't have raped Sylvia and gotten her pregnant with Adelle."

"Oh, yeah? Why not?"

"He had testicular cancer when he was younger and was made infertile. They had to adopt all their children."

Arden stood before me, blinking fast. "I'm sure that's a lie," he said. "Her way of covering up for him. She's worried about herself, that's all."

"She has the medical reports and is giving me the doctor's name. She will have him tell the truth. She's not lying."

"Yeah, well . . ."

"I had these dreams—at least, I thought they were

dreams—of you standing outside the first Audrina's room and whispering through the door while Sylvia rocked in the rocking chair. You impersonated my father and told her to do things. You told her she had to keep everything secret. It wasn't a dream, was it?"

He didn't reply. He stood there looking at me.

"You're the one who raped my sister, Arden. You're the one who took advantage of her. Did you do this for your own selfish pleasure?"

"No," he said, maybe too quickly, because he wasn't quite finished trying to deny it. "I mean . . . Oh, what are you so surprised about, Audrina? We both wanted a child, and you couldn't give me one. It worked out well, didn't it? Now we have a child who carries your father's blood and my blood. It's almost the same thing, and besides, everyone believes it. That woman won't convince anyone of anything."

"You raped my sister," I said.

"Stop saying that. I did what had to be done." He stared at the floor for a few moments and then looked up. "And maybe it will have to be done again. I want a son; you should want a son, too."

I stood up slowly. His words now and his confession, although anticipated, still struck me hard—but doubly hard when he threatened to have another child with Sylvia.

"You deceived us both, and you had me believing that schoolteacher was the rapist. It was all lies." A new thought occurred. "Did your Mrs. Matthews know the truth? Did she go along with it? Was it part of your plan? You don't have to answer. I think now that was why she was so disrespectful to me. She knew I was being a fool, and oh, what a fool you made of me."

"Now, you listen to me, Audrina—"

"No, *you* listen. You put the idea in Sylvia's mind that we'd both have to be pregnant. You set it all up, planning ahead for when the baby was born. Are you proud of yourself?"

"It was all part of the plan."

"Yes, the plan. I should have wondered more why you conceived it."

He sighed deeply and looked pathetically weak, wobbling and struggling to come up with a good response. "I did what had to be done," he said. "And yes, it was a clever plan, and I am proud of how well it was executed. Now, stop this indignation. You have a child to raise, and the world believes she's yours. You have a family. You should be thanking me."

"Thanking you? I have a family? Yes, I have a family, a family born of lies and deceit."

"That's not unusual for you, Audrina, or for Whitefern," he said, smiling. "Look at what your father planned and how well he planned it. Everyone in this house, including your own mother, followed his design. It was all a lie. They even had me and my mother believing it. To go as far as to install an empty grave with a tombstone . . . Don't try to make it look like your family was any better than I am."

"You're right, Arden. This home is hospitable to lies, but I don't intend for them to go on."

"So what are you going to do? Tell everyone Adelle is really Sylvia's baby? We both thought that would hurt the child and how she will be perceived."

"She'll remain our child, Sylvia's and mine," I said. "But someday she'll know the truth." I straightened my shoulders, just the way Papa would when he was going to make one of his definitive proposals. "I think it would be best if you left Whitefern, Arden. I don't want to share meals with you, much less my bed." I started to walk away, then stopped. "And as far as the company goes, it will remain as it is—in my control."

"What?"

"Go sleep in one of the downstairs bedrooms tonight," I told him.

"Like hell I will. And I won't leave here, either. You'll do what I say with those legal documents," he vowed, shaking his fist at me. "I'm your husband. You'll obey your husband."

"I won't," I said. "In fact, I'll be calling Mr. Johnson tomorrow and advising him of the same, so he'll know that if you try to forge anything, it will be a crime that he will be associated with, too. Good night." I started up the stairway.

"Audrina!" he screamed. "You're part of this. You can't escape it by sending me away or going to sleep or rocking in that damn chair!"

I ignored him and kept going.

"Audrina!" he shouted from the foot of the stairway. "Don't you dare walk away from me!"

Sylvia came out of her room and hurried to the

stairs. "Adelle is crying," she said, looking down at me and at Arden. "She heard the screaming."

"Yes. Well, she won't have to hear it much longer. Arden is going to move out," I said.

"Damn you!" he screamed. He rushed up the stairs. "You won't tell me what to do. And you will sign those papers."

I was nearly to the top.

He lunged at me and grabbed my arm. "I'm Papa here! I'm Papa!" he bellowed. He shook me hard.

"Stop hurting Audrina," Sylvia ordered. She sounded just like Momma telling Papa to stop hurting me or Vera.

Arden let go of my left arm to push her away from us, and I turned, freeing myself from his right hand. Before he could reach out to grab me again, Sylvia came forward with her arms out and pushed at his shoulder.

He tottered, looked at us both with surprise, and fell backward, his arms flailing out, his hands grasping air as he dropped onto his back and then flipped over, his legs flying over his torso and giving his body the momentum to flip again, this time coming down hard, his neck hitting squarely on the edge of a step. His body slid a little and stopped.

He didn't move or cry.

Sylvia and I didn't move, either.

"Arden fell," she said.

I held out my hand to keep her from following me and walked down to him slowly. As I approached, I was experiencing déjà vu. This was how I had approached Aunt Ellsbeth's body when she had fallen down the stairs. *She's not dead*, I'd kept telling myself, *not dead, not dead, only hurt*. She had been facedown, and I'd had to turn her body to look at her face. I remembered her head had lolled, unnaturally loose, and I had shaken her to wake her up, but she never did.

Arden was lying faceup. His eyes were wide open, already two orbs of lifeless glass. He had carried his expression of surprise all the way down and died with it. I knelt beside him and felt for a pulse nevertheless. There was none.

"Is he hurt?" Sylvia asked.

"Go look after Adelle," I said. I could hear the baby crying. It was the loudest she had cried yet. Maybe she sensed that her real father was gone. "Go on, Sylvia."

"Yes," she said, and walked back up and to her room. "Adelle . . ."

I stood and looked down at Arden. Perhaps I was in shock, because I didn't cry. I should have cried. I should have been screaming his name and begging him to be alive. Memories of how kind and loving he had been to me when I was young and just emerging from Whitefern were pushing away the anger and disappointment I had just felt. There had been wonderful smiles and laughter between us, too. They didn't want to be buried.

I sat on a higher step and continued to gaze at him. Sylvia came to the top of the stairs again, this time with Adelle in her arms. The baby was no longer crying.

"Did I hurt him?" she asked.

"No, Sylvia. He hurt himself."

I looked around at the dark house. Whitefern had done it again, I thought. Whitefern had exacted its revenge. The ghosts were gathered, whispering to one another and looking at Arden.

Papa, I thought. *Where are you?*

He was here; he was with us. I stood up again and stepped around Arden's body.

"Where are you going, Audrina?" Sylvia asked.

"To warm Adelle's bottle. Then I have to call an ambulance for Arden. You can wait in your room."

"I can warm the bottle," she said.

"No, I don't want you or the baby down here until this is over," I said. "Just wait in your room. Please, Sylvia."

"I'll sit in the rocking chair," she said. She said it as if that would make everything better again.

"Yes, go sit in the rocking chair," I told her, and went to put on lights in the house.

I called for the ambulance. Then I went up and handed Sylvia the bottle and let her feed Adelle while she held her in the rocking chair. It had never seemed more appropriate.

"Sylvia, the ambulance is coming, and with it will be policemen who will want to know what happened to Arden," I began.

"I pushed him," she said.

"No. You reached out to help him because you saw he was going to fall backward. Just like you helped Papa, remember?"

"Yes," she said, smiling.

"Arden drank too much alcohol, Sylvia. It made him dizzy. That's what happened, okay?"

She nodded and went about feeding Adelle. I could only hope that she would remember what I had told her to say. It would obviously be so much easier than having to explain why we had argued, how Arden had come up after me, and how Sylvia had instinctively come to my defense.

Less than half an hour later, the ambulance arrived, with a police patrol car behind it. The paramedics rushed in when I opened the door and pointed to Arden.

The two policemen looked terribly suspicious. How could I blame them? Another death at Whitefern was surely at the forefront of their thoughts.

One of the paramedics confirmed that Arden was dead. "Looks like a broken neck," he said.

"Don't move the body yet," the taller of the two policemen ordered. "We have a detective on the way." He turned to me. I was standing with my hands clasped and resting on my breasts. I was sure I appeared to be in shock. I felt I still really was.

"Can you tell us what happened here?" the shorter policeman asked.

"We were going to bed," I said. "My husband had been out to dinner with some clients. I think he had too much to drink at dinner, but he drank some more brandy when he got home. I pleaded with him to stop drinking and just go to bed, and finally we set out to do so. He was walking behind me. I thought he was okay. My sister came out. She's watching the baby in her room for me right now. She was the one who screamed that Arden was losing his balance. I turned. She reached past me to grab him, but he fell back and flipped over and over, until he landed like this."

Neither of them spoke. I gasped and tottered.

The shorter officer put his arm around my waist. "Hey, you'd better sit down."

"Yes, thank you," I said, and let him help me to the sofa, where the soft light had remained on. He went to get me a glass of water.

When the detective arrived, they told him what I had said, and then he asked to speak with Sylvia.

"My sister was born prematurely and had early development problems," I explained. "She's never been to a formal school, and she's what they call mentally challenged."

He nodded. He looked like he knew about us. When they had removed Arden's body, I went up to get Sylvia. Adelle was asleep again, so I asked the detective to come up. I thought it would be better anyway to have her questioned away from the stairway.

"Sorry to bother you," he told Sylvia, "but can you remember what happened to your . . ."

"Brother-in-law," I interjected quickly. "She's not clear on relationships."

He nodded. "Sure. Can you remember anything, Sylvia?"

"I remember things," she said with what sounded like indignation.

"On the stairway. What happened to him?"

"He fell backward," she said. "I tried to help him like I helped Papa, but I couldn't reach him . . . I was right behind Papa. I didn't have to reach him."

"She once kept my father from falling," I explained. "We made a big deal of it. I'm sure you understand."

"Yeah, sure." He looked at Sylvia again and realized she wasn't going to be much of a witness. "Okay. There'll be an autopsy, and we'll be in touch. My deepest sympathies, Mrs. Lowe."

"Thank you."

He nodded at Sylvia.

"Adelle is sleeping," she told him, as if she expected he would want to ask the baby questions, too.

He looked at me, his eyes like exclamation points.

"It's how she is," I said.

"Right. I'll call you," he told me, and left.

The silence that followed after everyone had left was the deepest silence in Whitefern that I could remember. I didn't imagine I would be able to fall asleep, so I didn't go to our bedroom, and I didn't lie beside Sylvia on her bed.

Instead, I returned to Momma's sofa, where I sat until the wee hours of the morning. Sometime before the sun rose, I did fall asleep. Sylvia woke me to tell me it was time for breakfast. She stood there holding the baby and looking at me.

"Yes," I said. I rose slowly, telling myself it was best to eat something. There would be so much to do now, so many people to talk to and repeat the same explanation.

"Is Arden coming back for breakfast?" she asked.

"No, Sylvia," I said. "Arden's never coming back."

She nodded, looking like she just wanted to hear it confirmed.

"Arden has passed away, just like Papa did," I said.

"I know," she said. "Papa told me."

Epilogue

It was a day without clouds when we buried Arden next to his mother, Billie, in the Whitefern Cemetery, exactly the wrong weather for a funeral. Everyone and everything looked too bright and alive. Arden's and Billie's graves weren't far from my parents' graves and those of Aunt Ellsbeth and Vera. Many of our company's clients and all the employees attended the service. Mrs. Crown looked devastated, as devastated as a lover of the deceased might. She cried harder than I did and needed more comfort than I did.

Sylvia stood beside me, clinging to Adelle. Onlookers thought it was one of the saddest and yet sweetest scenes they had ever witnessed. Afterward, as I had promised Sylvia many times, I took her over to Papa's grave. She read the tombstone and looked at the grave and shook her head.

"Papa's not down there, Audrina," she insisted.

"Maybe he isn't," I said, keeping my eyes on the headstone.

I had struggled through most of the day. I had

barely slept during the previous nights. I hadn't touched any of Arden's things yet. I intended to donate as many of them as I could to charity. In fact, nothing at all looked different in our home. Whitefern was invulnerable. The shadows in every corner were still there; the whispers I heard on the stairs continued. Some of the old clocks had stopped ticking, but I didn't remove them. The grandfather clocks in the halls still chimed, but I ignored them. Arden had hated them, along with the cuckoos in the wooden Swiss clocks. Now that I thought about it, he had hated anything and everything that related to my family. He had wanted to remake it all in his name.

We didn't have any sort of formal gathering after the funeral, the way we had for Papa's. Some people stopped by during the following days, people like Mrs. Haider and a few of the employees I knew. Mrs. Crown did not visit. For now, I agreed with Mr. Johnson to permit Arden's top assistant, Nick Masters, to run the firm. It took me a while to delve into real-world matters.

Arden's absence didn't appear to bother Sylvia very much. She was far too occupied with Adelle and, along with me, caring for the house. Occasionally, she would pause and look like she was about to ask after him, but then she would shake her head slightly and nod as though she really was hearing Papa.

Time closed wounds, but it couldn't prevent scars. There were so many at Whitefern. I could say we had a garden of them. Fall was rushing in. When we took walks, now with the new carriage we had bought for

Adelle, I could sense winter's eagerness. Leaves were falling faster; birds were starting to head farther south. A darker shade of blue seeped into the afternoon skies, and nights were beginning to drop with heavier darkness around us.

One evening after dinner, while Sylvia was looking after Adelle and playing some records on Momma's old phonograph, which Arden had once tried to sell as an antique, I went out and walked far enough away from the front of the house that when I looked back, I could see the entire house silhouetted against the stars.

I had been toying with the idea of selling Whitefern. We would sell the brokerage, and Sylvia, Adelle, and I would move away, to a place where no one knew us, the Whiteferns, the Adares, or the Lowes. It was a way to be reborn, I thought.

Could I do this? Could I finally leave the past, or would the voices follow us no matter where we went? It was an enormous challenge for me, even to consider it. Once, years ago, when I had tried to leave with Sylvia, she had revolted against it, and I'd had to stay. Would she revolt again? If anything, she was probably even more attached to Whitefern. It was here that she was comforted by Papa's voice.

It was impossible, I thought. Whitefern had a grip on us that even death could not break. Slowly, I walked back to the house, feeling like I was being chastised for the very thought of leaving it.

Sylvia was in the living room, cradling Adelle in her arms and dancing to one of Momma's favorite tunes. She paused when she saw me. Adelle looked comfortable and happy in her arms.

I walked to them slowly, smiling, and put my arms around Sylvia. Adelle was between us, looking up at both of us.

And we three began to dance again.

Now turn the page for a sneak peek of

The Mirror Sisters

Book One in a startling new series

By V.C. Andrews®

Available Fall 2016 from Pocket Books

Prologue

Haylee always blamed our mother for everything that happened to us and everything terrible that we had done to each other—or I should say, everything terrible that she had done to me. Many times as we were growing up, she would tell me to my face that whatever hurtful thing she had done wasn't her fault. It was because our mother wouldn't let her be her own person. I suppose I should have been a little grateful. At least she was recognizing that whatever it was she had done was wrong.

Don't misunderstand me. It wasn't that she was suffering the needle-prick pains of conscience. In fact, I now believe my twin sister might never have felt anything despite the agonizing look she could put on and take off like a mask. We were not a religious family. Mother never warned either of us that God was watching. *She* was watching, and she thought that was enough.

I knew in my heart that Haylee was just trying to escape her own responsibility by blaming Mother for things she did herself. No one could shed her guilt like a snake sheds its skin as well as my identical twin. And afterward, she could look as innocent as a rabbit that had just devoured most of a vegetable garden. But that sweetness could turn into a flash of lightning rage when only I was looking at her, even when we were still infants.

One time when we were eleven and our mother wasn't home and couldn't hear her, Haylee stood in front of me with her arms tight against her sides, her fingers curled like claws. She stamped her foot and screamed, "I am not you! I'll never be you! And you will never be me! Whatever you like, I will hate. If I have to, I'll scar my face just to be different. Or," she added, thinking more about it, "I'll attack you when you're sleeping and I'll scar yours."

The cruelty in her eyes stunned me so much I was speechless. She truly sounded as if she hated me enough to do just what she had said. Her threat kept me up at night, watching my bedroom doorway, and it set the foundation for nightmares in which she would slink into my room with a razor between her fingers. To this day, I am certain she did come in once or twice and stand by my bed, hovering over me and battling with the urge to act out her vicious promise.

To drive home her point this particular time, she seized the photo of us at our tenth birthday party, the party held in our backyard, where Mother had Daddy arrange for a party tent and had dressed us in identical pink chiffon dresses with pink saddle shoes. Haylee tore the picture into a dozen pieces, which she flushed down the toilet, screaming, "Good riddance! If I never hear the word *twin* again, that will be too soon!" She stood there fuming. I could almost see the steam coming out of her ears. My heart was pounding, because in our house, saying something like that was like a nun declaring she never wanted to hear the word *Jesus*.

If I had any doubt that Haylee could get into a great rage without thinking of the consequences, tearing up our picture should have convinced me, for how would we explain it not being there in our room, prominently displayed on our dresser? She knew I could never tell Mother what she had done. And she could never blame it on me. It was an unwritten rule or, rather, a rule Mother had carved into our very souls: we must never blame each other for anything, for that was like blaming ourselves.

Even if I did tell, it wouldn't help. Haylee was better than I was when it came to winning sympathy and compassion for herself and justification for any evil or mean act she would commit. I could easily picture her on the witness stand in a courtroom, wringing her hands, tears streaming down her face as she wailed about how much she hadn't wanted to do what she had done to me. She would look so distraught that she might even have me feeling sorry for her.

After she had calmed herself, she would quietly explain to the jury why our mother should be the one accused, certainly not her. She wasn't all wrong. Now that I'm older, I have no doubt that Haylee would be able to find a psychiatrist eager and willing to testify on her behalf. Even back then, I wasn't going to disagree with her about what our mother had done to us. I wanted to be my own person, too, but I didn't want to have to hate Haylee the way she felt she had to hate me.

Yes, I would blame our mother, too, for what eventually happened to me, just as Daddy would. And I have no doubt that anyone reading this would surely agree, but despite it all, I still loved our mother very much. I knew how hurt she would be over what Haylee had done and the things she had said. Her heart would suffer spidery cracks like the face of the porcelain doll her father had given her when she was five. I would hold her hand and I would put my arm around her. I would lean my head against her shoulder, and I would cry with her, almost tear for tear, as she moaned, "What have I done to my precious twins? What have I done?"

1

There was nothing Mother worked harder at than keeping either of us from differing from the other, even in the smallest ways. From the day we were born, she made sure that we owned the exact same things, whether clothes, shoes, toys, books, even the same color toothbrushes. Everything had to be bought in twos. Even our names had to be an equal number of letters, and that went for our middle names as well, which were exactly the same. I was Kaylee Blossom Fitzgerald, and my sister was Haylee Blossom Fitzgerald. That was something Mother insisted on. Daddy told us he didn't think it was very significant at the time, so he had put up little argument. I'm sure he regretted it later, as he came to regret so much he had failed to do.

Although neither of us had the courage to complain about our names, we both wished they were different. By the time she was a senior in high school, Haylee had gone so far as to tell people she had no middle name. When anyone looked to me for confirmation, I agreed. That was one of those little ways Haylee gradually got me to oppose things Mother had done. I was the reluctantly rebellious twin, practically dragged by my hair into the fiery ring of defiance.

Actually, when I think about it, we were lucky to have two different first names. We couldn't be Haylee One and Haylee Two or Kaylee One and Kaylee Two based on who was born first, either. Mother would never tell us who was first, and Daddy hadn't been in the delivery room when we were born. He'd been on a business trip. I don't know if he ever asked her which one of us was born first, but I doubt she would have told him anyway. She'd pretend not to know, or maybe she really believed we were born together, hugging and clinging to each other with our tiny pink hands and arms as we were cast out of her womb and into the world, both of us harmonizing a cry of fear. Whenever Mother described our birth, she always said that the doctor practically had to pry us apart.

"I thought there was only one of you at first. That's how in sync your cries were. One voice," she would say, and she'd look starry-eyed, with that soft smile of wonder that fascinated both Haylee and me when we would sit on the floor in front of her and listen to the story of ourselves. As we grew older, she wove the magical fabric in which we would be dressed, wove it into a fantasy about the perfect twins. There was one rule that if broken would bring about disaster: we had to be loved equally, or some dragonlike monster would destroy our enchantment.

Daddy wasn't anywhere nearly as obsessed about treating us equally in every way. There was never a doubt in my mind that it was something he believed

Mother would grow out of as we grew older. He humored her with his smiles and nods and especially with his favorite response to what she demanded be done: "Whatever you say, Keri."

He admitted that he was excited about having twins, but at first, he didn't see any additional burdens or responsibilities that other parents of more than one child had. Even as infants, we could see that he was nowhere as uptight about it, which only infuriated Mother more. During our early years, if he forgot and bought something for me and not for Haylee, or vice versa, our mother would become so upset that, in a violent rage during which I would swear I felt a whirlwind around us, she would tear up or throw out whatever he had bought. Haylee felt the whirlwind, too, and, watching Mother, we would cling to each other as tightly as we supposedly had the day we were born.

There was simply no excuse Daddy could use for what he had done that would satisfy her. For example, like someone else's father, he couldn't say one of us liked a certain color more or was more interested in something and he had just happened to come upon it during his travels. Oh, no. Mother would look as if she had accidentally put her finger in an electric socket and would tell him he was wrong and had done a terrible thing.

In his defense he pleaded, "For God's sake, Keri, this isn't a capital crime."

"Not a capital crime?" she fired back, her voice shrill. "How can you not see them for what they are?"

"They're little girls," he declared.

"No, no, no, these are not just two little girls. These are perfect twins. They see the world through the same eyes, hear it through the same ears, and smell it through the same nose."

He shook his head, smiling but concerned. I looked at Haylee. Was Mother right? To anyone watching us, it did look as if we liked the same foods, the same flavor ice cream, the same candy. It was true that when we were very young, anything one of us liked, the other did, too, and anything one of us hated, the other hated. Maybe we felt we were supposed to or we would lose our mystical powers. Nevertheless, Mother was shocked Daddy didn't realize that.

"I think you're exaggerating," Daddy told her.

"Exaggerating? Are you in the same house, Mason? Do you see your own children?" she asked him in what, even as a young girl, I thought was a terribly condescending tone. She sounded more like she did when she chastised us.

Mother also had a habit of smacking her right fist against her right thigh when she started her responses to things that upset her this much. Sometimes she did it so hard that both Haylee and I would flinch as if we felt the blows. After one of her more dramatic outbursts, I saw her thigh when she was getting ready to take a shower. It had a bright red circle where she had pounded it. Later it turned black-and-blue, and when Daddy mentioned it, she said, "It's your fault, Mason. You might as well have struck me there yourself."

Finally, Daddy always managed to stammer an excuse, but he still couldn't ever get away with "I'll buy the other one something tomorrow." Whatever it was that he had bought one of us and not the other, it was gone that day, no matter what he had promised. Sometimes he would take it back and have his secretary return it to the store, but most times, after Mother had destroyed it or thrown it out, he would go back when he could and buy two this time, so he could give both of us whatever it was he thought one of us had wanted. He never looked happy about it. That satisfied Mother, though, and brought what Daddy called "a fragile armistice where we tiptoed on a floor of eggshells." We were all smiles again. Our pounding hearts relaxed, and the electric sizzle in the air disappeared, for a while anyway.

In our house, stings, burns, and aches ran around just behind the walls and just under the floors like termites. Haylee and I were in the center of continuous little tornadoes. Sometimes I thought Haylee did things deliberately so she could see these storms brew between Daddy and Mother. It was one of the differences I sensed early about us. Haylee had an impish delight in causing little explosions between our parents.

But she was far from the main cause of it all in the beginning. It wasn't difficult to understand why this turmoil was happening around Haylee and me. In our mother's mind, a minute after we were born, all thoughts about one of us had to be about the two of us simultaneously. She claimed it was practically blasphemous to do otherwise, because the biggest danger for any parent of identical twins was that somehow, some way, he or she would favor one over the other and literally destroy the confidence of the one not favored.

It was one thing to praise one of your children because he or she had done something spectacular. Everyone knew stories about fathers who favored one son over the other because he was a hero on the football field or got good grades. The same was true for a daughter who might please her mother more by being more responsible, being talented in music or art, or maybe just being prettier.

But none of this could apply to identical twins, not in our mother's way of thinking.

According to Mother, Haylee had no talents that I didn't have, and I had none that she didn't have. Certainly, neither of us could be prettier than the other. Our voices were so similar that people never knew which one had answered the phone. Even Daddy was confused sometimes when he called. There was always a question mark in the air first. "Haylee? Kaylee?"

When we were a little older, Haylee often pretended to be me on the phone. I think she worried that Daddy liked me more and wanted to see how he would speak if he thought I was the one answering the phone. I suspected he did like me more than he liked her, and she knew it. Once she said, "If he doesn't know which one of us it is, he'll say your name because he hopes it's you." I didn't know if she was right. I didn't keep as close a count as she did.

Maybe it was simply because he wasn't around us much as he should have been, but if I suddenly came upon him while he was reading or if Haylee did, Daddy would look at whomever it was, and his eyes would blink for a moment as his mind settled on which one of us was there. Anyone could see that he was struggling with it because Mother had him terrified about calling me Haylee or calling her Kaylee. Mother insisted that he must know which of us was which.

After all, how could our own father not know us? He agreed, and when he did get it wrong, he blamed himself for not concentrating or paying attention enough. However, he admitted that there were times when he was actually mistaken even though he was concentrating.

"They're so alike!" he cried, hoping to be excused when Mother blew up at him for it, but all that did was prove her point and make her even more obsessive about how we were supposed to be treated.

"Of course they're so alike. That's always been my point. You have to try even harder, Mason, and be more careful about it," she told him. "You never liked it when your father called you by your brother's name, and you weren't even twins. He is two years older than you are, but how did you feel, Mason? Go on, confess. You felt he was thinking more of him than he was of you, right?"

Daddy had admitted that to her once, so what could he do but retreat with the look of a punished puppy? I always felt sorrier for him than I did for us. Sometimes I pretended I *was* Haylee if he called me that, just so he would get away with it, but if Mother was there, that was impossible. She never made a mistake. I never knew why not, except to think that it was true that mothers knew their children better.

There were so many rules of behavior toward us that Mother laid down, with the power and importance of the U.S. Constitution, our own Ten Commandments:

Thou shalt not call Haylee "Kaylee," or vice versa.

Thou shalt not buy one a gift that you do not buy the other.

Thou shalt not take one somewhere and not the other.

Thou shalt not kiss one without kissing the other.

Thou shalt not hug or hold the hand of one without hugging or holding the hand of the other.

Thou shalt not say good morning or good night to one without saying it to the other.

Thou shalt not ask one a question you do not ask the other.

Thou shalt not introduce one to someone without introducing the other.

Thou shalt not tell one a story without telling it to the other.

Thou shalt not smile at one without smiling at the other.

Because of all the rules, I often thought our house was more of a laboratory than a home. I think Daddy did, too. Even Haylee admitted to feeling as if we were under observation in a glass bubble while strange and new experimentation on bringing up identical twins was being conducted. Many of Mother and Daddy's friends often looked as if they believed that, too. I once heard someone whisper that maybe Mother was giving reports to a special government agency. I know that, like me, Haylee felt this all made us seem strange to anyone who witnessed our upbringing. There were other twins in our community, even on our street, but they were not identical, and they seemed no different from kids who had no twins. They were permitted to wear different clothes and do different things, and their mothers weren't so uptight about potentially devastating personality complexes.

But our mother would point or nod at them and say, "Look. Look how competitive their parents have made them. They enjoy making each other feel bad. You'll never do that," she would add with a confident smile. "You will always consider each other's feelings first."

She had no idea about what was coming, crawling along on the tails of shadows toward our home and our family as we grew older.